John Muckle was born in the village of Cobham, Surrey, but has lived most of his life in Essex and London. In the 1980s he initiated the Paladin Poetry Series and was General Editor of its flagship anthology, *The New British Poetry* (Paladin, 1988). His previous books include *The Cresta Run* (short stories), *Cyclomotors* (a novella with photographic illustrations), *Firewriting and Other Poems* (Shearsman Books, 2005), two novels, also from Shearsman, *London Brakes* (2010) and *My Pale Tulip* (2012), and a critical study of British fiction in the 1950s and 1960s, *Little White Bull* (Shearsman, 2014)

Also by John Muckle

It Is Now As It Was Then (with Ian Davidson)
The Cresta Run
Bikers (with Bill Griffiths)
Cyclomotors
Firewriting and Other Poems
London Brakes
My Pale Tulip

CRITICISM
Little White Bull

Falling Through

a novel

JOHN MUCKLE

Shearsman Books

Published in the United Kingdom in 2017 by
Shearsman Books
50 Westons Hill Drive
Emersons Green
BRISTOL
BS16 7DF

Shearsman Books Ltd Registered Office
30–31 St. James Place, Mangotsfield, Bristol BS16 9JB
(this address not for correspondence)

ISBN 978-1-84861-535-9
First Edition

Falling Through

ONE

Graham looked up at the sloping ceiling above his single bed. It was four in the afternoon, the winter darkness had fallen suddenly, and a blueish glare from the portable TV struck his ceiling obliquely, which created an odd pair of linked reflections up there. They looked like a model glider: a stick for a fuselage, wide billowing wings and a slender, spill-like tail somebody had twisted out of a sheet of file paper. He wanted to get up, pick it off the ceiling and throw it out of the window; watch it drift over the gardens, lift above chimneys, trees, and float away over the braided railway tracks that wove on down to King's Cross Station.

He wondered sleepily if he should make a new one of a similar design ... but any thoughts of gliders he'd previously stuck together and the awful prospect of doing it all again tired him out; he stretched out his limbs until they loosened, relaxed, and drifted off again into sleep.

Once he was properly asleep, the dreaming began. Always the same one. He sat in the begging chair, begging for forgiveness. The shadow of the larger man loomed over him, and then the tall man struck him hard in the face, again and again, first with the back of his hand, then with something harder. He was used to it. He almost liked it. It was no less than he deserved. He began silently to cry. There was a deep crease at the corner of his right eye, a conduit for a steady stream of salty water. He tasted it on his tongue, almost comforting: a pleasant-unpleasant dream he expected to be living in for the rest of his life, probably.

He awoke from it without fuss and peered at the alarm clock. It was after six o'clock. Dark outside. Swiftly he got up and dressed in his suit, his brown interview suit, splashed some water on his face in the bathroom, briefly combed his hair, picked up his bag and let himself out of the flat into Rathbone Avenue, its long curve of Edwardian terraces stretching down a hill for a while before climbing towards the shining blocks of council flats which he vaguely associated with Harringay itself, whatever self that was. Beyond them a small library was tucked away on a corner, a quiet building mainly containing crime thrillers and children's books. Somewhere along there you could pick up the New River;

it ran somewhat unimpressively along the backs of the houses of Wightman Road.

He turned in the opposite direction, walked up the short rise to Tottenham Lane, turned right at the top and walked purposefully downhill to Hornsey station and First Capital Connect. He recharged his Oyster card and hopped on a train heading in the opposite direction from Kings Cross. Alexandra Palace, Bowes Road, Palmer's Green. He hopped off at Winchmore Hill and hurried down the long hill, past the fancy Victorian shopping hub and on to his appointment.

He rang the bell of a large semi-detached property in an avenue which was a bit better appointed than his own – bigger houses, bow-fronted, mostly in that suburban style of the twenties, of which there were two basic sorts: teapot trad, and teapot moderne. Quite a few, including the one whose bell he was currently pushing, had skips in front of them, recounting their stories of improvements in progress. On his first visit here, early himself, he'd walked around the corner and found Edmonton cemetery, full of nineteenth century Poles and Jews, and glanced cursorily at a few of the impressive stones. Nobody in his family had ever been deemed worthy of a headstone, so far as he remembered.

Mrs. Anstis loomed behind the louvred glass of the front door, stooped slightly to open it and smiled up at him on the step. She was a small, solicitous woman of Italian ancestry who had once studied psychology, about the same age as the tutor. Her son Paul, at the sound of Graham's approach, had once again locked himself in the upstairs toilet. She apologized for his poor behaviour. "I am embarrassed!" She ushered his tutor towards the large living room and called upstairs plaintively – "Paul! Paul!" – going up sideways as she attempted to cajole her son away from his ablutions.

He walked over to their cluttered dining table, sat down at a chair and pulled his folder and a couple of books from his battered tan satchel. Their front room was crowded with piles of displaced kitchen equipment, piles of woks and pans, an expensive toaster jammed back into its dog-eared box. Mrs. Anstis' balding, elderly mutt approached him, woefully wagging its amputated stump of tail. After a few minutes the boy himself came downstairs, vacant and unprepared, and slid into the chair opposite. The lesson, if you could call it that, got underway.

He didn't seem able to spark any interest in Paul, not in W.H. Auden, Christina Rossetti, Daphne Du Maurier or Bram Stoker. The only novel on his syllabus he liked was *The Kite Runner* by Khaled Hosseini, which he had dutifully read and to an extent enjoyed, but couldn't quite bring himself to fully approve of. How likely was it really that the head of the Taliban was a blue-eyed half-German Nazi who was running a gay paedophile ring on the side? His study of the relevant Wikipedia pages had revealed the author to be the son of a diplomat. Like a lot of them he'd written himself down a social notch or two, and the whole thing was a love letter to America, more or less. His actual relationship with the impossibly loyal Hazara boy had been somewhat more distant and formal than implied by the tear-jerking outcome of his book. Typical novelist. Just another self-serving, lying little prick.

Still, none of this was Paul's fault. He felt himself to be a complete failure as a teacher. This perfectly normal boy, English, middle-class, with a builder for a father – who incidentally had doubled the size of the back of their teapot with a kitchen extension complete with Roman tiles and underfloor heating – had preoccupations other than passing his A levels. He'd just learned to drive, wore his trousers halfway down his backside, wasn't so sure he needed to go to university anyway. Forty years earlier, he himself had felt much the same.

Afterwards he walked back to the station. It was fucking cold, so he stepped on it, feeling in his pocket for the hand-warmer – the crisp sheets of a couple of banknotes, a ten, a twenty. He refused to dwell on anything in particular about the lesson. As usual the session had been like pulling teeth. Plainly the boy was not interested in the subject; he was just going through the motions to please his mother. Either out of stupidity or contempt he never seemed to remember what had been said from week to week. His notes and all of the interesting essays his tutor had copied for him were always left behind at school in another folder, or lost somewhere in his chaotic bedroom.

On the short train journey he flipped through a copy of *Metro*, read his horoscope and a five minute interview with a twenty-three year old TV actress whose favourite programme turned out to be *Twin Peaks* (before she was born surely) and he worried a little as the shrouded landscape of this little stretch of suburban London trundled by into the recent past. Alexandra Palace. Ally Pally. He hadn't been up there for ages. He wanted to go. No reason, none whatsoever. Just that he had a vague feeling that a glance through the telescope towards Canary Wharf would do him some good. Clutching at straws? He was getting worried about this peculiar little job of his. It wasn't much, but it was all he had been able to obtain in part-exchange for his careless, half-baked sense of how things go.

TWO

Next morning, Saturday morning, he got up at a reasonable hour and wandered down towards Crouch End. Succumbing first to the temptation of a hearty breakfast in Wetherspoons, he popped into Flashback Records, a cramped shop opposite the Harringay Arms, bursting with memories – his own and other peoples – to clack quickly through a few racks of pre-owned CDs. Dinah Washington, classy, withheld but passionate; Sonny Rollins, still trotting along like an old cowhand; Marc Bolan, dug up at the root, lost through a hole in the soul of his suit; Mary Hopkin's gloriously infectious Russian polka. *Those Were the Days.* Mary Hopkin, shy, beautiful, Welsh. Balalaikas, orchestral arrangements, children's choirs – these were the things that did him in.

But he soon found himself shoulder to shoulder with half-a-dozen other gold prospectors; so he left them to it and strolled off to the library to check his emails.

Viagra from Canada, Big Willy; a showing of *Jonah Who Will Be Twenty Five in the Year Two Thousand* at the National Gallery; *À Bout de Souffle* in French at Hornsey Film Club; a Word-a-Day; another request from persistent Taryn Buster asking if he wanted to be her FuckBuddy; a wide selection of photos of the more grotesquely overweight customers of Wal-Mart, kindly forwarded by a childhood friend who now lived in Houston, Texas. He deleted the lot of them. A flying bird had brought the message. It is better not to strive upwards. It is better to remain below. He threw away his *I-Ching* reading too and clicked around a bit in a well-worn but non-random way, compulsively checking on all three or four things he routinely checked. They were still happening, those relevant, irrelevant people still existed. He was just glad they weren't gathered in his courtyard, which only meant trouble, unhappiness, revolutions, demands for immediate payment.

On the other hand, he quite often clicked on The Cobham Blogger, enjoying his accounts of pizza franchises and restaurants opening and closing on the High Street, speculation about what might be next on the site, controversy over the disused buildings of the primary school Graham had once attended (should they be turned into a homeless shelter, or demolished to make way for luxury flats?); the poor condition of the outside garden of the Fairmile Hotel; the preponderance of WAGS in 4x4s since Chelsea Football Club's training ground had been relocated to nearby Stoke D'Abernon, and their arrogant behaviour; floods, washed out bridges – in memory and in the present; and the annual Christmas lights turn-on, with sardonic comments about what astonishingly cheap celebrity might be afforded this year.

Back in the day it had been Ronnie Carroll opening Fine Fare supermarket. "Are those roses still red, Ron?" somebody had called to him. "Of course they are, red enough for me," the briefly popular Northern Irish crooner had replied. He remembered how his mother had come home with a PG Tips album, featuring a chimps' tea party on the cover, for him to stick in the cards of animals and birds and wild flowers and flags of the world which came with every green and blue quarter packet. On it an Indian lady delicately picked tea and cast the resinous buds into a basket suspended on her back by a leather thong around her forehead. Just as it still was, always would be. "Imagine doing that all day long in the blazing hot sun," his father had said, "just so we can have a cup of tea whenever we like."

He quite liked reading the blog, but it seemed to be dribbling away: a fracas; a car accident; an unsuccessful ram-raid on Barclays Bank; a few more demolitions and rebuildings; road widening; unaffordable housing and the perfidy of Elmbridge council. Gerrard Winstanley dragged in as most famous Cobhamite: the irony of it, had anything really changed? And what would they think of him now, etc? He was casting his bread, but the commenters weren't biting. About the only things biting around there were bloated, genetically-modified chub with which the Mole had been stocked by the local angling club. Graham suspected he'd given up, been told to desist by his neighbours, or by what he called 'the powers that be'.

But today his favourite blog was telling a different tale: a body had been found in a wheelie bin in Hamilton Avenue, a woman's dead body. Under a heading which read 'Where are you Peter and how did this happen?' he'd simply reproduced a statement by the Surrey constabulary:

A man who may be able to assist a murder investigation is being sought after the body of a woman was found in a wheelie bin in Hamilton Avenue, Cobham.

Surrey Police was called by a woman at around 3:20pm yesterday (Saturday 6 June), after a human foot was seen protruding from the bin.

Scene of crime officers carefully emptied the bin to preserve forensic opportunities, recovering the full intact body of a white woman believed to be in her 30s, which had been surrounded by rubbish.

A post mortem at the Royal Surrey County Hospital in Guildford was inconclusive as to probable cause of death.
It found signs of a serious head injury, but could not confirm that this had caused the death.

Detectives are focusing their inquiries on locating a previous resident of the address where the body was found, who may be able to provide useful information for the investigation.

33-year-old Peter moved out of the address roughly three weeks ago and his whereabouts are currently unknown.
He is described as a heavy-built white man with broad shoulders, roughly six feet in height, with slightly-receding brown cropped hair and brown eyes.

He clicked other news sources and filled in a few details. The murder had taken place on the road where he'd grown up, in a newly built block of flats called Hamilton Court: a set of eighteen two-bedroom family places capping the avenue of semi-detached fifties council houses, which were somewhat more attractive properties. The Styles family had been awarded one of them after their two girls grew too big to share a room, thereafter ceasing to be landing neighbours. Tish no longer came in with her Elvis records and put her ear down to the spindly radiogram to listen to him breathing and to practice hula-hooping with his mother. There had been a row of shops, a grocer, a newsagent and a greengrocery, knocked down since to make way for more housing. Hamilton Court still stood, but what had once been a brand new block looked knocked about now; some flats didn't even have curtains up, and he had heard it was a dumping ground for single mothers and benefits claimants.

The similarity of its name to Hampton Court had not been lost on him.

Peter Wallner was a former chef at a local hotel, a German apparently, and the body was soon identified as that of his wife Melanie, a South African woman who had once looked confident and alive, her blonde hair done up in an old-fashioned, somewhat regal style: she wore a large brown velvet jacket, looked sideways at the photographer with a full, toothy smile. Another photograph showed a bloated-looking man with a short pudding-bowl haircut and a sparse goatee, a cropped image in which he was sitting slumped on a brown sofa, his left arm behind his head, peering at something or somebody, his eyebrows raised imperiously above gold wire-framed glasses. He seemed to be watching television. An unidentifiable object which might have been a surfboard was propped against the white wall behind his sofa.

Of course, it had all been different once. He had launched his first gliders outside on the green, on towlines and lengths of shirring elastic stretched between cricket stumps. He remembered how one such hopeless homemade contraption, unsightly, slapped together by instinct, had caught a freak gust above the rooftops and kept going, disappearing from sight towards the lazily circling sprayers of the sewage farm on the far edge of the estate.

In the local and national press photos, Hamilton Avenue looked much as it always had. The neat fifties council houses, the clipped privet hedges: a fully realized version of somebody's idea of lower middle-class heaven; order, tranquillity, and very nice too. A little tent stood in the front garden of one of the semis, presumably to cover the site of the wheelie bin. There were police standing in yellow jackets, beside cars, and swathes of neutralising plastic incident tape, everything about their deployment suggesting an outbreak which had been successfully contained, reassuring the public of its restored security.

Turning into the estate from the alley behind the police station, where above the tall brick wall an air-raid siren had stood freshly painted on its pole in readiness, he had once daily crossed the front of the lock ups whose dented doors concealed no less dented cars, had turned again at the corner onto the estate proper past Norman's house where the school clarinetist would be forever practicing his scales, composing his sonata for clarinet and piano;

a shy, bespectacled, isolated boy with a deep dimple in his cheek when he smiled.

On his way out of the library he caught an unwelcome glimpse of his reflection in the glass door: a tallish, dumpy man in late middle-age with a shock of sticking-up white hair, not what he was inside at all, but there you are, there you go, he felt totally worn-out, and that he was definitely ambling towards the departure lounge.

Up at the top end of Tottenham Lane he spotted Ray Davies, frontman and songwriter of sixties pop group, The Kinks. Graham loved their music, he'd had the right kind of childhood, prancing around the next-door neighbours' sitting room. Ray's studio, Konk, was situated at the corner of a semicircular parade of Edwardian shops, semi-derelict, then refurbished, but still mostly unlet. The studio's wood-panelled door was topped by a small blue neon sign, which said KONK, lit up when the facility was in use. He sometimes wondered what was going on in there and if Ray Davies was in residence, rerecording his great hits with a children's choir.

Once he had seen him buying a packet of salted peanuts at the corner grocery, looking slender and youthful, as though this was all he was going to eat that day; another time he had been passing on the street and had noticed his awestruck stare through the window of the kebab shop as he lifted a small cheeseburger to his open mouth, returning it with a wry smile; on yet another occasion he had been waiting and chatting with a shorter, younger woman by the bus stop.

Ray Davies was talking to a dog. "Alright mate? Alright?" Graham heard him say, bending almost formally to shake paws with a large ornamental poodle tied-up to a rail outside the betting shop. He passed before he could catch the dog's reply. But his spirits were lifted. His heart filled up with gratitude to see the insouciant giver of much pleasure and instruction so evidently enjoying the company of a dog. No-one was ever going to say Ray Davies was stuck up. All around him the pedestrian traffic of Tottenham Lane flowed past obliviously.

He kept going, propelled by this apparition, this celebrity sighting, past his own turn-off and down the hill, past Hornsey rail station and right onto Turnpike Lane. He crossed the over at

Wightman Road just opposite the West Indian Cultural Centre with its giant etched stainless steel mural of palms, and headed down to Wood Green, feeling, as always, a little different as the skin colour of the other pedestrians gradually changed and the procession of Somali internet cafes, Mauritian restaurants, Indian takeaways, nail emporiums, hair shops specialising in threading, exotic fish and vegetable supermarkets, law shops and dentists, thickened up quickly towards Duckett's Common. He crossed over Turnpike Lane and turned left onto the High Road, pace slackening as he loitered down its length, savouring its jostling difference, and indifference; losing himself in the usual weekend throng.

Everything was going on down there. First of all in Maplins, the electronics specialists. Rack upon rack of conjunction boxes and multiple networking connector hardware of all kinds, gizmos for turning vinyl into mp3s, coils of whip-like cable and differently-abled DVD players filled up the centre of the shop, whose walls were lined with sentinel plasma screens of various dimensions, usually quite big. The shop wasn't however filled with customers – most people appeared to possess most of those things by now, and he himself wasn't in the market.

Instead he sought out a pyramid of radio-controlled cars and helicopters which usually dominated the window space, slavered over them for a while, and sought out the ever rarer twin-propeller aeroplanes. They were getting cheaper all the time, but also disappearing fast. He could see only a scuffed box or two promising all sorts of elegant controlled curves and acrobatics from airily suspended contraptions of polystyrene foam at the touch of a joystick; but did they really work? He remained unconvinced – he couldn't afford to speculate.

There were clothes shops where everything seemed to be under ten or twenty quid. Poundland, its side wall embellished by a Banksy. Little prayer stalls sold cheap phonecards; next to them large transparent washing-up bowls out of which wind-up furry monkeys attempted to climb to freedom. Coffee shops. McDonalds. On one corner was a huge Vietnamese restaurant with framed numbered colour photos of a hundred dishes, closed. Stalls which sold a bunch of bananas, a clutch of oranges, or a pound of apples in a plastic bowl for a quid. A man and a woman arguing some point of theology, gesticulating wildly, enjoying themselves; further down West Indian churches offering to help you get ahead with lifestyle advice, ran courses in it. Everybody called you boss.

Traid. They sometimes had good clothes in there and all the money went to fair trade organizations providing help for farmers and producers in the third world. He ventured in briefly and saw a young woman alphabetizing the books. He peered over her shoulder, but there was nothing he particularly fancied, except her. Outside again. Outside was good ... but today it was all too much for him. It was all so generic. He turned back on himself just before Wood Green Shopping Mall.

He turned along a side street, past the trendy little bookshop and the big café he had never entered and the Jamaican barbershop, making his slow way back to Rathbone Avenue. It didn't take him long. He kicked his shoes off and divested himself of most of his clothes and made himself a cup of coffee. Ahhh. That was much better. He turned on the TV and rapidly manipulated the Freeview box onto BBC Radio – soft pattering voices, familiar music, from the past, that good old mulch of everything that had once meant something to him, to other people. They had him taped, he had to admit. Mix-taped. He blew on his coffee, feeling the blissful blow-back of caffeine as it bounced off his dry eyes.

THREE

Ray Davies was beginning to mildly enjoy himself in the studio. The ordinary North London house he had converted decades earlier was filled with young musicians who admired him and wanted to record an album of his songs, sounding, if that was possible, exactly like the versions he had recorded decades earlier with The Kinks. Naturally each generation had its own sound as well as its own ideas about things, and a younger person would naturally interpret one of his songs in his or her own way, but somehow they only sounded right when the harmonies were the same and the identical guitar breaks came in exactly the same spots as they did on those old records which had made him so famous.

What was a song after all? He wasn't sure he even knew, although he had given a variety of answers over the years; as far as most listeners were concerned a song was the song it was by virtue of quite small, quite precise moments in it: a break in the voice which broke your heart, or playfully threatened to so do: a rinky-dinky organ part which reminded you of some childhood fairground, a large flat knife thudding into a board only a hair's-breadth away from the assistant's quickly revealed small breasts; your own heart thudding along tumultuously with hers. Those were the days alright – everybody knew it.

Abruptly, he decided they didn't need him anymore and wandered out into the back garden. Nobody was out there, just a yard or two of scrubby grass and breaking up cement surrounded by high brick walls, a few old chairs and the stacked equipment cases of the TV crew. Ray sat on the paint-spattered yellow seat of a scuffed old wooden kitchen chair. The sun had come out and he was feeling a customary sense of enjoyment. Being there in the moment. He enjoyed his thinness and the way his loose t-shirt showed he was still a thin man. Eating next-to-nothing helped, also the shape of his head, especially the shape of his head, with its long lugubrious clown's face, his mouth extending its long expressive corners, as though carved into it with a sharp stick of greasepaint.

He didn't need a mirror to tell him any of this, he knew it if he knew anything, he was tall and thin and slightly stooped, leaning forward inquisitively into the things of this world. But there you are. He decided to piss them all off by sliding out of the back door of the yard, down the alley and out into the other road for a wander … yeah, it was time for Ray to wander off and have a gander.

He resisted the temptation to sprint away down the hill, kept his head down and propelled himself rapidly past the curve of terraces, away past the flats and down to the zebra crossing which led to the gaping mouth of the new estate and its guardian pumping station converted into a large restaurant he had never frequented.

He didn't enter the estate with its recent flimsy but elegant-looking blocks which seemed constructed for a mildly futuristic film set, grids of rectangular panels dappled in lime green and pastel orange as though assembled from a child's architecture kit from the mid-sixties. Instead he crossed the sluggish New River and pushed his way through the old iron lych-gate which led onto the path running beside it for a couple of hundred yards.

The New River now had a modest pipe running along its length, presumably delivering water at higher pressure than the eighteenth century canal, even though it looked healthier than it used to. Perhaps it saved North London from flooding, he speculated, or maybe it was like a heart bypass operation taking the pressure off. It wasn't particularly pretty, but then nor were rusty shopping trolleys and bicycle wheels, so some people said. Still, he enjoyed the moorhens with their ducking and diving antics and a couple of pairs of swans, drifting for a little then flapping up onto the pipe with a great and mighty effort of wings to huddle and bask in the mild sunshine.

Ray looked up towards the majesty of Alexandra Palace, sprawled at the top of its hill, a visible embodiment of beauty, harmony and enlightenment still lifting its mighty beacon to the sky to broadcast to the enslaved peoples of the Earth that, well, somebody was listening to them, or they were listening to us, and those of us who lived in its shadow were also somehow uplifted by those messages written on the air. He of course remembered when the new estate wasn't there, and when the sixties estate behind it was also unbuilt, just a few streets of older houses and small engineering works, and the gypsy horse fair had taken place in the long meadow which lay tumbled below what was now Alexandra Park. Not that he had been particularly interested in all this, but still, it had once been so.

He carried on between the wire builder's fences which protected the new site of what looked like a hydroelectric dam – or was it a small sports arena of some sort? Just as he crossed the bridge to get out through the gate his path crossed that of a young girl walking up from the direction of the estate. She had short ginger hair, cut in a severe alien punk sort of style, an open child's face, wore jeans and a short-sleeved t-shirt, which revealed her arms to be covered in a riot of recent and colourful tattoos.

Ray couldn't help but clock them; fat coiled snakes, cobras probably, were twined around the voluptuous torsos of a pair of large-breasted Egyptian goddesses in some ancient but contemporary expression of exotic sensuality, looking for all the world like illustrations to James Thomson's *The City of Dreadful Night*. The girl caught his eye, hesitated and smiled slightly. She obviously didn't recognize him – he was just some old bloke on the path. Ray smiled back shyly, one corner of his clown's mouth snaking up an inch or so, and she passed on, bouncing prettily ahead of him, on a mission of some kind to Wood Green, disappeared out of the range of his poor eyesight. Ray stood there, halted in his tracks, looking back along the path she had come down, up at the looming row of new play brick blocks of flats whose charming Mediterranean balconies, he was pleased to notice, had already begun to fill up with broken furniture and half-dismantled bicycles.

When she was gone, he continued walking, soon entering the narrow railway arch, which was richly dank and scarred with layer upon layer of elderly graffiti, so if somebody had been walking along right behind him they would have seen his tall moving back outlined against the sun pouring into the end of it, breaking him up finally as he disappeared with a pop into the bright spotlight out there in the Wood Green industrial estate and cultural precinct.

He emerged into the brilliant light at the end of the tunnel, stopped and turned slowly this way and that. He found himself presented with three clear choices. He could turn right, which led around to Bateman's Café, which would probably be closed today, but past which he had sometimes enjoyed walking; straight on would lead him past the Chocolate Factory – which was not a chocolate factory – and out past that Turkish pub, the Duke of

York; a left turn would take him around the edge of the estate, past a primary school, and to the edge of a small park which stood at the bottom of Alexandra Park Road. This was the direction, he decided, now with a sort of angry boredom, to take. He walked around the long circling road – completely deserted – and when he arrived at the small park he sat on a bench in the centre of it, one of a number ranged on a path curving around a trellis, a covered walkway which reminded one of the gardens of a ruinous temple. Only there weren't no ruinous temple to be seen. He leaned back, pushed a fried chicken box to the ground with an angry flick, noted the already overflowing litter bins piled with discarded copies of Metro and similar boxes, stood up briefly to toss the offending fried chicken box on top of the pile, sat down, placed his long head in his hands, and wept.

He cried and cried and cried. At length he pulled himself together, finally reassembled his long lugubrious clown's face and went on his way up the long hill towards Alexandra Palace Station, turned right at the pub on the corner and headed for the palace itself. He was winded by the time he'd climbed up to the row of telescopes which stood before its shabby frontage and fumbled in his pockets for a coin or two, which he pressed into the slot of the old iron contraption as it slid around with surprising ease on its greased gimbal. He could see nothing at first, just a green blur like the freefall landscape in a bad acid effect video, but soon he was able to make out the distant towers of Canary Wharf. Just about visible. Beyond them? A speck on the horizon. Perhaps it was nothing more than a scratch on the lens of this big sliding dinosaur, maybe the glint of a pair of binoculars in an impossible distant shrouded place on the other side of town, in Richmond Park.

He wandered back into the studio as dusk was falling. Being as how he was Ray Davies no-one dared to ask him where the fuck he had been. Instead it was Ray, Ray, Ray this, Ray that. We're ready for you, Ray. Ready for your masterly lead vocal. Do you want to hear what we've got so far? Of course he fucking did, or maybe didn't. He put on the headphones and listened to a rough mix of the choral version of You Done Me Up. It didn't sound too bad, even with a bloody awful schoolgirl vocal ensemble keening away down in the mix; but an irritating tinny high up rattle kept cutting in on his right earpiece.

21

"What the fuck's that?" he asked.

"That's you playing the mouth-organ, Ray," somebody said, laughing at him.

Laughing at him!

"Listen, you cunt. I taught Mick Jagger to play the fucking mouth-organ." Ray smiled inimitably. "You're fucking sacked." At this moment his eye caught the glint of a lens in the corner of the control booth. One of those BBC twats was filming him. "Unless you can do it better yourself, that is."

Everybody laughed at Ray's joke.

After they'd wound up the session and the BBC had packed up and gone back to Maida Vale with their equipment Ray called a cab and headed back to the ranch. His living quarters were modest, in a street like many others in North London, and anyone who had knowledge of where exactly he resided was sworn to the utmost secrecy. Anyone who happened to type "Where does Ray Davies live?" into Google would be sorely disappointed. Ray hung up his coat in the hall and slouched through to the living room where one of his living companions was watching *Hair of the Dog*, a programme, as far as he'd been able to make out, which had nothing to do with dogs. It wasn't that Ray was uninterested in what his living companions watched, but he'd found, over the years, a certain mutual lack of curiosity worked well where living companions were concerned. He didn't have to provide daily explanation or what he was doing or thinking about, and neither did they, unless they were children. Who was really interested in your doings at the end of the day? Just some obsessive fan. Okay, he knew they existed, but preferred not to think about them.

"Hair of the God?" he asked idly.

"Hair of the Dog," the living companion seemed unwilling to look away from a large screen on which …

Ray went into the kitchen and opened one of the cupboards. One of the living companions had opened a packet of Highland Shortbread and eaten two of them. He snagged another from the tray with his finger and ate it, lifting and shaking the kettle, then snapping it on. Cup of tea, cup of tea. "Cup of tea?" he put his head around the living room door and called to the living companion.

"Not for me," the living companion replied.

Just then he heard a stomp stomping on the stairs. One of the other living companions was descending. He knew from the tread which one. "Cup of tea?" he half-heartedly called.

No answer. He heard the living room door creaking as the other companion went through, to watch whatever portion remained of Hair of the Dog. The word 'portion' made him think of Highland Shortbread. Sipping his own tea, and feeling instantly better, more relaxed, he took another finger from the packet and nibbled at it more frugally than he had the last. There was no way he was going to watch any of *Hair of the Dog*, so he climbed the stairs himself and went into his bedroom. This was a room which contained his bed and a number of other essential furnishings. He lay back on the bed, finished the shortbread and put down his tea mug on the bedside table. He lay there in semi-darkness. He liked the door to be ajar and light spilling in from the hall, and he liked a gap in the curtains so he could look out of the window.

Due to his oblique angle of repose he could see almost nothing; but he already knew what there was to see, so wasn't unduly troubled. He just liked the way the darkness pushed up against the window yet was somehow kept at bay, although some of it always seemed to spill down the wall, into a shadowy pool in which he had once seen a school of minute fish leaping and playing. He also liked the suggestion, although not sure where it came from, that there was light out there in the other houses. Over the hills and far away. The only tune he knew how to play. He lifted his cup to his lips and drained it completely, definitively.

FOUR

The murder story developed quickly; or more accurately, had already developed, as they do, coming to light in set stages and playing out to largely predictable conclusions. This time he had to watch it happen. Wallner and his twenty-three year old Maltese girlfriend had hired a VW camper van and left the country on May 15th. Its registration plate had been captured on Automatic Number Plate Recognition (ANPR) cameras on the M25 in Kent and close to the docks at Dover on the evening of May 17 with two people inside. Wallner was known to have bought two tickets for a cross-channel ferry that evening. The couple also had three dogs with them – two Jack Russells and a Staffordshire bull terrier. It appeared he had kept his wife's body in the freezer for three years, and dumped her in the wheelie bin before leaving after selling the house. The bin hadn't been emptied for three weeks because the binmen said it was too heavy, then a neighbour, concerned about foxes around the bin, managed to knock it over and "the grisly contents were revealed."

There was another photo of Wallner in a stupid woolly hat, this time with his girlfriend, a slim young woman, sitting on his knee in a woodland setting. He thought this was near Wisley Lake. He'd walked across it with his father during a big freeze in his boyhood. He felt his childhood places violated, despoiled by all this. People on the estate were afraid, panicking. On the Cobham Blogger a commenter floated a rumour that a child's body had also been found in the house, others said they were afraid to take their children out, and a local wit suggested Wallner's wife had dived headfirst into the bin as a way of committing suicide. Others broke down into indecipherable syllables of rage and unhappiness. The blogger himself remained jocular, and even-handed, throughout, as if the situation wasn't particularly real to him:

> Well, what is there left to say about the crime of the century in Cobham? All eyes appear to be on our once sleepy town. Hands up if you live on the estate and haven't had your door knocked on by a reporter or TV crew. It seems like only yesterday we were innocently moaning about Chelsea flags.

His recollections of the estate poured back, as memories will after a death; it had always had its dangerous side: its share of people who might unexpectedly smack you in the gob when you were out walking the dog around the gasholders. But there was also the sweeter tug of the river Mole, which had lain at the foot of a long, sloping meadow, often waterlogged, and had sometimes contained a herd of cows that would run at you, on the weed-clogged stretch that flowed past the convent and a shady cricket ground within the latched, bar-gated lane of Burwood Park.

The Mole was a burrowing river, as the name suggested, but where it first surfaced he didn't remember. Just a weed-strewn and sluggish course along a broken path of mud-sluiced otter holes; funnels of midges; beige pillars of ash; crumbling paper towers of hexagonal seed pods, ready, close to the hand, to be crushed. Sometimes he and his childhood friends had swum in it, breast-deep in minnows. In a concatenation of memories, its roiling, rushing waters were bridged several times, glass-combed over a long weir beside the high wall of a hidden garden, with a rotten green door, which he now knew to have once been the property of Charles Hamilton, the 18th century owner and builder of Pain's Hill House and its gothic grounds.

Nowadays this pile was open to the public; in those days it had been wild, neglected and shut tight. Denholm Eliot, the actor, used to live in an apartment there, and his father had found an ancient Stutz roadster encased in vines near the old house; but they had been uninterested in him making an offer for it.

The river flowed onwards under the windows of a sixties-built estate, its penetrable, honey-coloured bricks – the same as those used for Oakdene Parade – named after Matthew Arnold, the Victorian poet and schools inspector who lived in a cottage there and climbed the hill for his evening constitutional and to play billiards with the contemporary owner. Matthew Arnold Close. He'd delivered newspapers there, hopping off and on the heavy trades bike on a round that had passed through bar-gated Burwood Park, and circled back again all the way down the Seven Hills Road – a number of spurts and freewheels, a final long no-hands flight down Pains Hill, over Cobham Bridge to the flats and home.

The stream flowed past some bushes clumped around builders' waste, away across some horse-fields, parallel, curling, and then was cut over by a sort of humpy bridge, turned into a green water snake crawling at the foot of St Andrew's church, where Gerrard Winstanley had held the office of churchwarden in later life, with responsibility for the poor of the parish.

It flowed past the end of the village, crackling over sharp gravel shallows, and at the old mill he remembered drooping willow trees whose pale green fronds had lightly touched the surface of the deep rushing waters; on the far bank blond wheat had stood bolt upright, bolt upright in a field they weren't supposed to set foot in, but which was too inviting not to wade to. In the floods of '67 an inland lake had lapped at the end of the High Street, stretching away as far as a horizon of elm trees that reached up, waving or drowning, beyond Downside.

Perhaps it was the River Mole which had suggested the underground stream of a buried life to Matthew Arnold, self-knowledge set free as a hitherto buried life-force breaks surface.

> A bolt is shot back somewhere in our breast,
> And a lost pulse of feeling stirs again.
> The eye sinks inward, and the heart lies plain,
> And what we mean, we say, and what we would, we know.
> A man becomes aware of his life's flow,
> And hears its winding murmur; and he sees
> The meadows where it glides, the sun, the breeze.

Arnold had sometimes referred to himself as the Hermit of the Mole, which of course wasn't true, he was just another affluent poseur with mutton-chop whiskers. Graham wished there had been a real one, a real hermit in a cave by the riverbank, wished it could have been him. Then Peter Wallner washed up again suddenly on Dover Beach. According to The Cobham Blogger: "He rang Surrey Police from Malta to see what all the fuss was about." They duly arrested him at Gatwick Airport, his girlfriend was detained on a secondary charge, and suddenly, predictably, it all seemed to be over bar the hushed delivery of a verdict.

The blogger had closed his comments section down following a stream of bile, distress and macabre 'jokes', but in the brief interregnum before Wallner's Old Bailey appearance, he decided to lighten things up by posting a humorous account of an historic crime:

Cow thief on his way to farmer's market
sentenced to death

Murder suspect Peter may have not faced the Old Bailey yet but here's another Cobhamite who had a brush with the law.

Old Bailey records from 1768 show William Cayley was spotted driving a cow through Weybridge on December 11 between eight and nine in the morning when the suspicions of a watching butcher's son were first raised.

He questioned Mr Cayley who said he had bought the heifer fairly for four guineas and a half and was on his way to Cobham Fair.

When the witness, Thomas Keen, went to Cobham Fair and questioned him a bit more, he did a runner.

Mr Keen later heard a heifer had been stolen from Hounslow. At the court hearing Mr Cayley, who was also accused of stealing a horse, did not say anything in his own defence.

He was found guilty by the judge and sentenced to death.

Nevertheless, it seemed the journalistic future of the Cobham Blogger was in doubt. His circulation hadn't been boosted for long by the wheelie bin murder, and continuing to inform a non-existent public had obviously become an onerous chore for him. The crime past and present feature seemed a bit obtuse. His most devoted reader thought it was a pity he hadn't gathered more local interest. And, once again, he was forced to wonder what any of this had to do with him, really. In moments of clarity it seemed a strange thing to do, an odd choice on his part to take an interest in this murder just because it happened to happen on the street where he'd tried to make a start on growing up.

Graham was moving around his flat in a semi-trance. He believed he was looking for something, just something he'd put down somewhere, maybe his glasses, maybe an envelope with a scribbled address on it, one of his students perhaps, his blessed tutees, a contact he was supposed to make firmly within twenty-four hours. He gave up and went through into the kitchen to run the hot water onto the stack of dirty plates.

He caught sight of a small darting light brown mouse with a stout more-than-a-baby tail whisking after it as it scuttled for cover under his cheese-encrusted sandwich maker. He froze suddenly, looking around for a handy shoe with which to bash it. Of course there wasn't one. He wondered where it had come from. It seemed to be aware that the hole under the water boiler had been securely blocked with a plastic bag, which is why it hadn't made its usual long, highly visible break for safety around the rim of the work surface. It was cowering under the sandwich maker as expected. "Boo," he said loudly. But the mouse didn't stir. "Boo," he said again, fully aware of, and actually enjoying, just how pathetic he was being. He silently placed the cups in the washing up bowl, reached out towards the sandwich machine with extended fingertips – like it was going to run out and bite him – and moved it slightly to one side.

The heroic rodent took off on its run, confused at first, but not making the mistake of heading for the boiler. Instead it darted under a clutch of crumpled plastic shopping bags, which rustled mightily but failed to entangle it. On a previous occasion a mouse had run into an open plastic bag and thrashed around fiercely and ineffectually. He had been forced to bash and bash at it with his shoe, killing it until it was stone dead.

This time the little mouse made it through the bags, jumped off the edge of the kitchen unit and disappeared behind the large overflowing bookcase he had lugged up the stairs years ago, empty. That was it. There was definitely a real odour to mice. Definitely. He smelled it now. Pungent, sour. Still, he could do what he was able to disperse it. He ran the sink full of hot water, cleared and mopped his work surfaces, and washed up a few things.

FIVE

He found himself on the top deck of the 121 bus on the way to his Saturday afternoon tutorial. The journey ground on interminably through Southgate with its village green, ye olde half-timbered pub and pricy restaurants, down a tunnel of greenery, past a golf course and open field vistas which made you feel you'd left London altogether, until you dipped down into Enfield Chase, another affluent village with a tucked away millionaires' row of new luxury dwellings thrown up behind it, bulbous new teapots with clusters of large black retro-looking 4 x 4s on their forecourts, roads with names like Vermont Drive, luxury apartment blocks christened in honour of social elevation and traditional values with old names like Marlborough House and Claremont Mansions.

At the end of one of those avenues lived Yupar McMannus, a tiny Burmese girl who wanted to be a fighter pilot and an engineer. He taught her while her lovely parents drowsed on the couch. Her father was a wheelchair-bound actor and writer, her elegant mother who sometimes sewed spangled costumes for their productions of musical dramas in traditional dress. Her mother met him at the door, and Yupar would sometimes bowed him out in front of a tall, flaking theatrical mirror. On the mantelpiece stood a Burmese harp, which Yupar played, never for him, and through the doors at the back of their ground floor flat a screened landscape sloped down behind its traditional mask of trees, of tumbling vistas driven over by golfers from the nearby clubhouse.

Yupar had soon caught fire with English. She was already confident, and had only to iron out her tendency common amongst peoples with ideogrammic languages to leave out articles. Several Burmese characters looked like purring cats with curly tails, and their women did indeed seem to possess insinuating, feline qualities. Yupar was soon high-spiritedly mimicking Curley's wife in *Of Mice and Men*, a foul-mouthed, ignorant creature, unravelling the intricacies of traditional English love poetry with creased brow. She wrote a piece about her Burmese grandmother, how she made chicken curry in a traditional oven and threw most of it out for the birds; and once, when she was over on a visit, he had met this tiny, dignified, bent over lady, who silently placed a glass of water before him.

Yupar showed him some photographs on the computer of a man who had risen up to heaven in a balloon, and of herself in RAF cadet uniform, considerably shorter than the others, strutting along, eyes right, looking for all the world like a young devotee of Kim Il Sung. She couldn't wait to be a pilot in the British air force, when she would be proud to blast those fucking Taliban scumbags to Kingdom Come. Her eyes flashed dramatically as she said this.

He enjoyed his visits to this outpost of the Republic of the Union of Myanmar, but today he stayed on the bus as it crept out further, past the squashed Rolo tube stations that were dotted along those ends, alongside ribbons of straight road and stretches of dual carriageway, thrown up warehouses and prefabricated business and retail parks. Here the landscape took on a dusty, flyblown look, until, taking you by surprise, Enfield village itself appeared – a bustling home counties small town with a shopping centre – and beyond it were row upon row of Edwardian terraced teapots strung between a succession of one-horse settlements: a couple of pubs, a few cafes and takeaways, shops selling fitted kitchens, white goods, lampshades and various other kinds of thing which he never bought and could scarcely register even in passing.

Somewhere in the middle of this nowhere a nutcase had got on the bus and sat behind him, speaking the names of various warehouses they passed – B&Qs, Asda, Debenhams, a major pharmaceutical chain – and weaving them into an ad hoc conspiracy which had resulted in his recent incarceration in a secure facility. What scum they all were, these tinpot lying doctors and their fucking Jewish paymasters.

Finally, excruciatingly, they ground past a sign which said Freezywater. He hopped off near a roundabout, crossed the road and walked down another long street (all roads in outer Enfield seemed to stretch along like this, to infinity, and strewn with empty bottles and discarded drug paraphernalia) to the home of Caprice Blount. He straightened his tie and ran a hand through his hair, hoping he still looked sufficiently like a teacher to pass the fortnightly audition.

Caprice's mother was concerned about her poor performance in AS level English. Her daughter was doing the AQA Language and

Literature syllabus, with which he wasn't particularly familiar, but he had decided to rely on strong eye contact and a knowledgeable manner. She was a pleasant, comfortable, buxom girl who had just begun to discover she had something there, smiling, friendly and straightforward. A little withheld maybe, slightly lacking in confidence, and after he had tried to explain something she would always say: "Thank you, I understand that now." Sometimes she complained about her regular teacher, how she had refused to mark some of her work or had snubbed her in some way. Caprice suspected her of incompetence because she was Russian and didn't seem to speak English properly.

Her handwriting was large and irregular, which looked a bit scruffy, but when he read her pieces through there were seldom any grammatical or spelling mistakes. Like many teenagers she was unsure what she wanted to do with her life – perhaps she could be a psychologist (she liked the subject at school), or a psychiatric nurse (she thought that sounded interesting), or perhaps she would go to university and study English literature. She enjoyed reading. Poetry was a little more difficult for her – she couldn't always see what Carol Ann Duffy and the rest of them were getting at; but when he talked her through a poem she usually said: "Thank you, I understand that now."

As part of her AS English she had to produce commentaries on excerpts of transcribed reported speech from ordinary conversations or from the media. In these exercises you had to note features like ellipsis, repetition, stalling, parallelisms, or face-threatening: a direct insult to the speaker), He hadn't heard most of the technical vocabulary before, but it was fairly easy to pick up and explain on sight.

"Thank you," Caprice would say hesitantly, with her charming smile. "I understand that now."

He thought the excerpts needed interpretation and she should try to read them like poems. Try to see what was going on under the surface of these interactions between people – a conversation which revealed all too clearly, for example, what boys thought about girls; an odd, gnomic exchange about the availability of a Wi-Fi connection in a Greek taverna, but she explained quickly they had been told not to do this. All that was required was to identify speech features correctly.

They worked together at a large round dining table in an immaculate room which opened onto their luxurious open-plan fitted kitchen and the allotted hour soon slid past. He thought of it as the Immaculate Conception as he slid into his halting dictation on the subjects in hand – Harold Pinter, Tennessee Williams, Angela Carter. He was as ever concerned to be helpful and to give full value for money, but Caprice always stopped him right on the hour. On one occasion her father had walked through the room to get to the kitchen and shot him a quick smile; another time her younger brother walked through the room, and dropped a twenty-pound note from his back pocket on the polished wood-block floor. He called after him and pointed it out: "I'm a teacher. I can read the serial number from here." The boy smiled at him, thanked him and repocketed the cash.

He couldn't help noticing that her family – and many of the others – usually spoke to him as if they thought he was of a higher social class than they were; but although he had a compulsion to disabuse them of this misperception, it was a game not without risk. Being well-educated was associated by an overwhelming majority of people with middle-class status, with being well-spoken and all the rest of the malarkey. Why else would they trust him and employ him to help their children? Because he was capable of writing her moving reminiscences of her grandmother, a woman she had hardly known.

"It's called creative writing," he explained.

Outside again he reflected that there probably wouldn't be too many more sessions with Caprice. He was sorry about this. Somehow he took a shine to some families, he just couldn't get enough of them. He liked being a guest in their houses and wished he could hang around with them forever. But the long and short of it and the fatal truth was that Caprice didn't need him any longer. He would again be a victim, not of his success as a teacher, but of his tutee's clear-sightedness.

Back on the main drag he decided to walk down into Freezywater and see what it had to offer by way of entertainment. Nothing much, it seemed at first. He checked his emails again at a rickety computer in a ramshackle internet café, then walked a little further along the same parade. Here, to his joy, he discovered an ultimate rarity: a model shop. He pushed in through the door; a bell clanged, announcing his presence to the two men behind the counter. They scarcely looked up from their engrossed conversation about model aeroplanes.

Hanging from the shop's ceiling and ranged around its walls was a wide selection of radio-controlled models, some prefabricated, some to be built from scratch from wooden or plastic parts; some with gas or electric powerplants the likes of which he had never seen before. White hot glowplugs and highly inflammable Jetex engines were obviously things of the edgy, unregulated past. But a closer look around showed most of the old stuff still to be available; a small outfit in the West Country turned out replica kits similar to the old Keil Kraft lines, computer cut for greater accuracy and ease of assembly – and the serious modeller still tended to prefer a miniature two-stroke engine to anything else.

The bigger kits were as prohibitively expensive as they had been when he was a kid. It was the German lines which now interested him most (hadn't they always, really, been better at everything?) – light, strong, prefabricated, electric-powered, with cheap microchip radio controllers. On the wall a screen showed a silent DVD of beautiful, elegant gliders made of space shuttle materials with a rear-pusher electric propeller, soaring and pirouetting in the ozone-laden skies of the Black Forest, piloted by a slender technician who had had to do no more than clip it together straight from the box. These were relatively cheap too, prices were plummeting as if any slashing of profits were justified in order to lure young people away from the evil war games and towards this enchanting poetry of imaginary flight.

Post-lesson he found himself waxing super-articulate, as usual, in his head, too late to be of whatever use super-articulacy had ever been to anybody. He left the shop, largely to get away from his own voice in his head. The men behind the counter – one old, one young – had already spotted him for a nut-case and quickly resumed their animated conversation about a forthcoming WW2 replica fly-off in which Stuka and Spitfire would soon be contesting once and for all who would be master of the skies over Enfield Lock.

He walked on further down the High Street, raging with hunger now as the lesson faded, deciding a sausage roll would be his choice for damage limitation, and popped into Gregg's the bakers at the corner of Turkey Street. Here he queued at the hot counter, ignoring a young man who had been laid out with his jacket under his head on the floor by staff. The guy's head turned slowly from side to side, half-closed eyes flickering in rapid eye movement as he dreamed the other dream of flight, slightly more affordable, almost effortless, apparently, and quite popular in these parts.

He ate the hot sausage roll delicately as he walked to Turkey Street station along a deep trickling culvert which was the only sign of water, freezy or otherwise, to be seen here. Mounting to the empty platform above a road bridge, he waited for the train to glide in from cozy old market town Bishop's Stortford. Then he would jump off at Seven Sisters, wait for ages at a crowded, jockeying bus stop where some of the jostling people seemed to have found time to fall asleep in camping chairs on the pavement, and catch an interminably slow 41 bus back to his crib.

SIX

In the aftermath of the trial a leaked police video of Wallner's interrogation was posted on YouTube, presumably by the police, so everybody could judge him for themselves. He couldn't see why this was either necessary or good, but watched it all the same. "I'm not going to lie to you," Wallner said. "I just don't remember." This was about the sleep mask found over his wife's face, which would have made it impossible for her to have been chasing him with a steak knife as he had claimed. His own wounds were self-inflicted. Still, it was also impossible not to conjure up the image of a blinded woman attempting to wreak revenge on her husband, and the husband beating her to the ground with a heavy Le Creuset pan. There still no explanation as to why a killer of such deviousness and cold-blooded cunning as to bludgeon his wife to death so he could spend his birthday with his girlfriend, buy a freezer from Asda, transport fake ashes from the barbeque to her parents in South Africa, tell them she had died in her sleep from a brain aneurism, all the while enacting the most heartfelt grief (perhaps genuine as he realized the likely consequences of his act?) could also be so stupid, three years later, as to dump her frozen body in a house he was moving out of due to unpaid rent. He had a new young girlfriend, but his life was falling apart.

He remembered feeling something like this. A confession, one last leap into oblivion, a fresh start he no longer believed in. Sentencing him to twenty-five years, the judge said he had displayed calculating deceit from start to finish, but what reasonable person could possibly think a woman's body would be overlooked by the dustmen, crushed and disposed of painlessly, unidentified, and why so easily give himself up? He was sick of running? His new girlfriend's parents watched Sky News? The services of Holmes and Watson had not been required. Melanie's parents, articulate people whose pain and loss had been compounded by his lies and treachery, were "heartbroken and angry at the same time", gratefully praised the police for their tireless work. Wallner had lied to so many people over such a long period, his colleagues, his girlfriends, and them, for whom he had woven a tale that his own parents were dead, as a way of gaining their sympathy, and so distracted them from his inability to produce her death certificate.

The Cobham Blogger was no longer posting on the subject, his last word being a story via the *Daily Mirror* reporting on the "sickos" who had been traipsing around the house as soon as it was put on the market. He thought them to be innocent would-be home owners rather than ghouls. How many people have moved into a place where somebody recently died, in a sense because of it? A lot of us. How many of us had speculated wildly and got all the details and the outcome wrong? A rueful majority, who were no longer following him.

He typed the names of several people he hadn't seen for thirty years into Google and rapidly scrolled through the first few entries to see if any of them had been up to anything interesting, or more to the point, anything publically visible. This would have been impossible in ages past, although, of course, the impulse had always been there. Nowadays you could sit in an Internet café on Tottenham Lane and just do it. One of his old girlfriends – or rather the successful company of which she was CEO – had been awarded a gigantic business grant to help them further extend their already near total hegemony in the Smoothies industry. He wondered how you would go about doing that – getting that – but he didn't know anything really.

He remembered her as a game girl with a jutting chin, but only vaguely now, and, as he fully realized, she was therefore somebody who no longer actually existed. He would give anything to be sitting with her in some pub in Kilburn, or anywhere, even in one of those instant neon cocktail bars of the day, near where she used to live, boozing and chatting the night away in a conversation sustained by nothing except a sort of good feeling they'd managed to keep going between them. Except they hadn't, they didn't. Another acquaintance of ages past twittered away like a song thrush, preening himself on his daft opinions to an audience of no-one, or ninety-nine to be precise.

He remembered this man as witty, self-mocking, and responsive to him. Could it be the light you saw in people's eyes was just a trick of the mind, something they turned on, or maybe no more than a blue flickering reflection like that produced by a computer screen?

Screen-burn. One of his old PCs had had it badly, now everybody else did too, he thought. The Internet revealed new things about people, anyway new to him. When you met up with one of them they recycled a selection of their recent tweets, which somewhat undermined previous impressions of being personally addressed. It was so banal, as was all this middle-aged anguish. What did it all amount to? Nothing!

He'd been quite willing to take somebody like Julian Assange as a hero, a Gary Numan lookalike for the digital age: the man who sold the world back to the original owners, or gave it away free, or something like that. Somebody who defied the most powerful people on Earth to tell us what our governments were really doing. But now he was supposed to be a rapist, just another sleaze bag. Like everybody else. Che Guevara, he was so-called iconic, women at the bus stop still sometimes had his picture on their everyday shoulder bags, they loved him. He knew he'd never see anyone carrying a Julian Assange shoulder bag, not any more, not ever in his actual experience, but still, it was all a great pity.

The internet seemed infinitely more fragile than paper. Unlike Guevara, he thought, Julian Assange was going to disappear without trace, not publically mourned, nor remembered. No longer to be anybody's amigo.

He went back to the flat and lay down on his bed. He turned off the lights and listened to some music on the radio through his TV set. He looked up again at the shadow of the glider on his ceiling; its wide looped wings and tail-plane shining brighter than ever before, he thought, in the light of his new Halogen heater, soaring higher and higher in the synthetic thermal this glaring appliance instantly created. It was like taking part in a rallying event as a rabbit in somebody's headlights. They should give out a free pair of sunglasses with these things, he thought, but couldn't quite bring himself to turn the thing off. He needn't have bothered. One by one the filaments burned out, and within a fortnight the last one had popped like a giant flashbulb. He didn't bother to replace them, just threw the heater away.

He went back to rereading Graham Greene's wartime thriller, *The Ministry of Fear,* an orange sixties paperback he'd found in a local charity shop. He wondered what he'd most liked about Greene, what had always made him so readable, so returnable to, apart from having the same name friendly English name as himself. Mainly the locations, he realized, the London squares, shabby boarding houses, the Lyons corner houses, dark trains, antiquated tailor shops, sausage rolls, clichéd greenery, Mass Observation and Esperanto: the thousand details of contemporary life in his books, their apparent nostalgia for times which had been present at the time of writing. It seemed gross somehow that whatever had been going on in the world – the Spanish civil war, the Second World War, the thirties seaside gangsters, postwar reconstruction – this ubiquitous novelist's ever-fertile if repetitive brain had been on hand to offer up in his latest thriller with its appropriate backdrop and formulaic plot devices.

In this one his protagonist might definitely be called nostalgic. He had been born before the First World War and was living through the second as a guilty amnesiac who remembered croquet on the lawn, vicars with floppy sun hats, and mercy killing a rat with a broken back, and doing away with his sick wife, with a glass of warm milk. But for the present reader – and he guessed there weren't many left – it was the atmosphere of times past, of years in his own family's past but beyond the reach of his own recollection, which made them so compelling.

Greene seemed to know all this and more about his reader, but maybe he himself had been aware of the transitoriness of the present, enough to always regret its passing, hyper-aware of the temporariness of his moment as it rushed away into the oblivion of yesterday. It was this he had wished to capture, and all the conspiracies of spies and their unlikely McGuffins – the cake, the vacuum cleaner, the message which must be forwarded or stopped, the watered-down penicillin – were simply a vehicle for this chase after fleeting senses of things, hopeless romances with unlikely young women, things passing like shadows.

He'd known what people wanted, anyway, what kept them turning his pages; but had he really been so morally profound? Guilt wouldn't do nowadays. It was considered to be a great evil. He raced through the brittle, yellow pages and tossed the novel off the end of his bed, wondering briefly if it would ever be picked up again. Probably. Arthur Rowe and Harry Lime would still be going strong when he had faded. Sometime in the future those succinct, vivid evocations of everyday life under aerial bombardment, and how it might have felt to accept possible death by fire every night, would be springing to life in somebody else's head.

SEVEN

Ricky Greaves fed his arthritic cat – called Molly – and let her out of the back door of his flat, which led down a narrow flight of stairs to a cat flap into the backyard, which was paved in spanking pale pink flagstones. Ricky's flat was immaculate, but the back stairs (the toilet stood at the top of them) were pure cat country. The carpet, which had been torn to shreds by Molly's claws, smelled rank and stood up in electrified tufts from top to bottom, and to his occasional visitors seemed like a clogged back passage of his mind overgrown with some horrible fungus, leading to inner darkness, maybe. But in Ricky's scheme of things it was simply Molly's space.

Coming out of the toilet Ricky glanced down – she was paused at the cat flap, a justified and ancient being who had temporarily forgotten her purpose – "Molly!" he called encouragingly – and the cat came instantly to life and disappeared through her flap, dragging her limp tail behind her. At the sink Ricky quickly cleared the washing up, then loaded the cafetiere, poured in hot water, and leached a fragrant cup of Brazilian coffee into his favourite small white cup. He found big mugs were too much for him nowadays.

He went into the living room and drew back the curtains on his wide expanse of first floor window. He didn't bother to look out at the quiet empty street. Nothing much ever disturbed the peace of Mortlake, not even a broken bottle or a pizza box, and nothing, he concluded with an elastic yawn, ever would. The giant plasma TV screen with its flanking pinhead speakers – more powerful than the Titanic's foghorn or the sound system of the early Isle of Wight festivals – rested silently, as though waiting for a crowd of kids to file in for Saturday morning pictures. They would never come, a pity. On his shelves were rows of DVDs, a book library of sorts – H.P. Lovecraft, August Derleth, every word which had ever been published about the exploits of Conan the Barbarian – and, a stack of very old driving licences stretching back to the twenties (these had belonged to his father); on his walls were photograph-based portraits of Charlie Parker and John Coltrane, meticulously pencilled for him by a Czech lady he'd once met; a coloured etching of the relief of Mafeking (he was no simple-minded imperialist);

opposite the plasma screen stretched a large comfy sofa, a couple of nice looking chairs positioned on either side of it; on the floor was a lovely old alto saxophone which gleamed invitingly, invisibly within its closed plush-lined case.

Further to vigorous tooth brushing, meticulous flossing and a brisk go round with his hair-brush Ricky went back into his bedroom, put on a sweatshirt and a pair of vinyl cycling shorts, and hung a pair of binoculars round his neck. He was ready to go out for his morning constitutional. By the front door he sat on the stairs and – first checking them for smooth running – strapped on his roller blades. Closing the front door behind him, affixing a grin of embarrassment to his face for the sake of any curious neighbours who may have noted his eccentricity, he skated away down the leafy street in the direction of nearby Richmond Park.

Such a beautiful spot, a lovely stretch of the river, just about as good as it got, with a preserved bridge, a station, a great old village stuffed with pubs and delis and restaurants, a green, and a snaky old road leading off towards Barnes Common. Ricky liked to jog along the towpath; nodding at and offering a warm good morning to any female joggers he passed, contemplating the braced scullers and the opposite bank in the early morning mist. He particularly loved a watercolour of Tom Girtin's (the painter of whom Turner had said that if he had lived he, Turner, would have starved). 'The White House at Chelsea' must have been painted a bit further downriver, actually: a dream landscape of unearthly delicacy, its windmills barely touched into existence, the blazing white paper of the house itself showing through; a strong focal point like the iris of God almighty. A framed print of it hung on the wall of his bedroom.

Struggling into the park, he got a second wind and treated himself to a victorious elegant twirl. Richmond Park with its clouds of distant deer, toppled trees and managed wildlife, an undulating ribbon of grey road running through it, a ribbon down which cyclists and other roller-bladers sprinted and freewheeled, each enclosed in his or her own bubble of concentration and self-communion. He lifted his binoculars and checked out a young woman – tall, splendid and proudly erect – as she sped down the distant incline from the far gate. She was wearing gear identical to his own, relaxed, self-possessed, and with an air of effortless deserved riches Surrey women seemed to possess as a gift. She was also a foot taller than him, but at least the roller-blades and plenty of practice lent him something of her speed and grace. He skated out onto the road and began to labour up it in time to see her go past on the opposite side and she glanced at him with a friendly half-smile on her lips.

Ricky put his head down and strove manfully on, going for the burn (no point coming out if you didn't do it properly, didn't suffer for your moments of joy) until he got nearly to the top of the hill, where he stopped, gasping, for a short rest. This was the spot in the park he liked best, the point of greatest vista and vantage. He stretched his aching calves and steadied himself against a neatly lopped tree trunk to survey his domain.

He put his binoculars to his eyes and looked away into the distance. Over the hills and far away. The tall young woman had disappeared; others skated around at the foot of the hill. More cyclists approached from both directions, dedicated exercise fiends like himself; a few morning trampers in buttoned up Barbours were following the paths of badgers and foxes; a cloud of what must be small deer darted like midges at the periphery of his vision. From where he was positioned the river was invisible, as was most of the rest of London, just a residue of thin consommé in the bottom of a soup plate, and the furthest, highest points looked like white palaces on a wooded hillside. One of these, he thought, must be Alexandra Palace, high on its distant summit. For a second he thought he caught the glimmer, the speck-like flash of an answering telescope pointed in his direction. Somebody else looking across the city and seeing nothing, really, just the hazy limits of things.

He let them drop against his chest and struggled back onto the road through Richmond Park. He pulled his sunglasses down onto his face and powered down the slope in racing posture: this was what he had really come out for, the most satisfying moment of his week, which otherwise consisted of a daily commute to Bracknell, in Berkshire, to tend a no longer state-of-the-art aspect of his firm's computer system on which he was an acknowledged and well paid expert. They couldn't get rid of him without replacing the entire system at a cost of millions.

In the evenings there was mild cookery, desultory takeaways, rubbish films, usually dealing with hand to hand combat, and, more often than not, early to bed. But why should he die? Why should he give up? He was still fit and healthy, the power of reason hadn't yet deserted him, and there was a massive – and healthy – rush to be got from powering downhill on a pair of roller-blades. Fucking right. The clean air bucked into his lungs and he felt himself soaring, soaring, clear and hard and high above it all. Where the fuck else would he want to be? The deer he might have chased were irrelevant now, the girls might even turn and admire him, and none of it really belonged to anyone, except him, or to him as much as anyone else. After all, he was a member of the fucking public and a fucking taxpayer in this fucking country, wasn't he?

At the bottom of the long ribbon of downhill road he coasted to a slow halt, turning his toes out and flexing his knees into what ballet dancers called a plié position in order to draw a firm circular full stop below the long exclamation mark of his run. Ahh. Ahh. Ahh. It was absolutely great, like hearing a massive peal of bells clamouring in his head. He straightened up and skated in that position, arms clasped behind him, out through the lower gates and back through the streets of lower Mortlake to his empty flat.

Indoors again he peeled off his skating clothes and showered quickly before dressing in jeans and a fresh sweatshirt. He put on his album of the early Miles quintet and savoured its splendiferous post-bop arabesques while sitting on the middle of his couch with one ankle cocked up on his knee, his head raised slightly as through sniffing the air, twirling a lock at the back of his hair in a compulsive gesture he had retained from his teenage years. He was soon bored and restless again, it was always this way, and as usual he felt a stirring towards mischief of some kind. He wondered whether he should boot up one of the computers and give somebody a hard time – really take the piss out of him – online, but most of his victims had grown wary lately, or maybe just weary of his aggressively self-important antics. And now here was nobody left to do anything with or to.

It was a shame really, he wasn't such a bad bloke at bottom, just a bit obsessive about winning at everything; but he wasn't a terrifically popular man. He collected for charities sometimes, set up webpages off his own bat, did sponsored runs, and made reasonably handsome donations of his own to get the ball rolling, but somehow it never seemed to roll very far. His good qualities weren't noticed, or not properly rewarded. His generous impulses were real, and they just kept rolling, kept welling up in him, but something equal and opposite always seemed to cancel them out. That's the way it had been with Lana too – she'd found him obsessive, almost grasping, always wanting more, too much really. All she had been after was a roll and a tumble now and then when her husband became particularly irksome to her, but Ricky hadn't been able to see it clearly. He couldn't look at any situation as it was and make the best of it – and now Lana (he had loved her passionately for many years) was a situation which no longer existed for him.

Reluctantly he stood up and went into his bedroom, and pulled out his latest toy from the bottom of the wardrobe. It was a radio-controlled helicopter. His sister – how did the silly bitch get away with her greedy, selfish life? – had bought it for him last Christmas. He carefully pulled it out of its box, eased away the protective polystyrene, switched it on and stood it on the bedside table. He turned on the controller and pointed it at the helicopter, pushing the joystick forward to obtain maximum upthrust.

The rotor turned and almost at once the machine flopped feebly off the table, kicked around violently on the floor, and attempted – almost successfully – to crawl away under his bed. He released the stick and patiently picked it up. Tried again. Same result. Again. This time it headed for the wardrobe, but not for even a few seconds did it soar towards the ceiling as it had on Christmas morning at his sister's house in Camberley. It was fully charged though. He wondered if the rotor was out of alignment, but it seemed absolutely fine to him. Batteries were fully charged. He couldn't fathom it. Perhaps they designed these things to work only once.

At last he picked up the miniature chopper, easily crushed it to pieces in his hands, crammed those broken pieces back into the box, into which he also forced the radio controller and battery charger, carried said box before him like a piece of dog doings in a plastic bag, out of his flat, and downstairs, where he dropped it into the open mouth of his wheelie bin.

EIGHT

Graham got off the bus outside Tottenham Hale rail station and crossed into Ashley Road, signed in at the desk and threaded his way through to the back of the suite of offices where Yemi was putting her Back to Work tutor group through its weekly paces. Yemi, their life coach, liked to improvise, to ask questions which were easy to answer. One of her hits had been to get everybody in the class to talk about their favourite ice cream and why they liked it, and she liked to set riddles about who deserved to survived on a leaky lifeboat - everybody deserved to survive in her view - and he and the others went along with it, they had to, admiring her, encouraging her mildly to drift off topic, which she did readily, telling them all about her recent holiday in Dubai.

Today, as usual, they were in groups of three or four. Paul was in the group, a short scruffy guy with long dreadlocks whose hobby was racing model cars and who had once worked as a runner for the BBC. The others were a woman from Mozambique and an African guy in a baggy car coat who always laughed at everything he said: a charming man. In a sudden burst of friendly energy he managed to persuade his group that it was the one-armed man, the pregnant woman and the retired police officer who should man the radio by the wrecked plane, while the others hacked through surrounding jungle. There, he had once more taken charge. They gave him a round of muted applause.

"Graham," said Yemi. "I feel you really should be working as a teacher."

For Yemi multi-culturalism meant sampling different kinds of food in exotic locations, in magnificent portions, and then retreating to a beautiful, air-conditioned hotel. Her ideas about how to get a job involved contacts and family connections, as well as an easy charm and a sense of entitlement, none of which they possessed. A slender woman in her early forties with newly soft curly beaded braids, she was a mystery to everybody; her fellow employees at Working Links were in awe of her. But, like all of them, she was only going through the motions, dishing around print outs of non-applicable and unappetising jobs they should apply for.

Still, Yemi was okay, Yemi could be fun. "In Dubai," she said, after a long description of the scrumptious fresh local produce and the delicious – and cheap – dishes they made from it, "one thing I was told, is they have this rule there that nobody, no foreigner, can set up a business unless they take somebody local onto the board of directors – as a partner – so they can be sure some of the money will remain in the country, local people will be employed and benefit from the business. Not just the foreign businessman. I would say 'or woman' but women are not allowed to operate businesses in Dubai."

"Maybe they should do it here," he suggested. "You have to have an English partner. But all the foreign businesses would just leave, wouldn't they? Pulling down the Arsenal stadium on the way out." A few people laughed. "But they probably do have English partners, I don't know."

"I think you're right," Yemi said. "You know – my grandmother is the most amazing businesswoman. She can't speak anything except pidgin, she can't read or write, she keeps all her money in one of those bum-bags around her waist. But she can't leave the house without buying or selling something, and she always comes back with more money than she started out with." She laughed lightly.

Everybody, all the others, turned and smiled at him, partly because they thought his attempts to engage with Yemi were some sort of flirtation with her, which amused them, but only slightly.

"You're really quite multi-cultural, aren't you Graham!" Yemi said.

It was true that he liked her; he liked her lightness of touch and her absence of authority.

Afterwards he went to browse around the retail park. He looked at the radio-controlled helicopters in Maplin's, priced laptops in PC World and finally lost himself in the bright, heaped toy aisles of Asda. There were wonderful little carts now, he thought with dull envy. Little electric-powered replicas of VW Beetles they had which a kid could sit in, dirt-cheap. Also, there were plenty of jobs for teenagers in these places, well-drilled holders of them would approach you and ask if they could help in any way. Radio Asda was advertising a volume of working-class memories of Harringay, an enjoyable chink in the corporate armour.

This really was a meaningful community space. There was nothing in it for him except to walk down the long plaything-festooned tunnel to the CD racks. Elvis, Eddie, Roy, the Everlies. The ones he would always look for were just about still there, gasping at the end of their long road. Mark Duggan shopped here, he thought, his mum had picked up his baby clothes along these aisles, and now the mother of his children bought toys and clothes. Right here. Was this miserable early shopping experience the reason he was carrying a gun? Jesus Jesus. He shook his head quickly, as if to dislodge something which had become stuck in there, something impeding his previously good eyesight.

He often browsed the charity shops of Crouch End. Oxfam was good for books, Shelter for clothes, Cancer research for general bric-a-brac, North London hospice for shoes, and the Children's Cerebral Palsy shop was a chaotic cornucopia of all these things, as well as being by far the cheapest of them. He'd picked up a number of things in all these shops over the years: lots of old paperbacks, a few CDs, shoes that scurfed the skin off his heels before stretching enough to wear, and one day a couple of unmade balsa wood aeroplane kits – a glider and a rubber-powered trainer – fresh in their long rectangular boxes from thirty years ago. He'd never made them, just rattled them and felt their weight, their lightness, before replacing them in his kitchen cupboard.

The jigsaw was an impulse buy from the cerebral palsy shop, which has staffed by a couple of French women who had a *laissez-faire* attitude to pricing, especially if they liked the look of you. Apparently he aroused their sympathies, or perhaps they were simply more interested in turnover than the others, catering for a poorer shopper. The contents of their shop were less artfully arranged, more heaped in zones; there was obviously a far greater throughput of stock, and in one corner a box of unsaleable bric-a-brac was to be found. He sometimes sifted through these items – a pair of salt and pepper shakers slung in straw baskets on the back of a painted wooden donkey, a spiky lampshade or two, chipped willow-pattern breakfast bowls, and – one day – a jigsaw puzzle of hundreds of cardboard pieces in a transparent polythene bag which somebody had labelled with a handwritten yellow post-it note: No Box.

He teased the bag out of the crammed junk box (it was trapped against one wall by a rickshaw and its sprinting driver folded out of heavy black wire, its bare ends, or all but one, capped with blue and red plastic globes) and examined it carefully. Impossible to tell what it was, or indeed if there were enough pieces to complete whatever scene it depicted. Somewhat shamefacedly he took it to the counter, fingering a twenty pence piece and a fifty in his jacket pocket. He held it up to one of the Frenchwomen, who waved him away with an exasperated look, and he wandered home with his catch in his pocket.

The polythene bag of jigsaw pieces wasn't his strangest acquisition: that dubious honour went to a Tupperware box of miniature plastic black bulls, part of the packaging of a brand of heavy red wine of that name. An old friend of his had left them as a gift when he moved to America some years previously, just hadn't been able to throw them out, and now he was the possessor of forty-three of them, each garnished with a coloured ribbon on the back of its neck. He had lined them on his kitchen counter before sweeping them into the spare Tupperware box, sealing the lid and casting them into the back of the drawer beside his sink.

He began by emptying the jigsaw pieces onto the floor, turning them picture side up and counting them carefully. There were exactly 1000 pieces stamped out of card, coloured in blue, blue-grey, black, green, yellow, white, purple, brown and a seemingly wide infinity of combinations of these hues. In shape they were the usual jigsaw configuration of male and female ends waiting to be conjoined, one way only, bubbles and uteri, straight edges, curves, and only two were joined together. The jigsaw had been thoroughly disassembled, or perhaps never attempted, but when he examined the two joined pieces more closely he noticed that they didn't fit together properly, nor did the colours match at any point. He prised them apart and put them down again on the carpet.

His next task was sorting them into piles, but the pile on the carpet, although not deep (he'd found it in a skip, carried it back to the flat over his shoulder) was none too clean: encrusted with dust, ashes, spent matches. That stumped him. He got up to stretch his legs, found himself teetering over the spread pieces, treading on them, and the break in his concentration brought him to his senses and he abruptly decided to give up on such a stupid occupation. Jig-saws were pointless and boring, he remembered just in time. He squatted, gathering the pieces in one hand and threw them into the mouth of the polythene bag he held open in the other.

He considered putting the puzzle in the drawer along with the bulls, or maybe tossing it on top of the Keil Kraft kits in the kitchen cupboard, or throwing it away. But he didn't. He threw it onto the cluttered ledge under the early fifties utility table which his neighbour had given him, on top of a small plastic comb, a few unpaid bills and crumpled lengths of toilet tissue.

Patricia Lumumba lived out in Edgware, a long, winding and bumpy bus journey out through Southgate, Bounds Green, Finchley, turning and turning in the widening teapots, stopping at thirties masterpiece landing saucer tube stations as kids swarmed off and on, at bus stations, shopping centres, old pubs turned into Harvesters, or else decaying at roadsides, once a late night stop for the fast set, now a scrawled boarded-up Halloween threat which had recently offered satay sticks smothered in peanut sauce, Thai cuisine. Nom de guerre. Somewhere along those humps of ancient scarp, twisting and folding into clearings tricked out with off-licences and cake shops and faded kosher cafes from the seventies, lived Erin, an Irish girl who had been excluded from school for threatening a teacher; a mad, allegedly musical creature whose parents were from County Mayo, who went on a sponsored sky dive, to whom he had explained the meaning of Poe's *Ligea*. How the first wife is reborn through the dying body of the second.

Erin nodded glumly, her hair still wet, bundled up in her white fluffy towelling bathrobe. At the far end of the big room, a mini-banqueting hall, a log fire leapt and crackled. Her parents were well-heeled builders, their luxury teapot one of a secluded pair tucked behind an evergreen hedge. There was an elaborate old-fashioned doorbell arrangement and an ancient baronial feel to it; a place where it was always nearly Christmas, and this time it actually was. He wouldn't have minded laying open her bathrobe and tasting her creamy flesh on the rug in front of the fire, and at the precise moment that this thought crossed his mind a lean uncle with a plane in one hand and a screwdriver in the other had put his head around the corner.

49

Another second generation Irish girl lived out there some-where, a girl who fancied herself as a photographer, her polite parents embarrassed she wasn't home for his 11am session. He remembered sipping tea with them in their luxurious kitchen with decorative Irish plates on the wall, until the girl deigned to turn up in her sports car – a cynical little lady who expected him to write her coursework straight off, with no input from her. Her father insisted money was no object. He was obviously somewhat perturbed by his uncontrollable little shit of a daughter, but seemed unable to grasp how she was mostly his creation. No amount of money, he replied politely, after an hour in her company.

Still, they were all recommendations of Chris Sekibo, a kid who at least tried hard, and was a real pleasure to work with. They all went to the same Catholic school and it was a little strange to be producing all of their coursework for the same beleaguered, gullible teacher. A good teacher, Graham thought. Better than him for sure. Patricia was simply the most beautiful of them. She was buxom, enchanting, a real African princess.

The Lumumbas were a large family who lived in one of the bigger teapots tucked away around a labyrinth of bends off the dual carriageway somewhere out that way. There was a minivan pulled up to the front window, a working vehicle stuffed with daycare equipment and cheerful bendy toys. Patricia opened the door smiling. The kids were all eating dinner off their laps, watching a big TV, two little boys eager to show off their bicycles in the back garden. Their mum only spoke kitchen Congolese French, which Patricia spoke to her, their father a forceful, sharply-dressed man who was in the motor trade, a car salesman perhaps, a manager or a team leader of some sort. He interviewed the tutor out in the conservatory on his second visit. He was none too sure Patricia needed a tutor, doubted it would do her any good, didn't believe she really deserved to go to university. "So what's your strategy?" Mr Lumumba asked.

Graham said a few hollow sounding things, his folder and his books balanced on his knees as he perched on a creaking wicker chair. Mr. Lumumba swung on the office model in front of the PC from which he ran his business, and on which his eldest daughter did her English homework. "She seems like an intelligent girl to me," he said. "I'm sure she's going to do very well."

"Intelligent?" he grimaced in a disbelief which seemed to have the potential of an uncomtrollable anger. "Come on, please don't try to fool with me. I know my own daughter." He smiled. But he was resigned. Under sufferance, he would be permitted to tutor her.

Patricia was keen on his visits, and at first they seemed to be progressing by leaps and bounds. They were shut up together in the conservatory having intense conversations about *Othello* and *The Duchess of Malfi*. He corrected the spelling in her Gothic coursework, pointing out that spelling an author's name wrong didn't usually go down very well: there were two 'e's in Shelley, and more than one 'l'. Sey hell. Soon they were racing through the two pages of Othello questions on a photocopied sheet he had been sent by a friend in Grays. They weren't essay questions but fairly probing either/or character assessments. Soon she was pouring out her thoughts about Othello in the way people did when they knew all the characters and had understood the storyline.

He enjoyed these jousts with nascent literary scholars; he would set them traps: what if Desdemona is just a brazen little harlot who had taken in a gullible black man who was out of his depth? What if A.C. Bradley was just an Edwardian sentimentalist of young women, and of people from different cultures ... well, as he said, can they ever really understand one another in that easy, instinctive way necessary for a good marriage?

Patricia became delightfully animated as he put her through her paces, frowning and pondering, coming back at him fluently when he provoked her. Most girls did. It was a trick played on their instantaneity of response to being led. She seemed to have read the play. But was Desdemona as pure and innocent as A.C. Bradley said she was? Was Graham? He had quickly discovered black and white kids had polarised attitudes to the play. Some white kids thought Iago was flat out justified in hating Othello, who was an over-promoted pompous buffoon, while all black kids loved him, identified with him, and were heart-broken when this evil racist shit brought him down. The white girls, Erin for example, were sure only of one thing: they never would have trusted him or gone anywhere near him. Perhaps the moor shouldn't have married a white girl, he would sometimes suggest provocatively, especially one who flirted with all and sundry. It was as though Obama had hastily got married to Britney Spears for the sake of spending one night with her. But neither side would shift their ground, not much anyway.

She was reluctant to admire the Duchess, and at first seemed to share the 17th century view which held she was an irredeemably bad girl with kids by several different men, so deserved whatever she got by way of retribution. But what really got her laughing were the Duchess's perverted brothers. She loved the story, had no problem with that at all, but the language was hard, impossible for her. Her student guide, like most girls', was so extensively highlighted in bright yellow little of the text remained unmade-up and so she'd negated the point of marking important passages. But where the Duchess was concerned, she proved more malleable.

The Duchess hadn't after all asked to be widowed. She was still young and her only crime was to marry somebody she liked, rather than go without a man for the rest of her life. Patricia particularly liked her dying words to the effect she would always be the Duchess: a proud death, she spat in their eye at the end. She, likewise, would always be Patricia Lumumba. He started to talk, again excitedly, about scheming malcontents, Iago and Bosula, how they were what made the plays socially interesting – these dissatisfied middle-class characters, forced to be go-betweens, to be running other men's errands. Bosula had worked his way up from galley slave to chief intelligencer … and just then the door swung open.

It was one of her two little brothers, wanting to show Graham one of his toys: an action man doll in uniform. The other small boy appeared and they both went through to the back garden. Cool air flowed through the conservatory. He sat back. He hadn't realized how hot it was getting in there. A dark wire of connection between them had heated the room. Patricia sat back, looking dutifully through her papers. His and Patricia's voices had been raised in intense confrontation, and there had been his cascading laughter. It was the laughter which was troubling, he knew why her mum had sent the boys in to call the session to a halt.

Another of her texts was *The Pardoner's Tale*. An allegory within an allegory, in which one allegory modifies the meaning of the other. An allegory about the destructiveness of greed, the vanity of thinking one could kill death: a noble enterprise the roisterers could only think of when drunk. Death, of course, has them all over quite easily by putting a sack of gold in their way. The pardoner flogs his relics, extracts gold from the credulous peasants by telling them his well-honed tale, forgiving them their petty sins. Perhaps the pardoner himself is death. He's a crook certainly, and the final curse he receives – his fellow pilgrim would rather eat a meal of excrement than listen to his crap … is er, the only good way to deal with Death.

"Yeah," said Patricia, glancing up from her notes.

NINE

He was pacing slowly up and down under the light in his bedroom, swivelling on his heels to catch a better signal as he pressed his vintage retro Nokia, a mock-Bakelite space lozenge whose silver buttons were worn transparent, to his good ear. At the other end of the line a young, confident voice explained its owner's urgent predicament. "My main problem is that my sentences are too elaborate," said the boy with precision. "In addition to which I have acquired a pronounced tendency to employ words my teacher suggests are too sophisticated for my level of understanding."

"That doesn't sound bad," he said. "Not really the worst problem I've come across. Just shorten the sentences slightly, put in a few full stops."

"No," the boy said. "This a genuine problem I will have to surmount in order to obtain a higher grade in GCSE English – my vocabulary is too sophisticated, my syntax too complex … and I don't always get to the end of one subordinate clause before commencing on another."

"I see." He paused. "Well, sometimes I've noticed people look up words on their iPhones. They find a nice long word which seems to fit and sounds good to them, but it doesn't quite make sense."

"No, it's not that," the boy insisted. "I use words correctly. But I need help organizing my sentences, and generally improving my grammar."

"I should be able to help you by reading some of your work."

"I agree," said the boy. "Actually, that's why I've contacted you."

The family lived in a split-level flat in a block amongst blocks, two streets away from Manor House tube station. Built in the seventies, it was a warren of stairs and walkways and numbered flats, daunting to the visitor, who could be seen coming from multiple angles, but comfortably home to many people, the kids smoking by the bins, who looked across at him, not unfriendly: a scruffy overweight man carrying a tan leather briefcase-cum-shoulder bag, with his index finger stuck in a page of an old printed thing, an A-Z. Somebody from the olden days who could only be a private tutor.

He had got used to such places, he enjoyed finding them and turning up at the appointed time, just before or during or after dinner. He had crossed many such thresholds and pulled out his black folder full of miracle tricks, many of them slightly familiar. The people who lived in them weren't really the urban poor, or at least they were the working poor. They were working-class, more or less, these immigrants or their descendants, and they were trying to help their kids do better at school by laying out thirty quid a week on somebody like him.

Their flats were generally beautiful inside, or as beautiful as the tenants could make them, containing the usual domestic things: tables, chairs, sofas, pictures of children, places, ornaments, sometimes a religious icon of some sort; always well-ordered (as they had to be), a whole sense of how things should go shoehorned into a small space: a capsule of human goodness and continuity. Or so it seemed to him. A family life, distantly related to what he had experienced as a child, certainly the smallness of the space, secured and doing its best to remain so, but very often fiercely aspirational in a way his own background hadn't been. Anxious parents determined their children should do well in a country which would never quite be their own, but was where their children had grown-up, learned to speak a language easefully and to be whoever it was they were becoming.

The door was opened by the boy who had spoken to him on the phone. Noticing a stack of discarded footwear in the hallway below where the coats hung, he bent to take off his own shoes, but the boy, wearing large Steve Tracy style plastic glasses with an electric blue flash on the sides, answered his questioning look with a shake of the head. He was pleased. He always felt at a disadvantage in household where he had to take off his shoes, and pad around in socks with the rest of them. They were at home, in command of their space, but he was disabled, enfeebled, and unable to attack them or run away before hopping around in the hall with his shoes. He walked through the kitchen, small, half-separated from the dining and living room by a hatch, and sat down at the dining table where the boy's books were spread, he glanced across at the glass-topped coffee table where a copy of Richard Dawkins' *The Selfish Gene* lay neatly with a book mark in it.

"Heavyweight reading matter," he smiled happily as the boy approached with his English book open for inspection.

"My sister's reading it," he explained.

"Clever sister," he said. He could bite his own tongue off with these facile, patronising remarks of his, but he was at ease with them, they flowed easily. They supplied him with a personality, one his pupils found easy to get and wouldn't mind kicking against. Glancing aside he noticed a small image of Jesus Christ's radiant head was stuck on the wall beside the fireplace, and relaxed slightly in involuntary relief.

Just as they were about to get going the boy's father came down to shake hands with him. He looked a bit like a Turk. A key went into the front door, which opened, admitting a young woman, his sister, who took off her coat and thereafter sat on the stairs, listening in on the lesson.

"May I ask where your family is from?" he asked. "It's one of my pleasures in doing this kind of work to meet people from so many different backgrounds."

"We are Kosovans," he replied simply.

His prose was beautiful, full of fine distinctions and paired opposites, expressed in a high-flown vocabulary only parts of which were wrongly defined, and as he read on he saw much of its sense could indeed be rescued with a few full stops, plus a few clarifications of tense and sentence structure. He set about supplying them, noticing an intellectual aspiration straining upwards towards A level, but which failed to quite resolve or make sense. Syntactically it was a tumbling house of cards; he also noticed a familiar opinion that Othello was a complete idiot.

"This is pretty good," he said. "But Othello isn't an idiot. You can't say that. Flawed yes, but if he was an idiot it would have to be a comedy. Some people think Othello is a comedy and Iago is the real hero, showing up the stupidity of the supposedly great Othello."

"Perhaps I might agree with them," the Kosovan replied.

They decided use the time available to write his English homework, which was to be a three-minute class talk about language and identity. He dictated the opening paragraph, but noticed the boy wasn't writing down his words exactly. He was translating them, not into Kosovan, but into the faintly archaic and supercorrect English he considered apposite for the exposition of one's essayistic thoughts. They fought over it amiably for forty minutes until the thing was done, Graham reacting with ever more demotic formulations, short punchy sentences right for a class talk where he would be speaking familiarly to other London teenagers. The boy fought him tooth and nail, particularly his contention that the best prose could be anything like everyday speech. He'd just read *1984*. He thought this idiot was suggesting he should write in some sort of degraded Newspeak, and that only precise, formal meanings were appropriate for the expression of ideas. He particularly resisted his example of the black London word 'boss', used not to mean boss, but friend, or mate: a word he insisted was half-respectful, and meant to express the notion that the person addressed was at the same level as you, not your boss at all. He made him scribble it all down. After all, he could always fix it later.

Eventually they were done, and the boy went to fetch the money from his father. On his way out of the front door, the boy's sister, who had been there all this time, still perched on the stairs, said "Goodbye" in a loud, cheery voice. He knew from her tone that the lesson hadn't gone too well. He would never see them again. He walked back to the station, somewhat crestfallen, wrung out, and sure enough, a day before he was due to come the following week, his phone bleeped and a polite, well-wrought text message from the Kosovan explained that, for financial reasons, they had decided not to continue with his English tuition. Good decision, really.

Portobello market. He was treading in the footsteps of Malcolm Mbulu. On his way home from school this lanky Nigerian lad had sampled, or at least sniffed at, every dainty on every stall along its entire length, Thai, Indian, Caribbean, African, Hippy Vegetarian and much else besides, zig-zagging between stalls; he had got lost in a mysterious shoe shop which Graham had never been able to locate, while his mother tried on pair after pair of glass slippers, and had taken it all in his lanky stride. His favourite Latin epigram was something about how all the women loved to go to the circus. Not bad for a fifteen year old.

The Mbulus, Cynthia, Malcolm and Alicia, lived in a small council flat in a nice old thirties block with landing neighbours who had a belligerent looking British bulldog on their doormat, although they were lovely people, so Cynthia said. She worked for the NHS as an administrator, and had amazing qualifications called things like PRINCE LEVEL III and SHADOW DEMON. They all actually meant something, she had assured him, trying to solicit his help with her MA dissertation. Graham had said it should have a three part structure: Beginning, Middle and End. Cynthia hadn't bothered him any further on the subject.

There was a strange Etruscan blue construction at the corner where they lived. What was it? A toilet? A bus shelter? A retail outlet? It cast the ambience of a retro postcard and a toy world over the whole area. Everything on sale in any of the shops was prohibitively expensive. OK, a pencil which will snap in half as soon as you apply its fresh sharp tip to a writing pad, a Kit-Kat.

Cynthia made him ginger tea and he and Malcolm buckled down to some intensive reading of modernist short stories at the dining room table. James Joyce, Katherine Mansfield. They unpicked the predicament of the country serving woman in a story by Thomas Hardy who married her ecclesiastical employer and brought up a surly, alien being in a lonely place far from everything she was familiar and comfortable with, and they read Graham Greene's story of feral bombsite kids dismantling a house from within. Graham thought the outcome should be short stories of his own. They were stories about being seduced by every emporium in Portobello Road, a bit like the boy in James Joyce's *Araby*.

Cynthia Mbulu was a pretty widow, a lively, slender woman who, in her slacks and bob, looked slightly retro herself, like a member of The Supremes, an observation he wasted no time in passing on.

"Which one?" Cynthia asked.

"Diana Ross."

He couldn't quite see why she thought these sessions with him were going to be of such enormous benefit to her children, but she evidently did believe it and he was perfectly willing to go along with this for as long as she wanted, although it was a long fag of a journey for a Sunday afternoon. He tormented Malcolm with poems by Bertolt Brecht and Ezra Pound, even one by a British Nigerian poet, who had written about his Irish mother.

"Are we supposed to be interested in this writer because of his ethnicity?" he asked coolly.

Cynthia's only admonition had been to warn him not to fill her son's head up with a load of stuff about being black. "That's the last thing he needs," she said.

Malcolm was an easy kid, who didn't mind their sessions too much; Alicia was a ten-year-old who'd already done well in her SATS, but apart from a brief ballet pirouette on first meeting him, he'd been able to elicit little response from her. He tried to get her to finish a humorous article about a fashion show for a magazine she was writing with a school friend; he printed out a number of mediocre short stories aimed at her age group, and got her to point out the boring moral in each one, which she did quickly without interest or effort when coaxed from the room she shared with her brother. She was being sent away soon to a posh school in the country; Malcolm was already attending an equally expensive establishment in West London, his springboard to Princeton.

He brought her oranges and lemons, old nursery rhymes, an article about girls boxing; but still she wouldn't crack a single smile. Finally he brought her a couple of poems from *Old Possum's Book of Practical Cats*, acting out Skimbleshanks the Railway Cat, The Old Gumbie Cat, the one about the do-gooding servant cat who tries to reform cockroaches and runs an evening school for rats and mice on her nights off. He desperately performed Growltiger's Last Stand, relishing its racially dubious depiction of orientals ("rats were roasted whole in Limehouse") and wrung a genuine laugh from her at the dramatic leap for safety of Growltiger's paramour, the Lady Griddlebone, when the Siamese hordes attacked his barge. His own family, he pointed out, had been models for Growltiger's absent henchmen, too busy lapping up the dregs in The Bell at Hampton to be of any help against the yellow peril at the battle of Molesey lock, and this episode at last wrenched a poem from her.

Patricia Lumumba had been another season, spring not autumn. The coursework had shuttled back and forth nicely, the revision notes steadily piled up, and the family had got used to him being out in the conservatory with their blooming daughter. Until one day he turned up – on the bus it was like a long tortuous excursion through outer purgatory – rang the bell, and nobody answered. There were raised debating voices until eventually Patricia opened up.

"I texted you a couple of hours ago?" she said irritably. "Didn't you get my message?"

"I left home two hours ago," he attempted to reprove her. "You're supposed to contact me the day before if you want to cancel."

"Haven't you got your phone with you?"

"I don't always carry it," he said.

"Well, you should," she seized on it decisively. "I'm sorry," she said, abruptly shut the door in his face.

As he walked away, and to his utter disgust, tears sprang into his eyes, he thought of himself self-pityingly as a useless old fraud, a near-pervert. Patricia had behaved to him like that, and it was never the same again. A few more meetings, a few more coursework rewrites and, as she hurried him out of the conservatory for the last time, he found himself wishing her all the luck in the world. Her father looked up from the couch, where he had a file pad on his knee and was patiently waiting for the occupancy of his office. He phoned in a long, slow wink: "Thank you, Graham. I would highly recommend you."

TEN

He sat on the top deck of the 41 to Tottenham Hale. He still liked riding upstairs, at the level of the shop signs, some of them in Polish, some in Turkish, others advertising African and West Indian businesses. He liked the cool black and white elegance of the sign for Okapi, a restaurant specialising in Congolese and African cuisine, partly because, when he was working as a census collector, he had retrieved a completed form from them as they were refurbishing their premises: he had seen the new sign being maneuvered into position, in two halves, and the crack in the middle of the letter K had marred the design at first then disappeared after final adjustments. Now it looked dusty, its metal shutters always drawn down, but the sign was still resplendent.

There were a lot of hair and nail emporiums, and he enjoyed the eye-level sultry looks cast in his direction by women modelling old-fashioned modern styles in which a hank of oiled black hair obscured one of their eyes. Another favourite sign of his featured large hand-painted bottles of Crown rum, one aged five years, another ten, and, at the top of the range, a fifteen-year-old bottle of rum. This rum, he imagined, was so strong it would take at least fifteen years to drink a whole bottle. How he would love to taste it, to take a long swim in it.

He liked to think of himself as an invigilator, or was Jim the invigilator? Jim the proprietor of Tip-Top Tutors. Jim's quiet explanatory voice on his mobile was followed by a text containing some contact details, usually presaging one of his brief, occasionally successful forays after tender prey in the outlying districts of North London. No, Jim wasn't his invigilator, more of a controller perhaps, and only really interested in his commission, although he did seem to have a vague idea of the social geography of the city: a large number of previous customers and contacts. Sometimes he would make vague remarks about nothing in particular. Sometimes not.

He liked to imagine him, bald, elderly, and friendly. But there was something he always avoided about his relationship with Jim, or at least in the way he had come upon the agency. Jim's address had been passed on to him by an acquaintance who had been just about to commit suicide. He didn't know the guy well, the ex-husband of an old girlfriend, and obviously barking mad. He'd met him one night in a pub in Wood Green, but after a couple of hours conversation he had found himself backing away and had been forced to run out of the place with a tightness in his chest.

This acquaintance – he didn't like to think of his name – had e-mailed him the following day, contrite, forwarding the web address of Jim and Tip-Tip Tutors. A couple of weeks later he'd thrown himself out of the eighth floor window of his council flat. Several months afterwards he'd sent his CV to Jim, mentioning the acquaintance's name, and so began the laborious application process. The acquaintance had said he liked working for Jim, the work had given him a real lift of spirits. It was only the recurrence of his mental health problems, entailing a further hospitalization, which had eventually forced him to give it up.

An invigilator was somebody in the background, apparently reading a book at the front of the examination room; but you never knew just when he would spring to his feet and patrol the aisles, just to check you weren't reading off your cuff or from the henna tattoos on your fingers, using a calculator when your own unassisted brain-power was being tested. Graham, he sometimes thought, was an invigilator of a different kind: a man sent to make sure you were cheating just enough, a man whose job it was to help you cheat at life's little game. Everybody cheating? Excellent, that's the idea, carry on. After all, everybody else was doing it, weren't they? Like the parents who could afford to send their talented offspring to the most expensive schools in London, and still hired a personal tutor to help them trick their way through the GCSE and A level exams.

He did all this of course, gingering up the coursework, supplying background and a slender grasp of syntax. He liked to dictate to his students – perhaps they'd pick it up somehow - but had noticed, over the years, that the ones who argued with him, who insisted on their own forms of words might be the ones who were really going to develop, although their sense of certitude was often equally a case of background social arrogance, or a temporary confidence borne of the high mark they'd got for his last piece of magic coursework.

The life of an invigilator wasn't easy; it was full of moral pitfalls, little compromises of the higher calling, but he was, after all, one of the anointed. The people would hide him and make excuses for him, and pay him what they could for his services. There was no doubt in his mind that the education system was fundamentally unjust, and if he put a finger on the scales now and then, well, then he was doing good work and he was thanked for it. Not particularly well paid however, which made his picturing of himself as an invigilator more attractive: a noble profession, a mug's game he had never stopped playing.

Once or twice he'd actually been a real invigilator. He remembered trying to read Gertrude Stein whilst he was supposed to be an active enforcer of the probity of final exams of some linguistics students, as if he could tell whether they were cheating or not. He sat at the front of the lecture theatre, glancing up now and then in case anyone wanted extra paper, each time losing his place in *The Making of Americans*, a bulky tome which hadn't often been taken out of the library. Not that it particularly mattered, but the master's permutations had had a hypnotic effect on him. He turned pages back and forth, looking for his place, because every recurring word had to be read thoroughly in its context of repeated phrases.

Eventually he looked up to notice some of the students were smiling at him. He was embarrassed to realize his contorted facial expressions had been registering every turn of clarity and bafflement in his public, silent reading of Stein. On their way out of the examination hall, one of the students had said: "Thanks – you were a great invigilator." Another time, a few years later, he had invigilated a GCSE exam at a school where he was doing a month's supply. There it was different: no reading allowed. He found himself patrolling the aisles, not to detect cheats but to force the kids to get through the exam by sheer force of will. He wondered why he seemed to love them so much – but he did, in his way, partly because everything still seemed to be so funny to them.

The journey to Kensal Rise was a long, dog-leg affair which involved changing twice, fleeing across a gravelled slope to change platforms at Manor House, where numbers of ticket invigilators often lurked on the waiting train. Well, not always. Swaying, trying to perch on those little upholstered ridges, apparently designed for somebody like Remi's mother. Mrs. Kuti, was a short, powerfully-built woman, didn't take shit from anybody. She was a social worker who specialised in trying to terrify junkies into cleaning up their act and looking after their children. "Fat chance," she said, "fat chance of *that*." He listened intently to her rapid African-inflected speaking voice, trying to take it all in and answer her questions. Did he think Remi would be able to get a B in A level English? He thought she would, yes, certainly. She'd driven him to the station after his first unpaid visit, where there was a cafe between the two station entrances. Well-dressed young women were reading vintage paperbacks, having heavy-duty conversations at outside trestle tables, wearing horn rimmed spectacles, Oxford bags, some of them sporting neat Louise Brooks-style bobs, towing or being towed by large poodles, even lurchers. He decided to scrub around it, scrub the overpriced coffee, go home.

They lived in the same road as the Mark Twain library, the one Twain had opened brand new when he briefly lived up at Dollis Hill House, working on *The Mysterious Stranger*. It was a squat mock-Elizabethan manor hall, or something, arts and crafts, a lovely building. Now it was closed and a few elderly staff were stood outside in the street, trying to rally the community, trying to carry it on with a polythene-covered stall and some interesting looking seventies reserve stock. It was pitiful, sad to pass them by. Many of the houses, flats mostly, sported save our library posters in their front windows, but it was obvious by now to all they had lost their jobs and the community's local library was gone for good. The building was too valuable not to be redeveloped into luxury flats, each of which would be sold for a large fortune to some greedy bastard. The council was doing the devil's work, as usual, and no amount of literary luvvies past, present or future, was ever going to change their mind.

In their first proper session he and Remi had written the best vampire story ever composed, based on a poem by Charles Bukowski. Remi loved vampire stories and owned every one of the Twilight series, a ton of Marjorie Blackman and several other multi-volume works in the same sorry genre. He himself had only read Bram Stoker and Poppy Z. Brite. Mrs. Kuti apologized for her daughter's time-wasting reading habits, but they had stood her in good stead. They sat together at the computer on the dining room table turning Bukowski's pleasant poem about bums into vampire prose. He was the old vampire, looking for new blood; she was ready to give it at a moment's notice. They met easily in a noisy, sleazy bar and made their contract without speaking too much. Occasionally he managed to elbow her aside and add a line which changed the direction of the story, mocking her, guiding her into the deeper waters of lust and death. She didn't need much encouragement. The trick was to keep going back to Bukowski's poem, he tried to show her, to keep its mood and shape there underneath her story. Mrs. Kuti sat on the couch talking loudly on her mobile throughout while her large wall-mounted plasma screen paraded the brightness of the world before their eyes.

Remi's doe-eyed younger sister, who had done very well at school with her essay on *A Midsummer Night's Dream*, occupied a high-backed chair at the other computer, in the corner, with headphones on, watching what looked like another vampire film. Remi's story plunged on into further degradation as we followed the old one back to his family home, a filthy slum somewhere extremely nasty, somewhere none of them had ever been. Except for Mrs. Kuti. He found himself trying to make the vampire more human, more sympathetic, but it was her story after all and she insisted on making him a ruthless predatory creature of darkness – which is after all what he was. It was soon done, came out well, he thought.

Remi trotted away to get the money from her mum, who had retreated to the kitchen. Mrs. Kuti came back through smiling with the notes in her hand. "Easy money," she cawed at him. "Easy!"

He scuttled down the street past the dark windows of the library, feeling like a worthless creature of the night. Perhaps he was one. Gliding through shadows, invisible otherwise, sometimes showed up against a splash of darkness, briefly there beneath a street light, in mirrors too, if he cared to look. But for the most part people walked straight through his body, a sour breath of chill air emanating from an alleyway, another day, another dull lair. What else to do but head off somewhere and try to prey on somebody else, somebody who probably didn't exist. Acton was close at hand. His last image of the place: a troupe of rats confidently filing across from the undergrowth on the traffic island on George St., heading on to where B&Qs used to stand in an old cinema building. He tried to accelerate away from the lure, the feeling of compulsion, almost running on tiptoe back to the bustling, affluent thoroughfare of Kensal Rise.

ELEVEN

"Mum – we're at Julie's place, can you pick us up in half-an-hour?" Lana's oldest girl asked, just like that. "Half-an-hour, okay?"

Daughters! Lana replaced the telephone in its slot. That's all she was there for as far as they were concerned. Personal taxi service to a pair of little madams who'd been running her off her feet since they were born. Lovely girls – she wouldn't be without them of course – but everything had its downside, and leaving childbirth until you were in your early forties was no exception to this sacred law. She should be their granny, nodding over her knitting and offering a few carefully honed homilies about her day, whenever that had been, not buzzing around like a blue-arsed fly easing them through every fucking detail of their teenage years. She put her coat on, picked up her car keys and wandered out into the backyard to look at the chickens. The Rhode Island Red was looking peaky; three of the Leghorns had laid. Lana gathered their eggs, took them back into the kitchen and placed them carefully in a bowl. Fresh eggs. She loved them. She loved chickens, always had. She would whip up an omelette for the girls when they got home. They would be more than delighted.

"I'm going out to pick up the girls!" she called upstairs. No answer from the lord and master. She let herself out to where her Nissan Micra was parked in what had been the forecourt of the Church, when it had been a church, a small Methodist building from the sixties which her husband, an ambitious builder, had converted into a roomy if drafty living space for them all ten years earlier. Lana liked the church too, but most of all she liked the yard and the chicken run. She got in the small car and set off for Camberley and her daughters' friend's parents' house. They had stayed overnight there, which she wasn't really happy about, but with Julie's mum and dad in attendance she didn't suppose they could have got into too much mischief at Julie's sixteenth birthday party.

Why was it people never got over their teenage years? Her favourite album was *Fire and Water* by Free – somehow Alright Now and My Brother Jake still did it for her, whatever there was still to do. Just the opening riff and she was back there in her parents' house in Milford, her father out in the shed brooding and running his giant train set around her mother's extravagantly landscaped back garden, her mother in the kitchen making another cheesecake, and she herself upstairs in her bedroom cutting out some more pictures of chickens to stick in her scrap book, or reading *Far from the Madding Crowd*. She smiled at the thought of it all. Playing the flute. Being so sure of where she was going – she'd always wanted to marry a farmer and keep chickens, and to be a teacher of some kind. The world had been laid out for her, her parents' pride and joy and only child.

An unwelcome thought of Ricky Greaves suddenly creased her wide brow. What was it he had called her? Not back then, but a few years ago. Intense. She was intense. Somehow she didn't really like to think of herself as *intense*. Serious. Organised. Single-minded, yes. He thought he was God Almighty did poor old Ricky. Bless.

No, no, no. It was always back to the sixth form or thereabouts. A pie and a pint in the Alma. And a pant in the churchyard. Against a tree with the top of her tights cutting into her thighs. You really did have to hand it to memories, although of course it had all been so unsatisfactory and frustrating at the time. Us seventies kids. Dear Sweet Horst, her shaggy-haired, bearded cousin. Horst from Frankfurt, somewhere up there on the genius spectrum of Asperger's as a musician, but it came to nothing, it always did, to bitter disappointments and careless smashes on the autobahn. Lana. Lana. Lana. She felt herself drifting off once more into the pain of it, once more into the pain my friends; it was like a sweet she sucked. The big turquoise woolly dressing gown she'd been painted in, spectacularly, in one long twelve hour session, with frequent interruptions for, ahem, tea breaks, loud knocks on the door. Gabby's Hitler youth badge, its silvery metal and red and black enamel still pristine in a grey velvet lined box. Something to be proud of no doubt, no doubt, no doubt. My brother Jake. Alright now. Free. And now she was as mad as a barrel load of monkeys.

Lana was out on the dual carriageway, sailing along at a fair clip in the small blue Micra like a small blue insect. The traffic was surprisingly light for Saturday, but she was stuck behind a large articulated lorry with foreign license plates and no way to see around it. She hoped the girls had been properly supervised at Julie's party. She would be able to tell within a few seconds whether they had been. Secretive though children often were, and understandably so, it was generally perfectly possible for the astute parent – or teacher – to discern exactly what had been going on.

And if so she would be giving them hell about it, daughters of hers, they must think she was stupid. She glanced quickly at her watch. Seeing nothing of course. At the clock on the dash – was there one? And, at the moment she looked up again, she saw the taillights of the big lorry in front flaring up close, and, for under a second, she felt the Micra's bonnet crumple as it ran up under the heavy steel frame at the back of it, wiping her from the face of the earth, dispersing her quickly, like a windscreen wiper clearing a spatter of raindrops or the remains of a number of dead flies, no longer exhibiting any mad grace.

TWELVE

He had once accompanied Lana on a birthday trip to the theatre in the West End. This had been his first date in town, his first formal date, on her eighteenth. It had been impressed on him by Lana and her mother that he must be on his best behaviour, if only for that one special night. Trussed into her new evening dress, heavily made up, she'd resembled a startled doll, a doll that blinked and had unfortunately been granted the power of speech. He'd worn a suit and tie which he'd thought made him look pretty good; but although they had both been adjudged lovely by Lana's mother, the atmosphere between them was edgy and sour.

Lana had taken the hint from the notion that this was to be her 'special night' to spend the whole evening bullying and insulting him. Humiliation was the order of the occasion on which everything had to be 'perfect', like a god-awful song of a decade or so later, a sort of rehearsal for her wedding day, although not the night she was to lose her virginity. The play they saw had been something by Thomas Hardy, Lana's favourite writer. *The Day After the Fair*, in which a lady had written love letters for her servant, leading the girl's suitor to fall for the wrong woman The theatre, and the play, struck him as an embodiment of every value he despised: stuffy, stuck up, bourgeois.

But maybe he was missing the point. Lana thought so. He hated the sense of himself being in public, his excruciating embarrassment heightened by the fact that they were seated next to Una Stubbs, who had played Alf Garnett's stroppy daughter in the famously racist BBC sitcom of the sixties, which was supposed to be combating what it actually promoted. Graham – like everybody else he knew – had been forced to watch this crap by a father who heartily agreed with Alf's hilarious sentiments. Una Stubbs was very likeable in the programme, forever remonstrating with her father ("Dad!") and sympathising with her put-upon mother, the 'silly moo' played by Dandy Nicholls. Una Stubbs was in reality a gorgeous and sophisticated woman, he remembered thinking in dismay as they sat beside her. Now he felt ashamed he could remember so much about *Til Death Do Us Part*, and so little about the play he had witnessed that night with Lana. Had somebody come in with a dead rabbit? He found it incredible that he'd later enjoyed reading books by Thomas Hardy.

He remembered squirming, imagining people were glancing at them, not because they were such a lovely young couple, but because they looked so fucking stupid. On the way home his comments were silenced, and he remembered not even getting a snog out of her, if he'd wished to kiss the thoroughly revolting creature Lana had revealed herself to be that night. Women! Yes, indeed. Still, they had their fun. He felt nothing but warmth and affection for her nowadays.

He remembered the long day on which he'd painted her portrait on a large sheet of grey card. She was ensconced in a wicker chair in her bedroom at Milford, bundled up in a thick woolly turquoise dressing gown, under which she wore nothing but her pale skin, perspiring in the early July heat. He had concentrated mainly on the folds of the long dressing gown, and her small hands, a tiring task which dragged on around the clock, a full twelve hours of meticulous effort, interrupted by endless bouts of sex on her divan bed until the room had reeked of sweat and come and pussy juices while her mother bustled past outside in the hall, occasionally tapping on the door. It was obvious what they were doing in there, but the painting continued to progress well. Echoing in his head were the words of Picasso as quoted by his art teacher, Miss Eddy: "I paint with my prick."

They were aching, sore and dry, but had still managed to do it a few times more before staggering downstairs to the kitchen near midnight for a couple of slices of her mother's homemade cheesecake. Lana's cousin from Frankfurt had been staying at the time. He had sat up for them over cups of coffee, a huddled gnome like figure with a big scrubby beard and lots of red spots, who looked like a member of Faust or Can or Amon Duul II, and was himself a musician. He was understandably sceptical of Graham. The panting was more or less finished apart from Lana's face which resembled an artist's manikin in a painting by De Chirico: a beige egg with a sort of black cross on it he was going to fill in later.

"I'll bet Lana wishes she had a dressing gown like that," Horst had commented in grudging admiration.

He couldn't remember how he'd got home with his picture and his bag of paints. Did he sleep on their couch? Did they recommence the following morning?

He had probably hitched back home along the dark tunnel corridor of the A3, which he did often enough, sharing the cab of a lorry driver or riding in the passenger seat of a salesman or some other generous lonely soul heading home through the funnel of the Surrey night with its ghostly silver birches and its scrubby flattened brambly grass. He didn't remember. But he had applied the finishing touches to his last painting, which he considered to be the best he had ever done, in the days following.

Lana's face had come out well – he felt he knew it so intimately that no reference was required: her jaw jutted forwards aggressively as it always had, but her features were blasted, staring, debauched and middle-aged, and more beautiful.

THIRTEEN

Ricky decided to make a start on deleting his unbeloved Facebook account. Deactivation was pussies; anyway, it just wasn't going to be good enough, as he knew from past escape attempts in which the faces of people he barely knew were held up to express their longing for contact with him then snatched away forever. He needed to take care of the fucking thing once and for all. He logged on and in. He felt his smile slide up a notch or two into a demonic masturbator emoticon and, not for the first time, regretted being unable to circularize his tongue and poke it out through a neat hole he had made of the side of his mouth. First to go was the useless webcam profile picture of him gaping insolently at a screen to the left of camera. Then his contact details, hometown, education, likes, groups and all the rest of the non-existent shit. Then his friends. All twelve of them. The apostles of Ricky Greaves. Goodnight forever, you ignorant cunts.

First of all that smirking supercilious bastard Mark Burgitt and his poxy travel book. Secondly, Andrew Drinkwater, Bracknell's answer to the Tremeloes. Thirdly, Wales Luna, whomsoever she had ever been. Fourthly ... would be Dave Boyce, bluesman and former dope-dealer extraordinaire. Fifth was Graham Bartlett, never liked him, couldn't take a fucking joke, always deeply justifiably unpopular. Number six was ... a prick he'd met in a pub. Seven was Lena Kertesz ... he still had her e-mail and phone number. Eighthly was his boss, who would understand perfectly. Ninth was his sister, oh well. Tenth was Bob Tender, his fellow Conan the Barbarian gamer. Eleventhly was a pleasantly unmemorable bloke, a vague associate from somewhere or other. Gone. Twelfth was of course Lana ... but she wasn't there, just a pale blue silhouette where she had once stood in her kitchen next to her eldest daughter. Had she unfriended him somehow? He knew this wasn't how it worked, but he typed her name in anyway and nothing came up. She was definitely gone from Facebook, she'd beaten him to it, damn. He closed everything down, ignoring the corporate pleas on behalf of indifferent, no longer extant friends, ignoring the change your mind option, and – bomp – gone forever.

He typed Lana's name into Google on impulse, just to check, and to his surprise it came up in a local news story on the *Surrey Herald* website. MIRACLE TEACHER ESCAPES UNHURT. A car crash. Lena had run her car under an articulated lorry on a dual carriageway. Mad cow. There was a colour photo of the Nissan Micra, unrecognizable, its roof shorn off, and running around it a gloating description of the terrifying accident in which a small woman teacher had so narrowly escaped injury due to being knocked back by her inflatable safety system to below the level of the back of the lorry. She had been imprisoned in the car for half-an-hour, barely conscious, before the fire brigade arrived to drag it free and cut her out of the crushed body shell. She'd emerged with barely a scratch from the accident, he read, but had been taken into Camberley hospital for routine tests.

Jesus H. Christ. Ricky stood up from the screen. Lana hurt. Or rather not hurt. He felt terrible, a squirming agony. He loved Lana, there was no doubt in his mind. If he loved anyone. He walked through to the kitchen and looked around for the cat, opened the connecting door and looked down the long furry tunnel which was the space he had left for her, her own place. No cat. "Molly," he called. "Molly!" He propelled himself down the stairs, opened the back door and looked out into the yard. But the elderly cat wasn't there; she was nowhere to be seen. Kaput cat. Oh no. He trudged back upstairs, then sat down at the computer and hammered out a long email to her, in which he poured out his anguish and concern for the poor girl.

He sat on the couch again, twiddling the back of his hair and looking up into the middle distance. All his memories of her had started firing up, little things they'd done together over the years, walking around various places in London with her while she'd been doing various early jobs, visits here and there; he remembered her learning to drive, passing her test, and the motorbike she'd insisted on getting a few years later.

Their friendship had been intermittent, but it had covered most phases of their adult lives. So when she'd finally started sleeping with him a couple of years back, it had seemed so right in a way, so like coming home to something which had always been there. And this was precisely why he hadn't been able to handle it for long without wanting more. She'd said so herself, it was understandable. She understood. She was always so fucking understanding. After a while he went back to the computer and saw an email from Lana had arrived.

My darling Ricky,

So lovely to hear from you at this difficult time! You're right, it was scary indeed. My neck is still very stiff. I'm wearing a brace and being fed through a straw (rather resentfully I might add!) but well and truly on the mend. I don't really know what happened. One minute I was there and the next I wasn't. I don't even remember being in the car, only setting out from home to pick the girls up. That's what scares me most. I don't even remember being cut out of the car, although apparently I was talking nineteen to the dozen (typical!) and telling the firemen what to do (typical!!) but I do feel a lot better for hearing from you darling Ricky my old friend. I woke up on a soft pillow in Camberley Hospital, which was the first I knew about it, and I thought, hang on, where am I?!! But I'm okay.

Lots of love,

Lanaxxx

(Phew!)

Ricky read it through again. He wanted to phone her, but it wasn't really on, not now it wasn't. He felt better anyway. Mightily relieved. At this moment Molly the cat came creaking around the door, her legs stretched out as if they were splinted. She paused in the middle of the floor, stock-still, staring at him fixedly, frozen there, without hope or interest.

He hadn't been twiddling long when he heard the phone ringing in the kitchen. Well, who could that be? His sister? He went through to the sonorous clanging of a thirties-effect ring-tone and slid the charging handset from its Enterprise-style holder. No, to his surprise it was Lana. He was shocked, found himself stammering and bluffing as if he'd been caught out being somebody else by a person he'd lapsed into thinking was only half-real. "Ricky?" she said. "You didn't mind me calling, do you? I know we said we wouldn't – but this is a bit different."

"Of course not, don't be so silly."

He grated on her straight away, and she wondered why she had called him. Because of Hugh. "I think Hugh has found out about us somehow," she said.

"How?" Ricky spoke immediately.

"Er, the girls?" Lana wasn't sure how much they knew, but somehow they did. Maybe they'd looked in her email account or history when she'd forgotten to sign out. "It's come to something when children are spying on their parents' computer use."

Ricky laughed.

"I don't think it's funny, Ricky."

"Well, it is your job."

It was. For the last few years Lana had been working as an ITC consultant in education, and it was always a theme parents brought up. Opening their minds with the internet was all very well but how were you meant to close them again, keep track of every nasty little can of worms the inquisitive little darlings prised open? Answer: you couldn't, not really. Not if they were determined little monkeys. She felt a welling of hysteria. She knew he knew, it was obvious, the whole chain of events lay before her on a plain, interconnected like one of the father's model railway layouts. The father. That was how she thought of him, she realized, as the mysterious bugbear of some other poor child's life. "Ouch!" she cried out.

"What is it?"

"I moved my head suddenly."

"Be careful."

"Anyway, I wanted to let you know in case anything should happen to me."

"What??" Ricky spat out the word. This was getting crazy even for Lana. "You don't think he …"

Lana chuckled drily. "Precisely Ricky. I do indeed think he. I think he interfered with my brakes or clutch or something. I can't remember properly, but I saw it coming, I tried to stop."

"Couldn't the garage check?" Ricky asked automatically, one of those questions you know the answer to as soon as it has come out of your mouth.

"They just pronounced it a write off immediately and sent it to the crusher. It was already halfway there." She paused. "You don't believe me, do you?"

.   "Well it does sound far-fetched," Ricky said. "But it's great to hear from you, Lana. I'm so happy you're alright." He caught himself twiddling his hair. "It's obviously been upsetting for you. I was distraught when I found out. I burst into tears to be totally honest with you."

"How did you find out?"

"I happened to type your name into Google."

"Oh." Lana laughed.

"Where is he now?" Ricky asked.

"Out," she said shortly. "You think I've gone totally mad, don't you?"

"No, no … you don't sound mad in the slightest. You have been through a traumatic shock. You're in shock, that's what it is." He felt suddenly angry – what a useless prick her husband was, he really was. "Hasn't Hugh been taking care of you properly?"

"Oh yes. He's been taking care to cover his tracks alright. Oh … come on Ricky, you know how it is with us two; nothing at all has changed one iota. Anyway. I'm okay for now. Listen, I've got to go. I just wanted you to know I was pleased to hear from you. Maybe you're right, I'm going a bit mad again. Bye, Ricky, bye. I'm sorry."

She hung up quickly. Ricky sat there without moving a muscle. He wanted to call her back, but unfortunately, obviously, it was out of the question, and – he realized – it always would be. He was just going to have to sit here on his own until the churning subsided.

Some men always seemed to get their own way with women, and some never did. Unjust, but there you are. Ricky was definitely in the latter category, knew it. Some lucky fuckers always got what they wanted out of women – they had what women always seemed to want – but they didn't deserve it. Scum mainly. Selfish, ruthless shits whom women were taken in by, and readily took in. Maybe they found their boorish shallowness and stupidity reassuring. Maybe they were just tall, although some, come to think of it, were manifestly shorter. Some were even shorter than him. It was enough to make you mentally throw your hands up; but would you be able to catch them again?

Ricky held his own well-tended set of grapplers in front of him, looked around in satisfaction at the well-furnished flat they had been able to grasp and manoeuvre into the winners' chute. He pulled out the case which held his alto saxophone from beside the sofa, unclasped it and took in an eyeful of the beautiful instrument darkly shining there in two pieces, nestling in its blue velvet recesses, waiting for its player. He didn't take it out, of course, knowing what the result would be. Scales, frustration, banging on the wall. He needed to be reminded he was once serious about something; although he told himself he had never been serious about playing the saxophone, he knew, really, he had been, stupid though that now seemed to him.

Spurious. This was a word he liked. Was he a blind watchmaker, such as Richard Dawkins had described? No, but only because he wasn't God. Anyway, it had all been a long, long time ago. Lana too, although in her case going back years and stretching forward into the present. Deep inside he suspected she was just trying to wind him up with all this near-fatal car accident stuff. But, as with the saxophone, he knew on another level he should have settled for what he could get with her. Backdoor man. Lover man. After all, what the hell was wrong with it?

As for Hugh finding out about them, he supposed this was possible, but quite unlikely, unless she'd told him herself. More than likely. Just the sort of thing she'd say when angry. In truth he liked the idea. Let her devoted husband know all there was to know, it wasn't any skin off his prick. At least fifty per cent of their time together had been wasted, he thought, on listening to her moaning about Hugh. Fucking Hugh. What a rubbish name. Well, wasn't it? It reminded him of Hugh Grant. But he knew for an absolute fact, far more certain even than the non-existence of Almighty God, Lana would never, ever leave its bearer – and, whatever his faults, Ricky loved her. As for Hugh interfering with her brakes, he didn't believe it for a second.

FOURTEEN

On the corner in Edmonton Green a tyre-fitting shop marked the turn off down to the Turkish school. He glanced deep into its open bay as he passed, savouring a dark rubbery atmosphere and the unamused glances of shadowy men in overalls who were bouncing pungent new tyres around or hanging about in anticipation of doing some proper tyre-fitting. One of the bow-fronted terraced houses about halfway down had been converted into a school. Two fully-equipped classrooms, one large and one small, front and back, and upstairs a flat where the proprietor, Sezin, lived with her almost grown-up daughter. In the corner of the main classroom, high on the wall, hung a small portrait of Atatürk, the great secularist founder of modern Turkey.

A phone call from Jim had led to weekly trips out to Edmonton, following an interview with Sezin in which she said that she didn't really believe in formal qualifications and wouldn't mind if he had served time in prison as, in her experience, so had a lot of the best people. In other words, he was to be the kind of employee she favoured. Failure, debauchee, black sheep – loyal! His moral defects made him both malleable and worthy of the contempt which would be meted out to him. All the same he sent her a copy of his teaching certificate and CRB check to prove he was as clean as a whistle, and got the job of teaching the older kids.

The younger ones always said hello when he came in, friendly often beautiful children. Girls skulking and sulking deep in the destiny of their wretched gender characteristics. Why couldn't he remember their names? He liked the back room, where he could get them within striking range of his hypnotic powers as he crammed the small whiteboard with his illegible handwriting and dictated comparisons of poems from the AQA anthology, poems which dealt with approved British history in approved ways or introduced the voices of 'the other', the colonial, even the occasional American poet. Other than this they endlessly ground through sample questions from paper three, developing the students' skills of summary and analysis. It was a well-meant enterprise. Sezin would appear at the back window, peering in. Making sure they were working and that he was sticking closely to the syllabus. Everybody got their heads down, as you had to do.

Sezin herself was often in the kitchen with her cronies – a group of Turkish women who had children in her school, one of whom spent a great deal of time rolling cigarettes from a couple of giant sacks of tobacco which Sezin had smuggled in on her last trip back from Istanbul, only a little over her allowance, she insisted, as the woman slipped menthol filters into them and packed them neatly into Sezin's old tobacco tin. This lady, a small stocky woman who wore traditional clothing and a shawl over her hair, as all married women were supposed to, had a roll-up stuck permanently in the corner of her own mouth, a smile braced against its curling smoke, and was often seen sweeping up leaves in the back yard and performing other small chores.

He was an outsider however often he came, and often had only the vaguest sense of how the little world of the school fitted together. He'd had her pegged as a member of the family, but no, just a parent of a quiet, delicate young boy whom he had once spent a spare ten minutes with, gently coaxing him through his little picture book of creatures he didn't understand, and when she came to pick him up she thanked him warmly in one of her few words of English, and he gradually realized these things about her.

The small kitchen was in an extension in the rear of the small house which Sezin had converted into a fully functioning language school, after-hours tuition centre, child-minding facility, and community home from home, often thick with smoke, coffee, Turkish cooking, its air dense with pungent conversations, or monologues whose listeners were conducted though the hell which was Edmonton by a wise Sezin's holdings forth, not a word of which he understood, by which most of them seemed sufficiently impressed. It was the mothers' union, he thought, also with a small table where Sezin would patiently work through students' essays in her one to one sessions

Whichever way he tried to cut her down to size, there was something irreducibly impressive about Sezin. She had instituted order and system and lo it had borne fruit in her life of endless work, guardianship, routines – a life constituted by the ring on the doorbell as the children continued to arrive and depart; she'd created a structure to her days which operated her to their own exhausting rhythms.

He was quickly introduced to all her hatreds, her misperceptions of ability, her sense of social place: a conception of 'good families' and the relative unimportance of girls which wouldn't have been out of place in the world of Jane Austen. She came from the same general class, he realized, large rural landowners, petty aristocrats, which many London Turks believed themselves to be, hence their sense of being a cut above other immigrants, of a disastrous fall in status, of being 'here on business' rather than desperate seekers of a new life. Not really immigrants at all. It was a word used with suspicion and contempt in the newspaper she read. The expensive furniture shops and sumptuous restaurants lining the way to Edmonton told the back story of what they could afford, as did the school fees they were able to fork out, and not only to Sezin, whose latter-day Dame school, only a stone's throw from the one John Keats had attended, inculcated contemporary values.

Comportment was crucial in her concept of education – slouching led to misbehaviour, to a deterioration of attention and a learning deficit. For her it was an obvious visual manifestation of sloth, the incubator of outbreaks of poor behaviour and bad habits. Maybe she was right. She was at war with her West Indian neighbour, who played loud Reggae music during school hours to taunt her, and had objected to her application for planning permission for the extension, her use of her teapot as business premises. Needless to say, Sezin had won, although the neighbour – whom he never saw – was uncowed, and his Saturday afternoon sessions were often accompanied by 'Kinky Reggae' drifting over the stout fence which had failed to make them good neighbours, "How can I be a racist when I am an immigrant too?" she spat angrily.

Without understanding he knew these were the subjects under discussion in a kitchen, where the *Daily Mail* lay folded beside the small woman who rolled her cigarettes. Sezin sympathised with the people who would have deported her. She was permanently unwell, with a hacking cough and contempt for the NHS, which had misdiagnosed her diabetes, and only a trip to a proper Turkish hospital had saved her life. She wanted to sue her incompetent doctors. Her fridge was full of medicines, her hideous screeching rising above the voices of the chattering children to threaten them with beatings and amputations. Her illnesses were not imaginary, her assessment of him as a freakish product of the laughable English education system – and a joke – was not without foundation.

Catherine – a black teacher who worked with the primary age kids – seldom spoke to him unless he forced her to say hello, her resentment based on the fact Sezin tended to employ one or the other of them, not both at the same time, or not for long. To Graham their boss was a natural stirrer who sensed potential conflict and drew it to an electrical point; a lightning rod for any minor bigotry hanging around in the air, she revelled in her ability to conduct and scorch somebody with invisible powers she believed to be everywhere.

All this was mitigated in his eyes by her intermittent employment of black women as teachers, which at least gave her an opportunity to treat them as second class citizens to their faces without fear of being answered back: a swerve which reminded him of her approach to discipline and slapping kids. "You are dead, dead – do you understand me?" She would shriek at them until they trembled in silent fear or skulked, heads down, waiting for her rage to blow over – containing her violent emotions, or the appearance of them, just enough not to leave marks on their plump little faces. She always stopped just short of actually hitting them, she just gently raked their peachy soft skin with her fingernails, while many a mischievous boy child singled out for punishment just met her squinting hatred with a steady defiant gaze, absolutely immobile, as though they were locked together in that moment, in a tryst of understanding, a spell that must not be broken – or else. When she started snapping at him in the same tone, he knew he'd arrived as a teacher, and also that his days were numbered, thankfully. He had been employed by a madwoman.

And yet she had read Dostoyevsky, much better than the crap English writers. She loved Scotland, particularly the area around Fort William, whose mountainous countryside reminded her of Turkey. Sezin had first been there as a student, when men in the pub had called her Turkish Delight. He liked her unkempt appearance. A short, stocky woman in her early fifties with an aggressive stance, he never saw her wear anything which wasn't a pair of jeans and a ratty old sweater, her aspect completed by uncombed hair, her eyes sunken in owlish circles, as though she'd been up all night crying over some private misfortune. "I am a child minder," she said contemptuously on one occasion, but the fear she aroused in her charges could quickly be turned around as she morphed into the all-smiles hostess of yet another kids' party, organized a Christmas game of levitating eager pupils in a chair by energizing the tops of their heads with a few swift passes, so that they shot skywards, chair and all, to delighted laughter.

This was a little known scientific phenomenon, she explained deadpan, but actually it was a real miracle. Sezin Guzen was a wonder-worker, justly respected in her community. Her scariness was all an act, he convinced himself; her puppet-show violence was the only way she knew of keeping these lovely kids in order

Travelling to and fro, back and forth, on the trusty 279, he was endlessly waylayed by the football traffic on Saturdays, starting early, finishing late as the great red chariot ground past White Hart Lane, inching forwards in the crush of cars, on diversion; battened onto by a Jamaican woman who wanted to tell him in detail about a dominoes tournament she'd once attended in Cardiff, to point out that a lot of coloured women had their wedding receptions in what had once been the old music hall on the corner of Bruce Grove, that she and her sons were all karate experts, and that this was necessary, to defend themselves where they lived; or he might be crammed down by the doors by people who were just too stubborn to move along inside the bus please, or find their way upstairs. It was company of sorts, as his satchel disintegrated, spilling worthless papers onto the floor of the bus as it was dragged from his shoulder by people who just wouldn't budge, the beautiful people of Tottenham.

Overheard outside Tescos: always go where the white people go, there you will find the best things, because they only go for the best, they know where the best things are, and what they are. Yeah. An African chuckle. What moral authority did they really enjoy? They had some, or thought they had, and this could be borrowed discursively, and they were sick of it, but he didn't think it was so much actually, that, and either way it could always be easily, righteously reclaimed if you gave the people on the bus a less narrow place to stand up in. We are here, they were saying, and we won't be budging up. Thank you, Miss Rosa. Not everybody, however, can really stand at the front of the bus.

On this return journey one day the driver had announced a diversion before the town hall and he hopped off, continuing on foot through what turned out to be a demonstration demanding belated justice for Mark Duggan. Mark Duggan, by now forgotten everywhere in the world except right here and in the history books. The guy who left the heater in the car – but they'd shot him anyway, in the middle of his fool's errand to the nowhere of his revenge, his deluded false authority. The road, the pavements were packed with people, TV crews, ranting demagogues who railed against police racism, hopeful *Socialist Worker* sellers whose small glinting spectacles hadn't changed in forty years, young black women waving their carefully produced placards, often, as ever, with the party insignia scratched out.

The cops themselves were cheerful, unworried, happily pointing people down to the demo as if it were the turnstiles of White Hart Lane rather than a political protest against them as the state licenced murderers of black people. The demonstration was winding down, the last speeches on the steps of the police station being made through megaphones. He stopped in his tracks, listened respectfully as the last drops of bile dripped into the festive Saturday afternoon air, soon vapourised by a good-humoured crowd; down the long road to the wide junction of Seven Sisters, the outside Colombian restaurant, past the weird African underwear shop.

He liked to lurk out in the back garden during breaks, to sit on a semi-circular wooden bench in the barbecue area in this place accidentally north of the equator where the sun rinsed the blue out of the sky; rubbing shoulders with milling cousins, dimly apprehending great loops of interrelatedness such as he himself had never enjoyed. A friendly young woman with a twitchy eye was still resitting her GCSE English at twenty-one, a confident person in every other way who enjoyed taking charge of the noisy children; there was a young Armenian woman; goofy harmless Sibel: all of them good to hunker down with for a few minutes in the pale Edmonton sunlight in an unkempt, scrubby yard where Sezin's poor cat had contracted its final illness.

What did he know anyway? Turks in the public libraries reading *Hürriyet*, which looked to him like a revolutionary newspaper – hurry it up, we're preparing an insurrection – and he'd imagined it was the *Isvestia*.of London, these coffee-drinking, moustachioed men in tweed jackets were pulling on their pipes to some greater insurrectionary purpose. More recently, when he was in the Whittington Hospital, a wiry little eighty-year-old in the next bed hadn't been able to stop talking, and with the urgent blissfulness of a lucky stroke survivor had told Graham his whole life story.

He'd come over in 1948 to run the marathon for his country in the Olympic games. His name was Sevki Koru, and he had come twentieth. Back the next year to run again. Because he'd been a long distance runner for many years; all his whole life in a way. And on and on through a restaurant career in the Midlands, memories of meat-cleaver armed street fights between the Turks and the others, yes he'd survived all that too, and here he was incessantly nagging the nurse about his mobile phone connection: an instrument into which his self-proclaiming words were soon tumbling endlessly as he lay back in relief, nursing his own knowledge that he wouldn't be around as long as this energetic octogenarian. Everybody in the transit ward had felt the same way about him.

But he was an outsider, not them; they never had been in his position, but he didn't resent immigrants and their children for this as Sezin seemed to think he should. In fact, he had little sense of England as 'his own country', although he knew plenty more about it than they did, and he was happy to pass on whatever he had gleaned of her language and customs. An old woman had been decapitated in the street nearby by a recent Islamic convert, but within the school everybody was on fairly good terms. They liked being there with other Turks, it had a genuine community aspect – but they had to pay for the privilege.

Sezin sold everything, books, paper and pens, and opened a tuck shop in the kitchen to further fleece kids, offering sweets and crisps and soft drinks, to keep them on the premises during breaks rather than let them go wandering up the road for half-an-hour. She ran it her way, with her own admirable qualities, putting the money in a large empty coffee jar as though it were a piggy bank which would later be emptied to pay for their further treats.

"I know you disapprove of my unorthodox teaching methods," she once said officiously as a prelude to an account of the miracle she had achieved in raising one of the kids to his current level. He'd made a serious, respectful face, feeling compromised as ever as the screeching abuse, threats and emotional violence he witnessed on every occasion he visited her school were reconfigured before his ears into some sort of progressive regime she had devised.

Sezin had compiled her own book of exercises which she sold, an impressive publication out of which she taught endlessly and punctiliously – tenses, idioms, model sentences, everything the struggling language student might require. It was difficult to square this with her grammatical inability in practice. She was incapable of writing a short e-mail, or even a text message which didn't include a number of glaring errors. But, again, he couldn't help admiring her for keeping the whole show on the road.

Pari, one of the older students, was a pale, reserved and somewhat aloof Armenian girl with neat handwriting. She didn't follow the GCSE syllabus but wrote instead in her notebook, telling stories of lovers' suicides, family disapproval, writing down the true predicament of women in Turkey with a gravity which suggested a belief that her momentary capture of these stories, the lightness of her touch upon the paper of her notebook, her thin perfect script, really did constitute the basis of justice, bestowing eternal life upon the victims of these everyday atrocities. She showed him the stories, insisting they were not stories at all but the truth, which he countered by correcting her grammatical errors or praising her clear exposition.

She would sometimes withhold her notebook, telling him she only wrote them for herself; on other occasions she admitted she was only practicing her handwriting, her grammar, and this was simply something to write down, something she happened to know. She would walk out of there into another life, a life he would never glimpse, a life in which the imperative was to forget about those kinds of things. It was not after all her own predicament she was describing. She would not be forced into marriage, into throwing herself or her newborn baby from a high river cliff. She was a Londoner, at least for now, and even if she went back – the possible fate of young women whose English did not improve sufficiently – it would not really be to anything as bad as this, not bad at all, in fact.

Usually she sat next to Sibel, a woman of the same age who was just such a hopeless language case, although a voracious reader. She had gained a temporary stay of execution by working in her uncle's estate agency, misfiling. Sibel wanted to be a policewoman and carry a gun: a dopey reader of romances for teens, still hopeful, and an Islamic novel about 15th century holy men. "It is good," she said, showing him the cover. "Turkish is a beautiful language. It is easy to read and to write, only two tenses which never change, and with plenty of good words to describe everything you need."

Orhan was a rich boy, beefy, prime stifado, his haircuts shaved in close to the neck leaving a slicked-down tuft of vegetation on the plateau of his skull, which imparted a fat, bovine sheen to his ample-sized head. He enjoyed looking up words on his i-phone, being a smart-arse and generally getting away with it. His mother was ambitious for him, his father had paid for the best schools, but his academic abilities stood at zero. They could well afford to employ him as a rewrite man. God knew how much they paid Sezin per item of homework, but the true author of his works only received a tenner a shot, however many drafts it took. Anyhow, Orhan was going to inherit their import-export business. It was amazing how they got away with it, but then, of course, it wasn't really amazing at all just par for the course. He was beefy, prime stifado, and his haircuts shaved in close to the neck leaving a slicked-down tuft of vegetation on the plateau of his skull, imparting a fat, bovine sheen to his ample-sized head.

He had come to quite like this young man, partly because the sheer stupidity of his comments as they huddled in the back room over Carol Ann Duffy and her compadres gave him a lift sometimes, and his resentment of writing Orhan's homework gave the hapless protagonist a perfect excuse to be nasty to him. He liked to get Orhan to look up Turkish equivalents for English words they didn't know on his mobile, but the rich boy punished him by forcing him to listen to his bigoted view of women and his conviction Moslems were going to take over Britain by stealth, a view shared with working-class conspiracy theorists across middle-England and the counter-butchers of Norway and drone-senders elsewhere.

He couldn't help pointing out that if stealth was their intention, he'd somewhat given the game away. His mother was fiercely pious, feeling aggrieved that the street butchery of Lee Rigby outside Woolwich barracks by a demented jihadi had received far too much publicity in the popular press.

And there were other kids corralled in the back room: a boy who came all the way in from Waltham Forest, a once pretty village now given over to drug-fuelled gunfights. He was a wide-browed, serious lad who wore small wire reading glasses which made him look like an intellectual, and bent over his notebook in earnest. He wouldn't let the teacher write anything for him, but liked to show his work.

He could do the trick of downloading recondite vocabulary from his i-phone into his writing better than Maral, mainly using words correctly, not too many outlandish near-synonyms misfiring into the roof there. When he got them to write stories in the big group, his was the best, descriptively rich and spot on, anyway containing the best line: "the girls laughed hideously." They had all laughed at that.

Another boy liked reading history books, his favourite subject, and could discuss the French revolution well, but again there was the sad evidence you dreaded – of cramped, pained letters, sentence fragments, only a couple of short, broken paragraphs of near scribble to show for all his assiduous effort; and yet another boy, haughty, with the common middle-class ambition to be a doctor, and the family money to back it. He was charged with straightening out his coursework, but he found it impossible to accept there was ever anything wrong with his arguments, his grammar, or that this scruffy teacher could possibly be more intelligent, or better at anything than himself. He was a smug young man he would like to have taken down a peg or two, rather than continually having to congratulate him on his genius and superiority to women – as appeared to be required for his emotional well-being.

Maral was a slim girl, fairly intelligent but highly strung, who was worried about her ever-burgeoning height. She felt she would never be normal. As she stooped to get in under the door-jamb, he offered her the mock-reassurance that if she kept growing, at least she would be able to get her clothes specially made for her. "That is so rude!" was one of her favourite expressions, and he often rose to it, flirtatiously baiting her until she threatened to call Childline.

He liked the way she spoke, in the accent of Tottenham's black kids, with whom she went to school: "Sah! Sah! Kin we do checkin out mi 'istry?" He enjoyed hearing this elusive argot, whose key items seemed to be "Whay?" and "Baey!" although he flattered himself that he could soon pick it up. But as they got to know each other he saw that to go along with her emotional difficulties was just to invite her to be a pest. She was another dominant type – full of herself, always trying to stop other kids talking, and making things worse; an attention seeker, a control freak, more trouble than she was worth. Eventually she refused to do any writing in his class, since hers didn't need his improvements. She didn't like writing poetry, because it wasn't on the curriculum, but he refused to see any sign of higher intelligence in this attitude.

Sezin was unsympathetic to her high strung outbursts, made her cry one day (actually she was already crying), withholding her sympathy as a kind of inoculation against her hysteria, and later got her to write a toe-curling glowing endorsement of her school, Maral's home from home. Like all teachers he tended to treat linguistic competence as intelligence, which it is, but not to any fantastic extent, and he would always be tempted to ascribe wider meaning to it – in other words, a potential to share his own intellectual pretensions. Well, you've got to try, he thought.

And as everywhere, kids had problems. Problems with English. They were articulate sometimes but unable to write well, a gulf between literacy and writing ability which is commonplace in people from all cultural and ethnic backgrounds, including the natives, but these Turks often displayed qualities of second language learners in near native speakers.

A Kurdish girl, Dersdar, was an exception. Her family lived in Hackney. She possessed higher language abilities, and enjoyed mocking the poor spelling of Turks, with their kebaps and pitsa She was having piano lessons, once brought a new metronome to the class, took it out of its box and bubble wrap and set it going on the desk, to tick out the minutes of her childhood, slow then fast. She was a small, pretty thirteen-year-old, and she reminded him of one of his childhood sweethearts, Katherine Stedman. She looked like a typical English schoolgirl, but she wasn't, like Adem, her male counterpart, who had the classic English schoolboy look, in his case combined with an impenetrable youth patois and poor written expression.

"Wilma! Wilma!" He had loved it when Fred Flintstone banged on the door after his unsuccessful altercation with the sabre-toothed pussy, and the disgruntled brontosaurus crane which lifted rocks on its head, and the hooter-bird which had squawked at the end of the working day, and the rack of dinosaur ribs which overturned the skate-car at the drive-in restaurant. Top cartoon. *Top Cat* had been only slightly better. Cool TC directed his gang of hipsters from a trashcan surrounded by skeletal fishes, fooling poor Officer Dibble again and again. Today's kids were deprived by comparison, having only *The Simpsons* left as a siren-call to rebellious youth. Maybe they would throw off their shackles or at least continue to laugh for a little while at the crazy adult world.

"It's the only good programme on television," said Maral's generally silent sister. "Why are they taking it off?"

He was forced to agree – it was a conspiracy against children of truly monstrous proportions. Keep *The Simpsons*, bring back *Top Cat*! In Tottenham, and probably elsewhere, Dibble was still bad boy slang for a policeman.

One hot summer day the front door had been open, and a strong smell of weed wafted in from outside. Several kids laughed, and he proclaimed this an instant citizenship lesson, reenacting the terror of two world wars. "Gas attack! Gas attack!" he shouted, and told them to cover their mouths and noses, as a single inhalation of the fatal poison could cause irreparable brain damage. Dersdar quickly covered her face with her school scarf, her eyes dancing with merriment: it was innocent, unfeigned, and it was enough.

SIXTEEN

He was ambling along side by side in quiet solidarity with Chris Sekibo, down towards the cashpoint outside Sainsbury's, where Chris was going to withdraw forty pounds from his account and hand it over to his tutor. They were Study Buddies. Whether it was the thought of parting with this hard-earned currency from his Saturday job at Gap in Brent Cross shopping centre which had reduced him to silence, or something else, he couldn't tell. He enjoyed it, that's all. Nothing else in his experience was quite like taking folding money from a teenager.

Earlier, in the small cloakroom beside their front door where they held their sessions, he'd been trying to impress upon him the subtlety and richness of Scott Fitzgerald's use of metaphorical language. Jay Gatsby's car was amongst other things, in Fitzgerald's description of it, he had noticed, a giant white penis. A flaccid penis. Flaccid? Limp. That had made the Nigerian boy laugh. But the money was hard to part with, being Chris's own hard-earned cash. Still, he took it, and they said goodbye.

He continued on his long stroll to Arnos Grove station. Nothing much crossed his mind. He entered what he thought of as the great acorn of light and descended to the platform, hopped on a tube train to Turnpike Lane and decanted himself through the left-hand exit to emerge by the 41 bus stop. He couldn't be fucked to walk home. He wondered what he found so likeable about Chris in his skinny, sagging jeans. It certainly wasn't his acute intelligence, nor any lingering sense that his people were oppressed. Like fuck were they oppressed. Chris had already bombed out of an expensive fee paying school where he had managed to achieve nothing but to break his arm playing rugby. Now he attended a nearby Catholic sixth form, and had put Graham on to some of his classmates following his sudden success in English coursework grades.

He was going to enjoy this job. He briefly toyed with the idea of dumping Jim and starting his own company. Study Buddies. Chris Sekibo had thought it was a great idea. He was a pleasant boy. He had his fun, his mates phoned him, he went skiing in Vermont with his family, the big apple was his oyster, and had a certain ability to surf along on uncomprehended bullshit which spoke of confidence rather than anything else, or perhaps just a desire to please, to do well.

Perhaps this was a strength in the middle-classes – their lack of any need for stuff to make overall sense. His sisters, as always, were beautiful. His father and mother stern. They stood in the large open hallway of their teapot and glared at the two miscreant children – Chris and himself – 'B' wasn't good enough. Chris had to get an 'A' at least, preferably an 'A*' in everything. Mr Sekibo had the air of a high ranking administrator of some kind: he knew how to demand the impossible. Nothing else was going to be acceptable. What else were they paying for? Chris looked at him with a bowed head, a slightly raised eyebrow. His powerfully-built father was obviously a man who always got exactly what he wanted out of life. A man who knew how to instill fear. Well, he knew what was required of him. He knew his place in this world alright, just chose not to take it too seriously.

He spent a lot of time listening to Radio Two, hoping they were going to play 'Mairzy Doats and Dozy Doats'. But they never did. He woke up with the radio still churning, trotting out its conveyor belt of audience-voted golden moments, and foggily disentangled himself from a dream about Chrissie Hynde, a dream in which the Pretenders frontwoman was a neighbour and a friend of his mother. His family were all whole and healthy, all still living in the large, comfortable country pile they inhabited in dreams, his brother still in his childhood room, a cavernous garage full of jealously guarded classic motorbikes. A quiet, friendly woman, Chrissie didn't really like being recognized as a famous singer, but when Roy Orbison came on the radio she smiled a crooked smile and pointed to her throat – and abruptly, unexpectedly, she kissed him on the lips.

He'd been doing a bit of supply once at Islington Green School in that hideous tower, and a girl of about thirteen had asked him what kind of poems he wanted her to write. She loved poetry and could do both kinds, love poems and hurting poems. "What's the difference?" he asked. "Well," she explained, "love poems are like I love you, I love you – and hurting poems are like –" she made an anguished grimace – "*you hurt me, you hurt me.*" He suggested she try some of both, and in a noisy, dangerously chaotic classroom she had reeled them off one after another, putting up her hand to show him each one, blinking in her eagerness to please. When he read through them he saw she was indeed fluent, if not proficient, in both genres. Thinking about this later he wondered if the two kinds of poems the girl had identified were indeed the only kinds, broadly corresponding to experiences of arrival and departure.

Hurrying up and down a long dark rainy street in Edmonton in search of an odd-numbered anomaly on the even side of the road, it was difficult to remember he was one of the anointed. Usually a welcome visitor, he was expected above all to be on time and to produce instant results – whatever the weather, whatever the inaccessibility of the location. After all, they lived there, and they had been able to find it quite alright. Sometimes he thought of himself as a door-to-door salesman, although it wasn't a close match. Sometimes his father had let them in, invited them in, just for the sport of talking to them for hours and hours. He still did it. Most recent was a one salesman with a case full of samples he had been happy to sample, although he was still more or less teetotal and definitely not part of the wine-drinking demographic. One of them had been an encyclopedia salesman, he recalled, and the old man had roped him in. Did he want a leather-bound set of the *Encyclopedia Britannica*?

Of course he did, and his father had come, it seemed, within a hairsbreadth of signing up for it. But it was not to be – no marvellous set of encyclopedias had been bought. What a boon it would have been in their sad, bookless council flat. Sure to have been a great influence and inspiration on him. He felt himself, once again, tumbling into gut-gnawing anger, a tired, bitter hunger for what he had never had, now never would. But it was stupid to blame his father, or anyone else, for his present ignorance of all that beautiful knowledge which the Britannica might have imprinted on him. He'd blown his chances, now he was standing on doorsteps, still nervously preparing to demonstrate a vacuum cleaner which could, in a trice, suck up the ground-in contents of a spilled ashtray.

Behind the front door of a council flat which reminded him of Cobham he struggled out of his shoes and into a pair of guest slippers. It was the end of dinner time as usual, and a slim mother dressed for work abandoned him to grind her son through *Much Ado About Nothing*, explicating every pun in the high-spirited sparring of Benedick and Beatrice, with a surly, confident boy who justified his lack of interest with the confession that he wasn't really thinking of taking this stuff up for a profession.

But there were certain corners, such as the bus stop at St Peter's church, where the world that seemed to jut from them like an upholstered shoulder needed to be discovered and negotiated at the last moment under the yellow street lights at dusk, his weathered *A-Z* peered at through 2.00 Boots reading glasses, rotated into focus. Cozy brown teapots were snug and radiating out in dew-decked spider's web rows from the tiled porch of the church, whose bells had clamoured in reassurance for matins and evensong since before teapots were thus sweetly arranged, dappled and stippled into the landscape of Enfield beyond Winchmore Hill, and fortunately there was somebody scurrying along in the darkness who would give him directions, who knew the area like the back of her hand, and when he rang the designated bell ten minutes early, somebody to answer in the middle of their evening meal, and he would be asked to wait on the once-white sofa and look at cookery books on a shelf opposite until they were ready for him. Somebody for whom this role-play of mansplaining urban saint just wasn't going to be satisfactory. A copy of Evelyn Waugh's *Vile Bodies* lay open on their sofa.

As soon as the plates were cleared away he worked with the girl at the table, while the mother sat retracted into herself on the sofa, listening to his performance. They discussed a few of her set texts, he looked at an essay for which she'd got a 'B', offering a judicious mixture of praise and suggestions for improvements. Beatrice was a drone of patriarchy, Hero little better than a whore. Bertram a nasty piece of work, Claudio an irritating boy who loved nobody. And the ending – how everything was covered up, papered over. Shakespeare was a hack, no doubt of it. If a thing could be said plainly, it wouldn't be. Was this a great national poet? She thought not. Gatsby was far from being great: a low-class shit, a gangster. Beverley (of *Abigail's Party*) was contemptible, her guests ugly. The working-class could only be a pale imitation of the middle. She had to admit, she was a complete snob herself. That settled it then. He struggled to parry her blows, admiring her vituperative flights.

"Gatsby has a lot of nice shirts," he objected weakly. "At least he means well."

As they bit into the poisoned apple of their second hour together, he noticed a reproduction of Christ's bleeding heart on a pillar which separated the kitchen area from the dining area. They were Catholics. The tenor of her talk darkened. She was a pessimist, she had to admit. People were rats: jumping, wheeling rats. The only book on her reading list she really liked was *The Road* by Cormac McCarthy: a work of great imaginative power. But he had to admit he hadn't yet read it. He couldn't fault her enthusiasm, her engagement with it all, but called a halt after an hour and a half. He extracted his money from the mother, who far from being asleep as her daughter hoped, had been monitoring every word and not liking any of his. "Well, I hope that was useful," he said, shaking the girl's hand at the door. The girl seemed happy enough. Mother disgruntled. Oh well, sometimes all it took was one lesson with the shadowman.

He retraced his steps precisely and sat in numb embarrassment on the same bus and train home as the empty landmarks reeled backwards emptily: the new-to-him MacDonalds in Palmer's Green where he had eaten his celebratory pre-class meal, now simply another instance, another link in the chain; the endless reeling, screening trees now indicators of not very much behind them. Whether this happened once or not very often, it seemed a repetition of humiliations from long ago. He awaited the girl's essay for editing for a couple of days, without much hope, completing other assignments, until finally Jim rang him with the bad news that the mother didn't wish to continue with tuition, because she had found him insufficiently versed in examination criteria.

"I think she's a bit mad, to be honest," his genial invigilator commented. "She's one of these people who think they know everything there is to know about education but with no particular basis. She said she sat in on the session – which I always find totally off-putting."

Graham knew nothing he ever did would satisfy those kinds of people, any more than he would be credited (by whom?) for any results he was ever likely to achieve for their eager, transitional progeny. He faithfully shamefacedly promised Jim to bring his commission up to date.

SEVENTEEN

The pupil referral unit was well-appointed, fairly recent, the way into it via two layers of glass, three if you counted the hatch at which you stated your business sand were issued with a pass. You were then admitted to the inner sanctum of earthly punishment, which had an eerily privileged feel. So few pupils were in evidence: those twos and threes materialising on the long wide corridor were accompanied by as many staff, supervising them through days in which obedience and accountability for one's actions were paramount. Any harsh words exchanged with another constituted an incident, an incident which had to be accounted for in writing, analysed in depth, so monastic training came to mind, if anything, as a model for what went on there.

The kids looked affable enough, kidding around with each other, if in more muted mode than usual. How had they got here? Was it simply a matter of failing the corridor silence rules in the academies, or were incidents of repeatedly punching others in the face required in order to enter this haven of quietude and consideration of the outcomes of poor adaptation, misreading the prerogatives of the other, failing to play well at games which others had mastered more easily than oneself?

Venting, swearing, lashing out. He imagined it must still happen. The pupils referred here would know this was their last port of call; they couldn't be moved on, so might tend to continue with their satisfyingly challenging behaviours, borne of poor home life, maybe, lack of boundaries, perhaps ... or whatever. Here were the buffers to shunt against for as long as the system had responsibility for you, on a minimal curriculum, and the teachers were people who were genuinely patient, liked listening to problems, setting you straight for the thousandth time. On the other hand there were kids who were relatively blameless, or unblameable, and those who would soon move on, move back into mainstream education if they could, into colleges for further education or training.

He met his referred pupil in a pristine, clean little room, its door propped open with a plastic chair, and when she appeared, smiling shyly, found it hard to believe she was any kind of miscreant. He asked took at her book, she showed it, and her handwriting was neat and free of spelling and punctuation errors. *Of Mice and Men.* Good work. Point, evidence, explanation. Pukka, if a little thin on the ground. They read a couple of things together, things he'd brought with him. Katherine Mansfield's story 'How Pearl Button Was Kidnapped' was one of them, her early classic about a young girl taken from the roadside outside her home, the 'house of boxes', by a group of passing Maori women, who feed her and undress her, make her one of their own children, taking her to the beach in their wagon or cart.

She has never seen the sea before, despite living quite close to it, and is having a beautiful time with her kidnappers until the little blue men appear on the horizon to take her back home. It was a lovely story, dream-like, with a buried eroticism which always seemed to hit the spot. Could his referred pupil work out any of its mysteries? She got how the little blue men were the police, but only after a few clues. He was looking for that look of pleasure, which he got, and perhaps was no more than an expected response she produced. He felt he was there to rescue her from this particular house of boxes and take her out for a jaunt on the open road in his gypsy wagon to look at the sea and a life without restraints, at least for once in her life, and for her part she wanted to get out of the pupil referral unit, where she couldn't do English Literature GCSE. This was more like it, a love match made in tutor heaven.

Entering her home couldn't have been more different than the trial of Palmers Green. Her flustered, smiling mum greeted him warmly at the door of their Finsbury Park place, her kitchen full of people finishing their dinner, a couple of three year olds said hello, a couple of sisters and a tall young black man smiled and gravely shook his hand. Then they all went away and let them get on with *Pride and Prejudice.* They are both full of pride, you see, and both of them are deeply prejudiced. But later they realize they were wrong to be like this, so much, although they were entitled to be sceptical, to ask a few leading questions.

All at once Yemi was gone from her job and it was all over between them. He had to return to the Job Centre and meet Christian, his new sustainability consultant, Christian, a devotee of the Steve Jobs (no doubt attracted by the name) approach to life. He was an avid reader of self-help manuals and pop psychology articles and was at work on a similar tome of his own. "People who succeed are mostly psychopaths," he explained his approach. "They aren't interested in helping others. They are interested in helping themselves, in walking all over the other. They are liars, thieves."

"I know," he said resignedly.

"But you have to be like them, you have to be strong and confident. Don't let them put you in an inferior position. Don't ask them for anything. Don't expect them to do anything for you. Why should they? It's the wrong approach. Show them you have something they need, which will make their life better, easier. Make their business grow for them. You've got to be pro-active. Go in there and demand an appointment with the top guy. There is a bad psychopath – he goes around ..."

"He or she," Graham corrected him.

"He or she goes around killing people. They have no remorse, no pity. They're not interested in the feelings of the other. Like a serial killer. They are only interested in their own feelings, feelings of power over others. Their sense of well-being comes from their power – from hurting people – but they're not interested in that particularly. They are ruthless, hard. They have no empathy. Empathy is an important human quality – but bad, in a way, for successfulness." Christian was smiling with pleasure, enjoying their conversation.

"Sometimes they do pretend to have empathy."

"Yes!" Christian's eyes gleamed. "They do pretend."

"They use empathy to manipulate others."

"Yes, they are manipulators." Christian sat back happily. "Graham," he said. "You can get any job you want, if you go about it in the right way. I know you have the ability – I can tell."

"I'm just too old," he said.

Christian brushed this aside, leaning forward. "There is a job out there for you, I know you can get it."

"By being a psychopath."

"Yes. There is a bad psychopath and a good psychopath."

"So, what's a good psychopath? What are they like?"

"Same as a bad psychopath – but not quite as bad."

"Why not?"

"Because they only use their powers for good."

In other words you had to look out for the McGuffin. The tiny spool of film in the cake, the missing part which will activate the nuclear device, the code to stop it. The thing most people will accede to as the key to an overriding moral imperative: saving the world. In a thriller it was often just some spurious item everybody was chasing after, the device that was just a device, which made the plot go along – although Greene was good at making his carry some moral freight, partly because of the real and evident threats besetting his early twentieth century world, which added up to a holocaust easier to believe in than putative nuclear annihilation, because absolutely real.

In a traditional poem it might be the body of the beloved, her restless limbs, her visage shining with news about something or other. God? Eternity? Mortality? The King's orders? Shakespeare's Sonnet 130, where the lady's breath stinks and she stomps around heavily on the ground, was the only one that proper girls really liked, not in his opinion set often enough, perhaps not as appealing to the middle-aged exam setters as those evergreen temporary darling buds of May.

Still, you could say, the down to earth woman doesn't altogether express the idea as well as the unearthly youthful beauty, transcendent object of all masculine striving. There she lay, her breathing a little fast, adjacent to the McGuffin, supplying a little moral meaning to your otherwise drearily self-interested tale. In Greene's thrillers there was sometimes expressed a moral intelligence of the beautiful young woman who has seen too much, of male greed and frailty, of the suffering it has caused, and who accepts this arena is where all of our small lives will take place; but the tender deer the haunted men were chasing could equally be an excuse, a pretext for the bloody mayhem for which you were actually deriving most of your readerly pleasure.

This was usually the case in physical action thrillers, including the worst book he had ever read, *Atrocity Week* by Andrew McCoy, in which brutal rape and murder of the protagonist's wife by raiders on his South African farm is a handy excuse for hunting down and killing a lot of renegade blacks. But the best book of this sort, *Rogue Male* by Geoffrey Household, he thought was a masterpiece of running, ducking, hiding, surviving, romantically defying the powers of darkness to the last gasp, to victory. All the same

Household barely touched his lost woman into existence, quite late, and in general tenderness was severely rationed in blood-spattered adventure books meant purely for men. Too much of it and your two-fisted reader would possibly cast your peculiar novel aside in manly disgust.

Graham Greene seemed to think there was something wrong with pity; it led to confused, monstrous acts, and was always twinned with cruelty, which sprang up to join it with a wolfish smile, and your marvellous mercy killing turned out to have a selfish motive after all. You put a broken backed rat out of its misery only because you couldn't bear to watch it suffer, but your own heart beat faster all the same as the stone – or in his case, the shoe – went down to finally terminate its small, pitiful, beat of existence.

Reasons to believe. Men needed them. The histrionics of Rod Stewart and Bruce Springsteen referred to something real in the human breast. Your lying woman. Your dead dog. Your moral compass. Your McGuffin. One day it would get up and run. Did the purveyors of these things actually believe them? Not in the case of Rod Stewart, surely. His apologies were cheeky self-endorsements … and the whole thing drivelled away into nothingness, into talk of 'the ideals of youth', a lot of patent nonsense nobody could really afford to entertain.

More generally, life had its double aspect. A woman he'd once taught, a pretty one with a lot of money behind her, became a fairly successful journalist. He'd met her for a cup of coffee in Soho, refusing to let her pay. Later he watched a couple of her online pieces. She landed in helicopters, rode across the African veldt on the back of a jeep with her long dark hair whipped by the wind, investigating some abuse, highlighting a conservation effort. In other journalism she exposed modern instances of child slavery in a way which seemed heroic, or at least principled. But it was the journey itself which obviously mattered to her, terrain seen from a certain elevation. How everything had changed for the better since Graham Greene's day. Nowadays far more women bolted together their own plots, deployed their own ingenious McGuffins. And, as a woman interviewing him in a Job Centre had long ago replied drily, in answer to God-knows-what, the jewelled lid of Pandora's Box had been flapping open for some time.

EIGHTEEN

Where was she? Who was she? Somebody on this bus smelled of sharpening, she was sure. Like when you sharpened a pencil; that pencil smell. Fresh and sharp. Maybe somebody was actually sharpening a pencil. She cast her hooded eyes around the upper deck, but couldn't identify the offender. A good sharp pencil could be an offensive weapon, she thought. But maybe it could be some other kind of cut wood. Somebody had been doing carpentry. Somebody had shaken their head too hard and the sawdust was falling out of their ears. She shook her own head, slightly, lightly, to stop herself from like laughing. But that pencil smell; it was something special, particular; it brought everything to a point, for sure it did: the strong smell of fresh sharpening.

The blue blaze of the sky was in one corner, the green of the land in another, and what seemed to be objects, buildings perhaps, constructions, or some another sorts of bulky thing he was unable to identify or classify, were roughly spread in the middle. It had taken ages to get to this stage with the puzzle, but without a picture to copy he felt he would never get any further along with it. The obvious thing was to find the corners, but firstly he would have to put together the straight edges that would frame whatever image he was attempting to bring forth from an almighty chaos of individual jig-saw pieces.

He fell to his task, and in another hour he had constructed what appeared to be the sky's curtain rail: a blue edge. He sat back and squinted, trying to guess what the picture was supposed to be. Nothing came to mind. A ship on the sea? A landscape? Where? It was at least possible that he had the jig-saw on its side; rotated perpendicular it would turn out to be the leaning tower of Pisa, complete with a miniature Galileo dropping a pair of different-sized cannonballs from an upper window. Or was that Sir Isaac Newton? He reminded himself to look it up next time he was in the library. On the other hand it might turn out to be a view of the Thames at London Bridge, or a hillside village in Tuscany. But ut didn't look like a photograph, he thought, the colours and their varied texture were recognizably those of an oil painting. He scuffled in the broken pieces of this hidden world with his fingertips, looking for more edges and, whenever he found one, lined it up with the others, higgledy-piggledy, in a long mixed row whose only criterion of affinity was possession of a single straight-ruled edge. He also found a corner, but putting it down for a second, immediately lost it once more in the central muddle of undefined world-matter.

Actually, he realized, this was hell. He was insane, locked up in an institution somewhere, eating flies, only imagining he was in this flat, carrying on with this strange precarious little existence, watching shadows pass on the walls of his cell, imagining a glider up there on his ceiling.

But he decided to plug on.

NINETEEN

Ricky never had liked Billie Holiday, nor for that matter any other female jazz singer. For him those corny songs they sang were boring, obviously phony crap. The tunes, the lyrics, everything about them was rubbish, and the musicians were just using them as a vehicle for improvisation; quite rightly they held the songs themselves in contempt. He made a mental yawn emoticon, in which one half of his mouth became a quivering open sack which his right hand fanned lightly, and this seemed to him to say it all, had anyone been there to watch him do it. What he admired about Charlie Parker was his technique, his speed, so he suffered Parker's renditions of the songs she had recorded earlier with Teddy Wilson and Count Basie with half-amused contempt, waiting only for the solos, really, if he was honest. Lover Man was a classic case in point. There were quite a few recordings of the song, and the last one – where Parker played it straight through with 'his Orchestra' – was by far the worst: plodding, undynamic, soft jazzy fodder in which Bird just fingered his way through a tedious tune on autopilot. There was another version recorded live in France, by an audience member on a home tape recorder, but this was so crackly as to be disqualified from serious consideration. And there was also the live in Sweden version, pacy and therefore correspondingly short, but which was actually exquisite, elegant, a beautiful throwaway gem.

But so-called jazz critics said the best version of Lover Man was the first Parker had ever recorded, sitting in with the Howard McGee Quartet for Dial in 1946. He was propped up in his chair, high on heroin (drunk, they said, held up to the microphone by Ross Russell, but Ricky thought it was smack), missed his entrance, sidled in with a couple of stray notes, wove around falteringly for a while, until Howard McGee's trumpet came in to support him, trying to save the take. Parker tried and failed to harmonize with him on a chorus, produced an oblique but beautiful solo, and spiralled to an abrupt halt. After the session, so the famous story went, he returned to his hotel room and set fire to it. He wanted it destroyed, eliminated – he wasn't much of a lover man any more – but the record company had put it out to embarrass him, for flubbing the session, which it did. He tried to record it again later, kept it in his repertoire and trotted it out from time to time. End of story. So how come everybody went on about it? It was another case, like Billie Holiday, of the perversity of jazz critics who knew nothing about music, just liked to embroider a nice tale for the public. They misread things. Mistook being stoned for inspiration. They found Parker's fumbling junk-numbed fingers and shortness of breath to be expressive of his pain. It was the singing of a wounded bird, the beginnings of free jazz. All that crap which was supposed to be so brilliant, which he himself had been taken in by. Miles Davis albums he had strained to make sense of were masterpieces sweating out a moisture of pregnancy. Whatever.

On one of the many Bird compilations Ricky owned, the song's title was misspelled as 'Lever Man'. It was just a careless error by some illiterate at the record company, but Ritchie had thought it was another song – until he got the record home and put it on his then state-of-the-art turntable. And discovered it was just Lover Man. The same fucking appalling take. He'd been had – and all the way home he'd been playing around with that title. A man who operated levers, in a signal box maybe, or a man who fitted tyres, or a man who was operated by levers. A man like himself. A strong man like Charlie Parker, who after all had actually managed to tilt the earth on its axis by means of the muscles in his arms. He'd levered himself into that studio, levered his way into the tune, lifted it out of the ordinary and into the realms of great art. By accident. By accident! What a crock of absolute shit these accidents of so-called genius turned out to be! And everybody who had ever since picked up a saxophone drove themselves round the bend trying to replicate them. Round Midnight. In Tunisia. Fuck. Off.

All the same Ricky took off the now ended Charlie Parker album – Volume 10 of the complete set he'd bought in his late teens – very carefully, examined it with minute attention for dust particles and slid it back into its pristine sleeve; and from there into its precise slot under P. He could play most of those tunes himself, even though, as he reassured himself once more, he had never taken any of it seriously, at least not his own playing. At least he could thank his lucky stars he'd been intelligent enough to give up on music.

TWENTY

The man had cut his hands off, or was just about to, and a body had been thrown on top of him. He felt around, breathing with difficulty, unable to distinguish the corpse's limbs from his own. He couldn't see the other man, but he knew he was still there, hovering just out of his eye-line, waiting to see what he would do. He squirmed and gasped and pleaded. He tried to throw off the inert, grasping limbs of the corpse, and did so, one by one. At first they seemed alive, actively strangling, passively smothering, but with an effort he managed to convince himself they were not. Then he was abruptly awake again. Too hot. The folds of his body were burning, trying to expel intense heat too quickly. He sat up, turned on the light and shook out his numb hands until he could feel them.

He remembered a final encounter with Eleanor B. in the street, dumped into his forebrain by the news of her death. It was after he'd stomped out of his job as a part-time lecturer, sick of her, among others, and now not even an invigilator. She had been half-pissed on gin, mid-morning at the bus stop, trying to pay her fare with a pocketful of clothes pegs. Her sharp once striking face wobbled, sunken into her shoulders in an attractively dishevelled old black coat. "Don't go back to teaching teenagers," she'd advised, "you won't be able to do anything with the girls." She left him there, or he left her, pointing, trying to make a point she couldn't quite express, speechless, about to offer him some non-existent consolatory word, and now she too was gone away into that silent land.

But that was a good reason as far as he was concerned. He hadn't been able to do anything with the girls anyway.

It was his anger at others which caused the head-convulsions, compulsive mutterings of rage and hatred, repeated arguments from years ago, which he could always win, as so many had noticed at the time. But it also ran its course into collapse and despair, and it was his mad sense that she had escaped justice somehow by dying which sent him tumbling into a dead lassitude, the kind where you just can't be bothered to get up, and then you can't, and then you've collapsed in the street and are in the Whittington

Hospital desperately trying to move, to speak. He should have hung on longer. It would have been better.

A man with inexpertly-dyed hair had taught a course in which he recounted opera plots and attempted to seduce young women – and actually seemed to have some degree of success with it; another, a bloated post-Marxist with a trsgic air lurched around the corridors with a vodka bottle hanging from his pocket, pursuing an identical mission. "Graham! What are you doing here?" Eleanor B. had exclaimed upon sighting him in the corridor. "I hope you realise there are politics involved in this!" The 'this' in question being his award of a couple of hours teaching. He soon realized she was their feminist equivalent, and a feeling of web-entrapment combined with a leakage of meaning, his own meaning, rose up in him, finally overcoming him a few years later. If only he had had the guts to walk out right then. But nostalgia is a powerful, evil drug.

Anyway, she was dead, as was that other person, and the other one, who hated him, and the tall guy who'd heartily disliked all of them, and the various professors had all retired on their pensions and borrowed authority into the netherworlds of death's waiting rooms. He hoped their strangulated colons, their cancers, their bleeding interiors would get them as soon as possible, in a lot of pain, and hospitals would run out of morphine to buffer them. Teacher's pets (sons and daughters of other professors or simply eager little shits) misremembered every lyric, turned a profit from it – with their false poetries of darkness and death, their empty comedies, their endless cheapness and venality: they were the dead letter of the living law of Satan. A young Asian woman had recently become chancellor of it now. He hoped she wouldn't just be a figurehead, but would institute the kind of swingeing changes necessary to turn the place into what it always should have been. Poor Eleanor, lone feminist on a corridor full of priapic middle-aged men – and she hadn't been getting any interest, any younger herself.

Not the sort of thing you could shrug off with a shake of the head, a laugh, a change of subject, or pace, but this was exactly what he did do. He knew dwelling on past injustices – were they? – did him no good, damaged him, in fact, as a person and as a teacher. Life needed your full attention. Victory was to those who jolted awake full of adrenalin after five hours asleep and set about filing other's hopes in the rubbish bin at the foot of their bed. They were buoyant and would win every encounter with 'the other', by spouting some plausible administrative sounding crap.

Underlying it all was a strict limit they placed on the degree of responsibility anyone could be expected to have for other people. None would be a fair estimate, one you could fully count on, anyway, and should ethically enforce, actually, because it was the boundary stone of our social dealings with others, the good fence, the trusted sword, an agreed marker we must learn to respect. And, at the end of the day, it was true. Whenever somebody walked towards you smiling, they generally wanted paying for it with some sort of extortionate rate of interest.

TWENTY-ONE

When he'd first started teaching he had made a lot of use – too much – of writing games: I remember; I used to – but now; wishes, lies, dreams; and secrets; and getting his classes to write lines which contained the name of a film star, a flower and something else, a place maybe, or an infectious disease. Perhaps it had been his naive enthusiasm, or the notion of anonymity he introduced, but the results had often been instant and spectacular. His apprentice mechanics produced miniature heartfelt love poems to their first car, the first time they got drunk, and the first time they dipped their wick in the inflammable matter to be found between a girl's thighs. His hairdressers spilled out erotic secrets, indefinable incidents of mysterious poetry, and general harmless naughtiness.

Sometimes the secrets people wanted to share with him and the others were painful, tragic – a little brother mown down by a car, the day their mother's hearse rolled into view – but there was definitely something about the process which seemed to suggest the circle had been unbroken, not bye and bye, but here and now. The bored students turned into a congregation; there was a church-like hush as he praised and read out their testimonies, and he thought he felt what a priest must feel on a good day – he'd been a conduit for some higher energy so powerful it was difficult to retain one's humility in the face of its manifestation.

Naturally there had been much scepticism in the staffroom of Carshalton College, especially when he began to excitedly praise the illiterate but highly graphic account of a young black girl who apparently remembered being burned as a witch in the fifteenth century. She described the agonies of being burned alive, of screaming and watching your own melting flesh in a language so splintered and agonized you felt you were there, and he suspected she must be experiencing some kind of abuse. The main scoffer was a trendy-looking, youngish teacher who wore Buddy Holly glasses and a fashionable short back and sides haircut; his name was Scott.

"You think Anthea Bradley is some sort of tortured genius?" he smirked openly at the hapless beginner. "You might be a good teacher one day, but at the moment you're an idiot pushing ideas which don't make sense – or rather they do make sense, but the wrong sense."

"I think she sounds genuinely disturbed."

"She probably is – and you think that's good, do you?"

"Well, at least it shows she has a powerful imagination."

"They've sat her down in front of some pirate video nasty, which she shouldn't even have been watching, and this is the result – unless you think she's regressed to a past-life." Scott had already shown Anthea's page of scribble to a few members of his court. Now he retrieved it and cast an owlish glare over it. "Yep – it's *The Evil Dead*. Disgusting drivel – if she'd managed to think of it herself you might have a point." He handed back the paper with a flourish. Case dismissed.

He'd looked around the room for possible support, but there was only the friendly old guy – according to Scott the worst teacher on earth – who had presently nodded off next to his yard-high stack of general studies photocopies, some of them dating back to the Mods and Rockers era. But he was foiled, and he knew it.

His approach to teaching poetry was partly based on the ideas of a once popular New York poet, Kenneth Koch, who had expounded them in a few highly accessible teaching manuals which were successful for a while, since they enabled kids to express themselves easily, to write attractive surrealist poetry to his formulas as well as learning complicated, antique forms like the sestina, before being dismissed in a backlash as having no educational value whatsoever. Koch's ideas were never widely known in England, so he had only ever experienced the backlash, as well as a widespread feeling amongst teachers that what children produced using these methods wasn't poetry at all. Koch had been a sophisticated, humorous writer with a strong democratic and populist streak. His ideas worked well, in Graham's opinion, you always got a result with them, and they were highly adaptable to different levels and purposes. He still liked using them.

Sometimes a kid's poem was so striking you had to keep it. He remembered a moment when Deniz, a shy, bespectacled boy with 'severe incurable dysgraphia' brought notebook up to his desk and it contained a fresh masterpiece. He had made an excuse to pass it over the face of the photocopier, musing later how this made nonsense of his supposed job, which some people thought was fairly laughable anyway, a throwback which in some way justified his original approach to teaching.

I am a gangstar
I live in a White Rich house.
    I am a boss.
I have a Black BMW JeeP.
    I am rich

I Could Go out and get Everything
    I like free.
I am the strongest Man in my
Gangstar Leaders and Team
Which is Colour Red Side.

Every day, I wear a new styles of
Clothes and Shoes and I get
Gassed every day.

This kind of stuff was a completely different thing from competence, or any capability of academic improvement. It defined something for the reader of it more than for the writer, although he also knew exactly what he wanted to say. At the same time Deniz was shown to be more than a dumb thing: he was a thinking thing, a being, if only a boy who wanted what other boys wanted. Which was certainly the case with Deniz, who had been elated by his praise as he read out his poem to the quiet class, and he raised his arms in the air, a boxer who has just delivered a knock-out punch.

Actually you could say any idea worked if you wanted, but for whom exactly did it work, what work did it do? Did it pull for the pupil, the teacher, or the administration? And within these categories there were different kinds and degrees of working. The teacher could learn from teaching many kinds of classes, mainly from the research and also from the feedback from pupils, but did the pupils derive the same things from the process? Not necessarily. Not if they had nothing in terms of other knowledge to which to attach the ideas or content – it was all more teacher's blather which went in one ear and out of the other. With Koch's poetry ideas approach, the genius was in the idea, and the teacher's sensibility to appreciate the result. What had the pupil learnt? It was a bit like completing those learning grids which had been devised to raise Ofsted ratings – a case of filling in the blanks, so it looked like you could write a sentence, organize a paragraph, had appreciated the main points of *Romeo and Juliet.* In which case it was a related idea which worked for the administration, gave you an acceptable result, ticked the box, not dissimilar to prefabricating a surrealist poem by building in juxtaposition and metaphor.

He tended to walk away happy from a class if he felt he'd got something over – but did the kids have the same experience? Had he really? The proof of the pudding wasn't necessarily in the immediate result, but in the eating. Did the kids put on weight, and how long was it taking them to learn the skills of summary and organization? It was all process, yes, but he still thought Koch's ideas were good if you concentrated on the process – an experience, a reflective experience, leading to a realization which put the ball back in your quadrant in an interesting way, leading perhaps to a process of self-development, self-education, thinking for yourself.

Grand, airy bullshit. But you couldn't really think for yourself properly without grammar, so the theory went, despite the fact so many could express themselves so very fluently without its necessary restraining corsets.

Back in teacher training he had baulked at the concentration on behaviourist ideas, which, in effect, said you could only judge by results, by the output of the black box, and self-development was impossible to measure, probably non-existent with its reference to a shadowy yet supposedly coherent interior which remained unproven. B.F. Skinner suited the administrators, the box-tickers, the social engineers, and that's why it had proved so popular. The key was to ask the right searching questions, and to throw those who hadn't been able to answer them on the educational scrap-heap. Where, he hoped, they would continue to outbreed the fucking middle-classes.

He preferred Matthew Arnold to all that – if only because he insisted we all had a buried self, one which was capable of being developed and providing us with access to things far beyond our mundane lives. We each had our own hidden portal into the hive of culture. Matthew Arnold, one of the first generation of state schools' inspectors, sounded like a revolutionary compared to the present government's educational pundits. And long may his balls continue to cannon around the billiards table of Pain's Hill House.

TWENTY-TWO

Arnold straightened up, creaking, from his last shot, which had bounced around his designated corner pocket, careened back on to the far edge of the table where it now sat against the cush: cushty-wooshty, quite unplayable. He failed to meet the laughing eyes of his host, a yahoo if ever there was one – a dodo with money, unfortunately not yet extinct. Charles Leaf. A gentleman, an Apostle and a dear friend. Arnold pulled out his fob watch, which failed to offer him the date of his host's death, and replaced it without noticing the correct time.

His own time was short, he knew that well enough. He arrived out of puff anywhere he walked to nowadays, whether up here or on his weekly stroll down Between Streets, past mean cottages and newly thrown up villas, along the now considerable length of the High Street and into his rear pew at St Andrews for Sunday matins. No more hacking with the dogs for him, doing the round of Burwood, no more winter skating on the frozen lake. Even the garden tired him out. His upcoming American tour would be his last trip to the new world, which, as he'd admitted to their newspapers, was all a bit too novelty-addicted for his taste. Ralph Waldo Emerson. That had been a name to conjure with, one of the true busy-bees of culture, a furry monster of nectarine light amongst a lot of prating spiders dinning on about the wonders of their racketting idiotic machines. Controversy! Arnold hated all this yackery-hackery. Sticky webs. But at least he'd managed to hack a few of them to ribbons in his time.

"Matt! Matt!" his host over-familiarly recalled him to the business at hand.

Arnold effortlessly triangulated his next stroke of the cue. Nothing wrong with his brain, but once again he failed to place it where it might have given his host pause to reconsider his social arrogance. Damn. His eye was still in, his co-ordination of hand and shoulder failing, failing with earnest rapidity. One last brandy and soda and it was time to say goodnight to old whatsit, not such a bad fellow, he grudgingly admitted to himself, although not to the person in question.

Matthew Arnold. Close. Long, horse-like head, accentuated by whiskers which gave him the appearance of a dray, a long-hauling beast of burden dragging barrels of nectar for the workers and their children. He staggered off down the hill in darkness. There is no spot of ground, however arid, bare or ugly, that cannot be tamed into such a state as may give an impression of beauty and delight. He wished he'd said that, perhaps he would one day, although he had always liked Surrey just the way he had found it; not too wild, but scenic enough.

His way home was devilishly pitch black. He'd decided to take the rural route, but the long snaking path down through the night-shrouded gardens of Pains Hill House seemed oppressive to him tonight. The barbarian with whom he'd shared his customary brandy and soda, who had also dispensed his discomfiting thrashing at the billiard table, had kept them in poor order, really. He'd let the place go to rack and ruin, and the eighteenth century layout was now a half-improved jungle of scotch pines and cedars whose grandiose ruins offered much to delight Arnold's eye in daylight, but at midnight seemed foreboding. Better not fall into the Serpentine, he thought. But just then the moon broke through its shrouding canopy of cumulo-stratus, a hunter's moon, and the whole spectral panorama was briefly revealed to him. It tugged at him, redolent of things of which he didn't approve and in which he didn't believe for a second. A few seconds of ghastly-ghostly and the moon went out again like a snuffed candle.

Roots were the main problem. You couldn't just wander down what there was of a pathway, thinking your own thoughts, you had to be awake to the darkness, alert and aware of snaking roots, which, he soon discovered, had a damnable will of their own, to trip you up and break your leg, and the tangled overgrown rhododendron bushes and sprouting ferns brushed your face, seemed to have sprung up in your path expressly to detain you with a long and pointless argument in the course of which you were reduced to asserting, over and over again, that they just shouldn't be there. Fie and fiddlesticks! He was in spider country and he knew it: a veritable arachnid paradise whose mighty webs of mechanical so-called thought were going to wrap you up good and tight. One of his more disreputable great uncles had carried a sword-stick. Arnold wished he had it with him now, if only to thrash any poachers he might encounter. He chuckled as he went on his way, amusing himself with all manner of nonsense as he cut down past the lake and headed towards the bridge.

The lake was like an enchanted realm at night, the scent of lilacs blowing across its still, dark expanse; swans, moorhens and Canada geese bedded down, hiding for the night behind its fine fringe of velvet bull rushes. A gentle breeze broke across it in the darkness, as if greeting the great man's progress around its somnolent shores. *In pastures green he leadeth me the quiet waters by*. It would do! Arnold reflected. It had done for him and it would do for everybody else who had some sort of brain in their head. Why not? Why not indeed, why not.

He let himself out through the door in the wall, outside into what he thought of as the world. He had his own key to the green door, a large key with a looping decorative head. The door swung open quietly, oiled by a gardener, and he repocketted his key after closing it firmly behind him and relocking it. That was kind of his host, he had to admit. He enjoyed feeling valued by the local gentry, whatever his reservations. He paused, unsure quite why, took the key from his pocket and unlocked the green door. Unsatisfied with the invisible result, he pushed it ajar. A few steps along the river path and he was on the bridge that had been erected for him: a simple affair of a few dozen screwed and nailed planks, but constructed to a fair design and employing the best craftsmanship Cobham had to offer.

Arnold fled across it as it creaked dangerously under his weight. One of these nights, he was sure, he would discover the village boys had partially disassembled his bridge, and it would give way, and he would get very wet indeed. After all, they could cross over it here themselves, just before its long lazy meander around the village; but they could not enter the gardens, oh no, that was obviously forbidden. Who could really blame them? A spot of sabotage. His bridge held, perfectly robust and efficient, as he'd always known it would be.

Back at the cottage the fire had fallen into the grate. Frances had retired for the night. Dear Frances. She had borne him six children. They would go on after them both. Except of course for poor Thomas and poor Trevenen. Out of a habit he could not break, he found himself praying for them before retiring. But that surely was what life had always been about too. Real life. Succession. Women were strong, little-minded but indubitably strong. Usually right about everything. One of his daughters had even married an American. People had lined the streets of Cobham and stood on their pews in St Andrews to get an eyeful, much to the vicar's disgust at this disgraceful display by massed tradesmen's daughters. He too would have awarded them Ds. Arnold had found it amusing, satisfying. Henry James had been deliciously squeezed in amongst them. Everybody he'd ever known had been there; at least everyone he'd remembered. He would be seeing her again soon.

His head was still buzzing from the brandy as he slid between the cool sheets and let his heavy eyelids droop. Soon they began to twitch as if he were rapidly reading something etched on their undersides; behind them he was running, running for a train to take him to some godforsaken school to hear them parrot out their lessons. The three Rs. Remembering to catch a boat. That was it, or meeting one at Liverpool. He was running for a retreating tram.

TWENTY-THREE

The Turkish girls enjoyed Secret Santa, an anonymous gift exchange game, a supposedly ancient yuletide tradition which had recently cooked up somewhere or other behind his back – he enjoyed no childhood memory if it. They got all this stuff at school, obviously, and they relished unwrapping the gifts and wondering who they were from, but there was no celebration at home, in Muslim households, and so the divided culture of immigrants was reinforced. Sezin liked nothing better than to express her contempt for Christmas, which went along well with her scepticism that London had ever been bombed by the Germans, her general disdain, her certain sense of looking down on them all from a great height, her steady instinct for domination of her own space.

Watching their children growing up as aliens, creatures of their new patch, Turks were forced to acknowledge their autonomy, or some did perhaps; others continued to impose their ancestral ways come what may, knowing something of them would always win out. You'll always be a Turk. They looked around at others' kids and saw their own going the same way. But they had their own busy lives to contend with and didn't necessarily care one way or another. At least, Sezin thought so. Sezin regularly criticized the poor parenting skills of the Turkish mothers, suspecting them of everything from spoiling their children to full-scale sexual abuse, her imagination fed from its own fertilizing springs deep within, supplemented by a diurnal dose of the *Daily Mail*.

Besides, they could always get their own back on him, and frequently did, babbling in their unknown tongue, talking over his head just as Sezin did in the kitchen. In fact, they found it difficult to believe he didn't speak Turkish, didn't understand a word. Maybe they thought everybody spoke their language, or should, just like the English abroad, but once they'd got over their delight in his incomprehension and the almost limitless scope it seemed to offer for disrespectful utterances, they realized it didn't have quite as much potential as they thought, since he didn't care what they said about him, and genuinely didn't understand it, therefore they would have to translate any offensive remarks in order to have the desired effect. Not being a proper teacher he permitted himself mild retaliation, like saying if it was up to him he would chop their hands off for watching porn on their laptops, a casual remark which produced an unexpected momentary hush of embarrassment in his young companions.

His attitude was they were all in it together. He wondered why he drifted so easily into the point of view of teenagers and children, liked nothing better than to entertain them, and found it difficult to identify with his contemporaries, let alone those generations of subsequent comers who now made up the majority of the responsible population. It wasn't anything other than the fact of his childlessness – he had never been a husband and a father and never would be – he'd once tried to be a nice boyfriend, was still and always would be a son and a brother. The child is father of the man, still looking out for the same old rainbow. No answer was the stern reply. Book of Job.

Yildiz was a tall, somewhat gawky, scruffy girl; a dark beauty who somewhat resembled one of his early girlfriends, so he thought, and so more meaning was leached from his precious past. She looked ridiculous in her ill-fitting police cadet uniform, a garb she'd been forced to don as a penalty of her exclusion from school. A pupil referral unit case with sugar-sweet eyes, she'd beaten up a smaller girl for 'being racist' (you had to say this to avoid the full wrath of the law), but had since managed to turn her turbulent young life around. Although she didn't like the police very much – who did? – she now saw they had an essential job to do. She shrugged, telling him all this. But what else could she possibly say?

Initially, she struck up a friendship with Dersdar, the Kurdish girl. Dersdar was several streets ahead of her, a different kettle of fish, and soon moved back into her own zone, where she had only her unpleasant little brother to contend with, which she did ably, ignoring him. This twelve-year-old Robert DeNiro lost no time in accusing him of thinking his sister was buff and of giving her high marks for it. Graham denied this crime: it was self-evident Dersdar could easily form a good sentence, read and write, whereas her dapper, cocky little brother would always be struggling with written language.

He was however an able noise-maker and manipulator of others, encouraging poor little Deniz to kick the German maths teacher under the table, then accuse him of some sexual misdoings, probably, which led to his resignation, or at least to non-attendance of further classes. Eagle-eye Maral, purveyor of whatever social justice obtained, had detailed the whole sordid business – sympathetic to the teacher – in what turned into her eloquent defence of Sezin and the methodology behind her marvellous school at which so many grateful Turkish children had found a happy home from home, as well as improving their grades. She was a pain in the backside. Yildiz herself was little trouble, she liked being liked by a teacher for once, and she was good at poetry – whatever that meant. She couldn't resist embroidering and changing some collaborative thing she'd copied off the whiteboard, and generally it was always for the better, but who would ever know or be able to tell?

Erda, Erda – how many men were going to drown in the pitiless pools of her eyes? Erda wrote about how she 'd taken off the cheap silver bracelet a Syrian girl had given her and threw it into the sea. She didn't know why she had done it, afterwards turned away and walked back to the family barbeque and had never thought about the incident again until this minute. She realized she didn't care after all, her friendship didn't mean so much, anyway the girl who had given it to her was no longer there – gone away somewhere, in Syria. He wondered if this reflected her parents' attitudes to Syrians, but her act of repudiation, her succinct, vivid expression of the moment he had asked her to frame, was the stuff of literature. He thought she was a bright kid because of it, and her flair at description, her instant easy possession of words and power of stringing them together was something he liked to encourage in all children.

Her brother's pieces always painfully described school dinners, different ones they were served each day, a subject he had suggested to him, and which the good-natured boy tackled with as much relish as he showed for anything, continuing in lesson after lesson. He was a thin, slight boy with intelligent eyes, a putative moustache and a Beatle haircut. His sister reeled off poem after poem, and wanted to collaborate on a play they could all act out.

When she got fired up, nothing was beyond her, she thought, and she would elbow aside others' suggestions, her eyes dancing to the teacher's praise as he drew her out until she was prancing and dancing around the room in delighted surprise. Only twelve years

119

of age, she hadn't yet acquired many analytic skills, and found those tasks designed to develop and test them as boring and intractable as anyone else. The two of them disappeared suddenly, unable to pay the ongoing fees, but it was obvious really, they had no problems, no reason to be there, would do just as well without his weekly input.

He wondered what it was he was recognizing, or misinterpreting in the kids, especially the girls, willing as he was to ascribe almost supernatural abilities to a pair of laughing eyes. He was the pole they pranced around, each clutching one of his brightly-coloured ribbons, weaving them together so perfectly around the tall tattooed stake, the magical maypole of Merry Mount.

They amused themselves by writing poems on their iPhones, or maybe they were just downloading them from the internet. Sometimes these were on classic school themes: bullying, for example, cheap homework from the ancestral online memory banks – but left to their own preference it would always be love poetry, for which they nursed an unhealthy obsession. Once he introduced the idea of collaborative poems they asked for it again and again, and if they had the luxury of the big front classroom, Assiye – a big, boisterous, stroppy girl who had somehow provoked Sezin's ire and fully reciprocated with her hatred of the bullying proprietor – would jump up and snatch the marker from his hand as other girls called out their lines. This was one of his favourite lessons, watching girls write poetry, and he would retreat to the back of the class, only occasionally calling out a suggestion or two. Sezin, however, knew it wasn't real work, that it had no educational value whatsoever.

On the 279 he'd made up a sentence of incrementally longer words, by one letter – he forgot the name for it – and thought he might write it up on the whiteboard. They could try and write a collaborative poem based on: *I am the four early rising magpies, brightly carousing, fluttering, quarrelling occasionally.* Could work well, so long as Sezin didn't get wind of it, but he could fairly easily predict who might be willing or able to try it out. The boys and the rest would have to amuse themselves for an hour, so probably she was right. He scrubbed the idea as too ambitious, and pointless.

Instead he told them about Poly Styrene, a great heroine of the punk era, along with her band X-Ray Spex, and how she had recently died singing Hari Krishna from her hospital bed. She was an English Somali whose great songs summed up what it was to be a misunderstood teenager. 'Germ-free Adolescents', 'Oh Bondage! Up Yours', 'Identity', 'I am a Cliché' – and, he reflected bitterly, no-one would ever again know how great she really was, no-one would remember, not even the BBC, who had made her a star. Somebody asked sceptically if she was really just an ordinary teenager. He said yes, but she had somebody behind her. As pop stars always did. Warming to a pet subject, the classic red herring thrown to a teacher, he explained all about Svengali, the evil Russian Jew who had hypnotized the artist's model Trilby into singing like an angel in George Du Maurier's novel, and how this character had given us the word Svengali, for a behind-the-scenes manipulator of young female talent. But who was her Svengali, her Simon Cowell, or her Phil Spector?

And he told them about Helen Shapiro, who for him would always be their contemporary, their big sister.

"Spector," Maral remarked. "Ugh – what a creepy name. You just know from that name he is not a good person."

Turkish children, like most children, and despite a panoply of teaching materials designed to alert them to the woes of the contemporary world, safely ignored of what went on outside the child-world. Protected, not necessarily by their parents, but by their own childishness, from what was going on anywhere else, they remained in the safe enclaves of their games, *Grand Theft Auto* for one, and the bland pop music they favoured, by Ed Sheeran and others, reading the heart-breaking stories of *A Boy Called It* by Dave Pelzer and *The Fault in Our Stars* and gulping down massive fizzy tranfusions of teen vampire novels. If pressed they were defensive, finding the latest ISIS atrocities atrocious if they were atrocious enough, but otherwise sympathizing with Islamic fighters. The Israeli attack on Gaza shocked them, particularly all the images of dead children killed by the Israeli army, bombed out mosques and houses, the relentless ruthless carnage of what looked to many people like an attempted genocide.

"Jews are evil," said Meltem, a plump girl with a fine singing voice who had been born in Exeter Hospital when her parents ran a kebab shop down in the West Country. At Christmas she had told him about this, now she had turned against him. Less sophisticated than some, she was always going to be a distractor, somebody who had turned around to pursue another conversation, who wouldn't get on with any work – and she blamed him for not having taught her anything, any of the basic skills she needed to know to pass her GCSE exam. Worst of all, he was a boring man who liked Jews. For some reason he felt a slight pang of guilt for his failure to engage her.

"Ed Miliband is Jewish," he said. "He might be our next prime minister."

"I would never vote for a Jewish prime minister. Never in a thousand years – they are evil," said Meltem.

"Not all Jews are bad," Graham said. "Roald Dahl is Jewish."

A twelve-year-old in the front row started sobbing silently.

"He is Norwegian, not Jewish," said Maral. "And as well he was a fighter pilot for England during the Second World War."

"In fact, the whole of *Charlie and the Chocolate Factory* is pure Zionist propaganda."

"How do you mean?"

"It's alright to use Negro pygmy dwarves as slave labour – because they symbolize the Arabs."

"Very funny. By the way, Negro is a racist term. Not that I care." Maral was sitting bolt upright, a twitching gazelle regarding him through slitted eyes as she half-turned away in an attitude of extreme disdain, studied but effective; but he couldn't let it go there, he had to tell them not to be racist, which meant trying to explain what he thought racism was, which they felt was the most over-covered subject in their dreary school curriculum. The problem, as he explained it, was to do with looking at political – and sometimes religious – conflicts in ethnic terms. Everybody groaned as they tried, not very hard, to follow his reasoning. It was important to understand what he said, because if they expressed their views in racial terms they wouldn't be allowed to state their opinion. It was fine to criticize Israel, he totally agreed with them on it, but Israel was a political entity, a state, not 'the Jews' as such; and the further problem, the main problem, was that it was a racially-based state, institutionalising racism – in among other things in the law of return – but mainly in the theft of Palestinian lands.

He explained its origins in ancient times, and modern Israel in terms of European guilt over the holocaust. For some reason he veered into the Catholics and Protestants of Northern Ireland, ethnically indistinguishable but with different origins, and the Tutsis and Hutus of the Rwandan genocide who could only be distinguished, it was claimed, by the relative length of their ears. They kids groaned, but he couldn't stop until he'd disgorged the whole sorry business, the business everybody was sorry about, in some of its details. They could attack Israel but not the Jewish people. How did they like it when ordinary Muslims were blamed for terrorist atrocities? Any questions?

Orhan said: "We understand. Just leave it there."

But no arguments were forthcoming, just sullen silence, and when he tried to break them into an open discussion, they could say nothing. Orhan repeated: "Just leave it, we understand."

Meltem looked at him with the grim hatred of somebody who knows she is right but hasn't got the language to argue.

Maral soon set to work on an essay about Israel and the Palestinians: a subject sufficiently important to be worthy of her higher attention.

"It's good," he said, when she showed it to him a week later, "but you don't need so many adjectives."

"I feel strongly about it," she said. "They express how I feel."

"I'm glad you feel strongly, but in this kind of writing you need to express yourself with arguments."

But he knew there was something wrong with his own arguments, just as with any line of reasoning which could only be allowed to turn out one way, questions to which there was only one permitted answer, one requiring the forcible removal or sequestering of everybody else's weapons, when those weapons, those arguments, referred to observable realities, obvious differ-ences of races and peoples who were probably always going to be bearing enmity and arms against each another.

Until the end of the world. Until the descent of Jesus on a golden throne. But of course he didn't say so – and a few months later there was the massacre of cartoonists in Paris for blaspheming the Holy Prophet, and the Jews in the supermarket at Porte de Vincennes, who were killed for being Jews; and Lassana Bathily, a Malian-born and Muslim shop assistant, who rescued some of them by shepherding them into the cold storage room in the shop's basement, for safekeeping.

All the Effs. Effnic. Effnics. Contract workers. Effnicities. The soft building blocks of nation states. Murder and melding. Equal parts thereof. Shaken, stirred. But it was invariably a white girl who came out on top at that failing school in Walthamstow, arrogantly bubbling to the surface in that ninety percent solution of latte and espresso. So the maths teacher had said. He decided to have a bust up with her in every lesson. Even our adored protagonist silently agreed she was a self-important little bitch, there in the cramped smokers' staffroom where the worst teachers gathered to fight a good game in five seconds retrospect. Instant revisionists. One and all. Although some just smoked cigarettes.

They had been still recovering from the riots of the previous year when bat-wielding West Indians had rampaged through the school, and the main culprit, the very teacher whose attitudes most exemplified evil for the parents who had gathered at the school gates carrying a homemade banner accusing the school of institutional racism, was a would-be proletarian novelist who'd climbed to safety out of the staffroom window.

Graham had taken part in an unwelcome conversation with him about all this while they stood next to the coffee machine in the main staffroom, earwigged by a crew of young besuited black members of staff at a nearby table. "I just don't fancy black women," he said. "Does that make me a racist?"

"Could mean you're gay," he suggested.

Which had elicited a cheap laugh. But the ethnic horse-race and the universal perception of it as such was an inevitable reality, he now realized. His clients disliked hearing about other clients, other people's children; they thought it unprofessional when he tried to create a mild, half-serious rivalry between two students who didn't know each other, pitting one nationality against another, as though GCSE English should have a friendly spirit of competition built into it, something like the Olympic games. Most of all they hated, if they were anything other than, their own children being compared to black children. Especially to hear that any of them were doing well. At the end of the day it flew in the face of experience. Was that racism? As far they were concerned his clients now were just buying a service.

There could be no more English child than Jack Daw. Where did it come from, this perceived danger that he was leaving out all the Es? Even the journey to where he lived with his mild schoolteacher parents was like a journey out into the past. First Capital Connect to the Emirates stadium with its wall-painting of the Arsenal's heroic present and past, a dive across a road and up through a labyrinth of pale blue Georgian houses made of cake, climbing and crossing avenues of discreet poshness, to a street of Edwardian blocks of well-heeled tradesperson's abodes, with arched ways back into courtyards where you could park your van or cart, built on the bevel, every blessed corner rounded off in a friendly decorative flourish, and now further sub-divided into comfortable flats. Nice places. Proper places.

He climbed up to their second and third floor flat on his weekly gig to do Jack's homework, prepare him for his coming exams. He passed a book-lined study with a music stand, an ascending gallery of comfortably indifferent art of personal significance, continued past a spacious dining room with a large bare wooden table, neat stacks of classical and light modern CDS, urged himself on past the fragrant scent of wholesome English cookery (a pie of some sort perhaps, a pie that Jack's father was about to sit down and eat). He continued to the small upper bedroom where Jack sat at his laptop, trying to conceal his impatience to be done and go downstairs for his own portion.

"Can I get you anything to drink?" he asked.

"A glass of water, please."

He extracted his folder, brimming with just the sort of rubbish he carried, and looked out over the criss-cross of slanted roofs which seemed like planed surfaces you might clamber across, waited quietly. Who was it talked about the kindness of kind? Why don't you love me like you used to do? It was because they knew you all too well. Jack had been provided with a library of rarely consulted reference books, hardy annuals, football books, and he reflexively scanned their laminated spines, neatly arranged on a shelf above the folded camp bed.

Jack was clean of limb, slender and well-made, fetchingly shorn, dressed in a style of boys' clothing that seemed to recall the early seventies. There was a certain balanced stiffness to the way he moved, as though he was swinging his upper body around a maypole spine, using those heavy feet in a pair of clumpy, tasselled shoes to kick himself around. By an ineluctable process of association that in the end reduced everybody who could be to a familiar who echoed another's physiognomy, he was reminded of one of his male cousins at the same age, about sixteen. Jack's parents and he were the same kind, and wanted to know if he would recommend his father's job, car mechanic, to him. In all honesty he couldn't recommend it, told the boy that he should try to be middle-class like they were. If only because he thought it was a much better deal. Worth trying for. He tried to inspire his killer instinct with a few tales of his feistier West Indian students and their do-or-die attitude to social mobility. Jack Daw was happy to contemplate gliding gently downwards onto what he imagined would be a safer, less demanding perch.

Jack was a mild boy, ready to laugh at feeble jokes, his brow creased by concerns over the holocaust and other stuff they were doing at school, his breast warring over more deadly and immediate ethnic rivalries ... that between Southampton and Portsmouth. His father was from the Isle of Wight. Jack attacked with vigorous elan the people and footballing skills of Portsmouth; he exalted Southampton, its football team and the incontrovertibly higher quality of its inhabitants compared to the motley scum of Portsmouth: they were chavs one and all over there, two miles down the South coast, and it was perfectly safe, all in the game, to abuse them gleefully and at length. It was a natural subject for his free-style essay, and they browsed a gallery of ridiculously stupid-looking Portsmouth supporters in order to get his blood up. They were England's equivalent of people of Wal-Mart. Jack could despise them harmlessly, fiercely, no need for any tact or restraint.

He didn't have the heart to tell Jack that he supported Portsmouth, almost by rote. Portsmouth was a Navy town, they parked warships there, the *Victory*, sailors staggered through its winding streets looking for a way to get out of it, they already had, but even all that had been allowed to go down the fucking drain. There were the council estates, the Irish community, a decent university where you could study something that might lead to a job rather than wrestle with somebody who was him or herself wrestling with intractable modernist poetry. Southampton was a terminal for more romantic departures, to places where new beginnings might be possible. He had watched his own father get on a ship bound for Canada there. He permitted himself a few feeble defensive moves to draw the boy out, feeling like a Portsmouth player who had been ordered to let Southampton win.

"I think the Portsmouth players are ordered to let Southampton win," he said. "Actually they buy them off one by one – Southampton must be made to look good, no other outcome is permissible."

Jack laughed. "How do they do that?"

"They've got loads of money. A bottomless pit of money, a slush fund."

Jack laughed even more. "For paying off the Portsmouth players?"

"Anybody who stands in their way," he said. "Has to take a dive or –" he passed a finger quickly across his throat.

Jack looked shocked. He had had him going there. He looked sweet, harmless. Which he was. He really did look like his cousin, spitting image of him, and the tutor wished they were at that moment reassembling the Scalextrix for a return match.

They buckled down to writing the essay, and he soon realized with some satisfaction that he had stymied Jack's simple enjoyment in his anti-Portsmouth bigotry. He was hesitant, nervous. There was a possibility he would start to feel guilty about it, which was something, maybe a place from which to start rebuilding his entire personality.

Unfortunately there was never enough time to do anything but initiate these epochal changes in people's lives. At the end of an hour, with his homework safely saved on the laptop, Jack went downstairs for his shepherd's pie. Jack was already tucking in as he descended to the street and let himself out into the fresh early evening dusk. Out to where a skateboard wobbled by as he retraced his steps past the St. Joan of Arc community centre, Highbury Grove and a grid of regency houses, until he reached a downward sloping end with the Emirates stadium looming at the end of it like a great gob-stopper – it was chancy every time, and a mild surprise to him when he realized that he'd once again managed to find his way back to Drayton Park.

There were black working-class homes he had entered where they had had a photograph of President Obama pinned on the living room wall: a ray of sunshine, hope. For these striving Londoners Obama was something to pull for, even here in far-off outposts where most white people, probably, couldn't really care a feather or a fig about who was President of the United States of America. Despite being goaded into caring. Despite the lack of choice about hearing about the fucking place from cradle to grave. It was actually quite moving, he thought, in the way that religious icons were on others' walls. Household Gods. The Buddha. Although he had ever seen *The Light of the World* by Holman Hunt on anyone's wall, he would definitely have liked to have done. He would have saluted its dark garishness, its friendly English face illuminated above the square, glowing lantern, peering into the barn in Surrey where it had been painted. Barack Obama was that for many people, in the way that you once might have found Martin Luther King or Malcolm X on somebody's fridge door.

But that was reading too much into things, things that people just did, and the problem of reading too much into things was that it kicked everything out of kilter, you encouraged yourself to look at things the wrong way, far-fetched perhaps, or even if not, a subtle skewing that was enough to screw everything up for you – and the others, the others, the other others. Well. Or not. Things passed like shadows in a world of aftermath, which was a kind of prison he felt he lived in, a bare place where nothing happened any longer, and to invite anyone to share in that (even by commenting on the pictures on their walls) was to invite trouble, distrust, and every probability of being taken the wrong way, or most likely, not at all.

TWENTY-FIVE

The mouse sauntered casually towards him across the carpet, sat up on its hindquarters and addressed him in a tiny but authoritative voice which could not easily be mistaken for squeaking.

"Graham," he said, "you've got to stop people walking all over you. Especially us mice." The endearing creature chuckled irritatingly. "I mean it, man."

"What do you know about me?"

"More than you do, evidently," the mouse replied. "Look, take us mice for an example. We scuttle around, but we keep at it – we avoid creatures who are obviously stronger than us –"

"Like me!" he protested.

"Yeah, right," scoffed the mouse. "OK, so we avoid most humans, especially ones which make sudden movements, but you're so pathetic … anyway, what I'm trying to say with what you no doubt believe to be my minimal powers of mouse-reason is that we keep at it – we keep pushing for what we want, what we need to survive. That's life for us – a short scuttle to calvary. But we keep coming back for more. We go where it is. We find it and we eat it. And what we can't eat we thoroughly piss on." The mouse laughed again. "We spread diseases. We do it deliberately, mate."

He remembered the night he'd woken up to find a whole family of these small grey fellows cavorting around on the carpet, gobbling dust balls with evident pleasure, recalling with chagrin that he had done no more than shoo them away before collapsing back to sleep, He'd dismissed the whole incident as a dream, but now realized it had been real enough.

"We're persevering, persistent – we are pests after all."

"Pestistent," he said.

"*Pardon?*" said the mouse in a French accent. "*Ne jouez pas avec nous, monsieur, s'il vous plaît.*"

He leaned forward slightly and banged the flat of his hand on the carpet next to where the mouse sat; a small cloud of dust rose up, but it didn't budge an inch, not this time.

"Look, I'm trying to do you a favour, you big useless lunk. Why don't you drag the hoover round, clean this place up thoroughly for once in your life? That usually discourages us for a while. Otherwise we think of it as our natural domain. We make dust balls and play fucking football with them."

"Why are you telling me this?" he asked.

"I'm not sure," admitted the mouse. "The others wouldn't like it."

"Where are they?"

The mouse sniffed, continuing to eye him steadily. "They are all dead," he said shortly. "They curled up and died one by one."

"But why?" Graham felt a surge of pity for the brave little animal. "Surely there's more than enough to feed a family in this flat?"

"I do not know," said the mouse with dignity. "There are mysteries I have not penetrated about our condition. Besides," he added, "we are not all related, although we doubtless look pretty similar to your eyes. Take it or leave it. We are a small species, but we do know how to run and hide."

"I'll do it tomorrow," he said absently.

"Do what?" asked the mouse.

"Hoover up. Like you said."

The mouse sighed, realizing it was useless.

TWENTY-SIX

Beilul was on her second GCSE resit and she had reached her ceiling in language acquisition. Or so it seemed to him. What was the point in doing any more coursework for her when she still couldn't string sentences together and would never be able to replicate his loan performance? None, of course. Financial considerations: twenty quid, or, if she was feeling generous after a particularly gruelling meeting of fingers to keyboards in Wood Green library, twenty-five crisp smackeroos. The interest of meeting up with her, an eighteen-year-old Eritrean girl, yes, but that faded with repetition and the evident simplicities of the transaction. Some political thing about helping Africans, especially if they might be refugees. He'd been impressed by her frail speech and her confident beating down of his hourly rate on the phone. "Is too much." Twenty quid? "Is okay." She'd sounded like a child; and he'd been nervous about meeting her alone, even in the public library.

He lay back and remembered their first meeting. She had been waiting outside in the library's vestibule, a small creature in a gold-edged headscarf, stepping forward with a crooked smile. They did a piece of coursework comparing two publications about social networking and the internet; a student newspaper webpage from a small university in the American south, which suggested all the glories of independent youth would be laid before those who remembered to log on in freshers' week; a leaflet reminding parents of the dangers of social networking, and the importance of close supervision of children who may be targeted by predatory adults on sites which did little to prevent grooming. There were a number of brief anecdotes in bubbles giving horrific experiences, and bullet points enumerating safeguarding steps to be taken, emboldened headlines and graphics of protection in which stick adults stood behind stick children who were seating behind rectangular boxes. Presentational devices which anyone should be able to decode and explain.

The second time he had been invited to her home at the top of Wood Green, and sat before a laptop on a child-size table on a creaking nursery chair. Beilul was beside him, her hands on her own lap, looking on at his adjustments, cocking an ear to his patter of explanation as he reworked her poetry essay comparing a poem by Lawrence Ferlinghetti with one by Simon Armitage and another … what had it been, he didn't remember. Beilul's dimpled, crooked smile, her wise gentle glances seemed to suggest she preferred Ferlinghetti; she seemed to like what he was saying about the self-ishness of Americans, so he found her some good words to do it justice. His back ached as he crouched in a tense typing position at her toy-like lap-top on her toy-like desk.

Her bedroom almost bare, her narrow bed with a faded cover pulled quickly over it, on the wall a small blurry portrait of Christ wearing a crown of thorns – which reminded him of an Ethiopian icon, although it obviously wasn't one. It was a white nineteenth century Jesus, and higher on the wall above it was mounted a slice of log with a flag and a name carved on it. "That is where I come from," she said. "That country!" She smiled again, her small, crooked smile, at which moment her mother knocked on the door. Beilul told her to enter and a small bent woman came into the room carrying a tin tray with tea and biscuits on a saucer. He straightened up from the doll's house desk and took gratefully a mug with a tea-bag floating in it. Worrying about his teeth and the pendulous belly he'd just been holding in as it floated before him, suspended in mid-air between him and her keyboard, he declined the biscuit proffered by her mother.

Next time it was back to the library, had been ever since. As so often with his clients one meeting seemed to define the relationship between them, one particularly successful working encounter. Part of some coursework where she had to write a leaflet advising parents about the dangers of the internet had included a first-person testimony, to be printed in bold, of a girl's unfortunate experience. She had agreed to meet somebody she'd met online in the park, but he had turned out to be considerably older than his Facebook age, and furthermore had a wife and three children. Once he had lured her to the park this maniac had pulled a knife on her and tried to force the girl to have sex with him. She had wrenched the knife from his hand, stabbed him with it and run for her life, and somehow, she wasn't sure how, she had escaped from the park. When they had finished writing, he asked: "Do you carry a knife?" This time Beilul had hardly smiled at all. "It is in my bag," she said quietly.

132

But it was the next encounter which struck into him. As always she sat there primly waiting for him with her laptop open on the desk before her, and he had to endure the slightly embarrassing process of approaching her in front of rows of people who were working at the open, bench-like desks, people who couldn't help but glance around in curiosity at this meeting between a diminutive young black woman and a middle-aged white man, a man with white hair, an old man really. Although that feeling soon faded once they got started, as did, he supposed, the interest of anyone earwigging their quiet keyboard encounter.

He liked the way she had always done the work, and simply needed him to improve it, which he did as swiftly as possible, while Beilul looked on as his revisions and additions unfolded. The shaping hand of the master craftsman, he thought ironically, who wanted to get the whole thing over with as quickly as possible. This time she had written a story: 'LOVE AND REVENGE'.

It was supposed to have been based on some photographs, and she showed him the image she had selected to write about: a young couple, perhaps in America, perhaps in Africa, on a motorcycle. They were lightly dressed, the girl hugging the man from behind as they sat by the sidewalk ready to pull off, and both looked deliriously happy. The story concerned a love triangle between two boys and a girl who were from the same village and had gone to university in the same town. The girl was married to one of the boys, but she remained friends with the other, who kept coming around to their flat and insisting on spending time with them. His motives were obvious. Eventually the girl's husband had killed the suitor on a walk in the woods. The girl hadn't called the police, but ended the relationship with her husband. A war broke out, and years later her ex-husband was admitted to the hospital where she worked as a nurse. He'd been badly wounded in battle, paralysed, but the girl painstakingly nursed him back to health, and finally she forgave him and they were remarried.

Her real English teacher had objected to the ending on moral grounds: the man had committed murder. She felt he should be punished; the girl in the story took murder far too lightly. Beilul smiled as she recounted this; she didn't really understand what was wrong – after all, it was only a story – but still she wanted him to change it so it was okay. He nodded as his fingers flew over the keyboard of her laptop.

"Where is this story set?" he asked.

"England."

"Why not Eritrea?"

"Is too difficult," she said. "I can't do."

Scrolling through it, he started to fill in details, of the town they were from, the courses they were doing, and just a few salient points of the kind she might have been able to pick up herself. He didn't mind that it remained an African's version of England, a thin fantasy: this added to it somehow, and would be expected by her teacher. She would be impressed by Beilul's observational powers. He made the girl into a drama student, and her husband's rival a computer studies type who had obtained a well-paying job soon after graduation. He attended all her performances, although they were only small parts, and always sat in the front row, applauding wildly.

Beilul laughed at this last scene, which she particularly liked.

"Okay?" he asked her.

"Is good," she said. "Drama student. This doesn't exist in my country."

"It's common here. All the girls want to be actresses."

"And they become?"

"Not always," he said.

"Ah."

"Not usually."

"Never!"

Now there was only the ending to be dealt with. "What shall we do with this?" he asked.

"Change it!"

Obediently he did his best to milk some pathos out of the nurse painstakingly teaching him to walk again and the murderer's slow, painful recovery from horrific injuries. They'd shared some memories of their early days, as children playing together in the old home town. This helped him remember who he was, helped him grow stronger, and her constant loving attention also gave him something to live for; but when he popped the question, she said … he hesitated, groping for the appropriate words, which were something like: 'No,' she said. 'Those were good times – but they are in the past.'

He wondered if this ending wasn't too abrupt. He juggled with it a little, said it aloud a few times, and glanced back through the narrative which led up to her final rejection of the murderer. It made sense, he thought, needed nothing further. She still loved him in her way, she had done her duty: there were just too many painful memories which would be sure to resurface later on. Both of them needed to move on.

"What do you think?" he asked, straightening up from her keyboard. "Okay now?"

"Yes, good," she said.

Next time he googled Cobham he discovered that seventeen Eritreans had been arrested after they were spotted clambering out of the side of a refrigerated lorry into the car park at the M25 services. One quick glimpse of glorious Surrey before being bundled into police vans, interrogated, recycled. He couldn't help but think of Beilul, little Beilul, her poor mother's hospitable tea tray, her elderly father looking up in greeting from the couch, beginning to rise, and her tall slender younger brother. It was her brother he saw when he looked at those shivering men with their pinched, bleary, aquiline faces. What could you say? They couldn't let them all come in, could they?

All the same he couldn't help being pleased Beilul and her family had made it through the thin blue line. He also wished she could pass GCSE English and he wouldn't have to see her again. Indefinite Leave to Remain. An odd phrase. Leaving was obviously the opposite of remaining, but here it was in its almost archaic sense of being allowed to do something. Indefinite meant, in this context, forever, without end, but a penumbra of uncertainty, a certain fogginess hung over it. A right to stay which could be rescinded at any moment, which, he supposed, was what it meant. It gave and withheld in equal measure. Anyhow, there were many shops along Wood Green high road offering to help you attain such a right. It was a talismanic phrase on their windows, easy to imagine an Eritrean searching hopefully for these words in a torn-open letter.

When they could remain no longer they stood up to leave and a young black man at the desk opposite glanced at them curiously.

An odd couple. He stared back. Beilul smiled up at him. Usually they walked down the library stairs in silence, but this time he tried to make conversation. "Where are you going?" Beilul beamed. She was going shopping. There was a nice relaxed feeling between them, walking close together as they left the library, which accentuated the difference in their heights: Beilul was perhaps half as tall as him. They obviously liked each other, and though it was poignant to the older white man, there was something momentarily intimate and double-jointed about the possibility of their relationship consisting of anything but a transaction, strictly cash.

"Now I can buy some sweets" He patted the notes in his pocket. She laughed. He pointed a finger in the opposite direction and followed it away from her, wishing her well – and, as usual, the conversation continued for a while longer in his head, perhaps in hers too. What was she saying? "My brain is not good. I have nothing to say." Nothing in any of their meetings suggested this was particularly untrue. For a few seconds he followed her on her shopping trip, wishing he could have gone along with her; he would have been happy to watch her buying the things that she wanted.

TWENTY-SEVEN

Graham Greene looked out of the window of his suite at the passing traffic, at least the tops of a few red buses and black cabs, then sat down heavily on his couch and fumbled for the silver lighter in his fob pocket. How monumentally boring London had become in recent years, or perhaps it always had been, if he was honest, which he tried to be, at least with the only person he truly respected. Holding the slim Calibri at an acute angle, he put the mouthpiece of the pipe into the corner of his mouth like a cigarette holder, clicked the lighter and let its flame play over the black lump in the pipe's bowl. A few judicious, pumping sucks and it bubbled and was alight, smouldering as he languidly fanned out the flame, glowing fitfully as he nursed at the blob of Limehouse opium he'd had delivered earlier in the day. So much more difficult to keep burning than eager hashish, but the technique, once learned, was never forgotten. He soon managed to ingest it all. Job done, he replaced the mouthpiece of the hookah in its clip and reeled back towards the bed. Greene sat down carefully, precisely, and heeled off his patent shoes, swinging his long, now distant, stick-like legs up onto the hotel bedspread.

Thomas De Quincey had been absolutely correct about opium: his moral sensibilities were certainly infinitely more acute under its influence, but – he giggled suddenly – in a proportion directly inverse to the possibility of doing anything about them. If he'd wanted to. He felt his limbs flowing away from him, an immense relief of mental pressure, and once more the delightful dance of memories, or rather of his fancy toying with the materials of memory, began in earnest. He felt a stupid smile begin to affix itself to his normally impassive face. Thank goodness nobody was here to witness it. The people in his books needed other people. So did he, in a funny way, actually in a lot of ways. Ho hum.

The telephone beside his bed rang and he picked it up languidly. He was expecting a call. "This is Graham Greene," a voice said on the end of the line. "To whom am I speaking?"

"There must be some mistake," he replied. "You have just telephoned me. I am Graham Greene."

A dry chuckle, a cough. "Graham," the voice replied. "I have become aware you are using my name and have assumed my identity. I'm afwaid this can't be allowed to continue."

Greene pressed the ear-piece close to his head, a technique he sometimes used in order to discern what was going on in the room beyond, the other room from which he was being telephoned. It was a large room, he realized, not an office, and definitely not a telephone box. In the far corner of the room, which was furnished in materials absorbent to sound, he could hear what sounded like small children's voices, giggling and conferring, then a faint clack, an exclamation of pleasure. They were doing a jigsaw puzzle, he surmised.

"Hello?" said the man on the end of the line. "Hello? I'm afwaid this can't go on any longer."

He strained to hear more. A faint gossamer-rustling sound. A woman wearing nylons had crossed – and recrossed – her legs, sitting quite near the speaker. "You're playing some sort of prank on me, or trying to, I suppose, but it won't work," he said. "My celebrity has provoked this kind of thing in the past. Your call is being traced as we speak."

"I know where you are right now," the man replied. "You don't know where I am."

"Not far away," Greene replied coolly. "Not far at all." He pressed the ear-piece harder into his ear again and fancied he could hear glass, a lot of it, of a door pleading to be opened, but actually shut, so the breeze beyond it could not be heard, only somehow sensed. Then he heard the woman's gentle voice, a clatter as the jigsaw pieces were put back into their box, the children's voices raised briefly in protest, the creak and closing of a door, and the breathing of his caller.

"Graham," he said. "I'm twying to warn you in a fwiendly way – desist."

Greene could hear a woman between them who was wearing white silk gloves, so she wouldn't get a shock from the electricity in the wires. She was the Mayfair operator. She was listening to their conversation, he could tell, and she was wondering what to make of it. He could hear her intent face, young, fair, slightly pinched in concentration.

"Sorry," he said, "wrong number."

He replaced his phone in its cradle, and in a few moments he'd completely forgotten the incident.

TWENTY-EIGHT

Ponders End: a whimsically named place, a place where all those endless, bottomless, perplexing questionss about the meaning of existence might finally let go of you. Here the lucky suburbanite would kick back in his newly built villa and contemplate the ripening of his grapes and the gentle drip-drip of the filling whisky jug: a bit like Arno's Grove, perhaps, home of Chris Sekibo, which he knew had been named after a real Arno who had planted an actual grove, whose steep sloping wooded park indeed suggested a hillside in Tuscany, now denuded of vines and replanted with the utilitarian arboreal kit favoured by English suburb designers. Still shady and attractive but.

Obviously it had been a village once, as he had discovered, wandering down its high street on the return trip from one of his meetings with Caprice in Freezywater; but arriving by train on a winter's afternoon was a different story. Towers loomed above a military-style academy with a wall to ceiling screen visible through glass frontage. Parade of shops including chips. He bought a portion and gobbled them, warming him up en route, still shivering from his cold. Park people were afraid to go into for fear of being stabbed by teenagers: a friendly woman advised him to take the long way around after dark.

Darkness came on. He found the address. Knocked on the door. An eleven-year-old girl wearing a flowery onesie opened it, prancing backwards to admit him. Her mother was close behind her. He perched on the couch, pulling his overstuffed folder of worn-out tricks from the battered satchel. The boy who'd been in touch with him was on his way: he'd sent Graham a text on the bus, still at the academy. The little girl was getting ready for her SATS. She showed her writing book. He read what she had written about *Charlie and the Chocolate Factory*. She liked this story, evidently. It was a story that every child had to like in order to qualify as even possibly normal. The mother appeared to speak no English, and looked at him with blank disapproval as sat there and attempted to get on good terms with her daughter.

After a time the boy, Murt, arrived – a hirsute handsome fifteen year old. He seemed bright enough. He knew what he wanted, explained himself well and honestly, but had to admit he was struggling with school work. Graham noticed, on the far wall, a large reproduction of the detail of God and Adam's hands almost touching, from the ceiling of the Sistine Chapel. They didn't mind that it was an image from the Vatican, many of them seemed to find it beautiful He had seen it before in a few Turkish homes, a permitted representation of God's relation to man, in which the face of the Almighty himself did not appear. Graham tried to find out what he could about what the boy needed, although to him it was obvious enough. Murt had left his fucking English book at school.

His mother asked bluntly, "How long his grades get better?"

"That's a difficult question," Graham said. "But you should see an improvement straight away."

It was also obvious to him that they didn't really want a lesson. The boy said he would have to ask his father. They tossed him a screwed up fiver for his travel expenses and he skirted the shrouded park on his way back to the railway station, well aware he would never be passing this way again. The mother thought he was a crook, a thief, maybe some sort of pervert, at least a charlatan. He couldn't bring himself to feel bad or annoyed about it, just glad he wouldn't be returning. It was the shoes, he thought. He should've taken off his fucking shoes at the front door. No deliberate offence, although Murt's alert mother had expected no better of an English.

Whenever he tried to remember Sinead there were always a few scenes and locales which sprang to mind. One of them was Production Village, a combined film studio and bar complex somewhere in North London, a place she had often wanted to go to go back to, , an eighties nightspot jammed with brightly-dressed and gelled teenagers, a place filled with cheap promise and the fine beginnings of things, the location of her own first steps onto the stage of her independent life. It was a sawdust sprinkled arena with an exotic one-eyed bouncer from Plaistow, a meeting ground where they'd stared into one another's eyes on their first dates. He had felt awkward, staged. You could eat an indifferent basket meal, star in your own movie, and buy a jug of some garish cocktail for a knock-down price. It cost something all the same, but, after all, everything has its price, especially fun. His girlfriend had been the same age as most of the staff there and for him they all represented some sort of confederacy of the young to which he was being admitted as a tolerated guest.

Another – this one really made him cringe – was a wire-enclosed netball court somewhere or other where he had once picked her up for an early date. The teams had still been playing, blues against yellows, wearing ribbon sashes over their gym kit, and it had been this detail, remembered from his own schooldays, which had first brought home to him the air of transgression and public disapproval which surrounded relationships like theirs.

He'd stood at the fence briefly and watched the end of the game. Sinead was a good foot taller than most of the other players, an obvious star of the court who strode amongst them, effortlessly outreaching her rivals, and often gratuitously clubbing them to the ground. It was to be her last season. The referee shooed him off with a not unfriendly grimace (he was distracting her girls) and he had briefly wished he had a date with her instead before he crossed the road to wait outside the pub. Sitting on a bench he'd realized Sinead had insisted he meet her here so she could show him off to her netball friends, but also she felt she had nailed him, exposed him for a pervert. She'd joined him half-an-hour later, freshly showered, her hair damp, and after a few early drinks in the pub they'd gone back to his flat, where they'd fallen upon one another.

She had been eighteen years old, fully cognizant, and he hadn't been teaching her when they began their relationship; but all the same one of his primal scenes was the classroom in that FE college in Watford where as a student teacher he'd made his first attempts at the profession to which he'd been unwillingly driven back a number of times. Unprepared for the role of whipping boy, he'd selfishly thought only of his own loneliness at the time, and allowed himself to be attracted by a tall, scruffy-looking girl with a mass of badly combed blonde hair, her awkward, coltish movements, her accent full of backwards clicks and hisses, which he'd soon learned was from County Mayo, and her forthright intelligent questioning. She was miles ahead of all the others.

He'd written poems to her, free verse and sestinas, poor stuff. How he had loved his idea of her – and, alerted to the perniciousness of such things, she had loved to contradict him, finally proclaiming it all to be a load of male shit, not before he had done his boyfriend duties of ensuring she got an A for her A Level English, finally dumping her in the second year of her degree at a prestige university he had helped her to get into. But, he remonstrated, he had tried to stay friends with her. Tried to keep her dangling as a reserve fuck, she replied.

Years later, not long before he came back to London, they had been in touch, and Sinead had unexpectedly phoned in response to his e-mail. Whatever their relationship had been at the time, it had hardened into a story for her, he could tell, a dark tale of his abuse of his position and her innocence traduced.

"Go on, go on," she said, her voice singing, "Why don't you put it all before the public, let them make up their own minds?"

"I could discuss my qualms."

"Your qualms?" she laughed bitterly. "Nobody gives a shit about your qualms. You won't be able to talk your way out of that one, Graham. Although it would be most entertaining to hear you try."

"I think we're experiencing a reality gap here,"

He held the phone away from his ear while she ranted on self-righteously about how you could say that, and his parents laughed obligingly. "Is that your parents?" Sinead's voice softened in memory. "Do they remember me? Say hello."

"Of course they remember you," he said. "I remember your parents too, they were great to me, and your sisters – " he named both girls without hesitation. "All of them doing well, I hope?"

"Mind your own business," Sinead said. "I don't want to talk about my family. You still seem to think I'm stupid. You're talking to me like a little girl. You know damned well you wanted to get all three of us into bed."

"Not at the same time. Oh come on."

It was more than he'd bargained for, and far less agreeable. Not long after they'd said goodbye and hung up – despite anything which had been said it had been amazing to hear her forgotten voice – he realized he really had broken an innocent young girl's heart and he would never be forgiven for it, not by anyone. Still, he reflected, at least she was rich and powerful. He had to admit that her strong mathematics abilities had after all proved to be decisive.

Sinead was a real life multi-millionaire, twice, three times over, one for whom the word millionaire was itself no more than a shrug, no longer had meaning. A woman who at a pinch would describe herself as being comfortable. But not for him.

TWENTY-NINE

The flaring toy-like money flues along the path of the Docklands Light Railway were great roaring furnaces of light, channelling surplus human product up into the groaning atmosphere. A cluster of glittery buildings designed on a laptop, extruded by a 3D printer and planted haphazardly in the soft plasticine of the riverbank by the giant laughing baby in the sun. They reminded him of those roman candles of flame above the oil wells of Kuwait, whooshing up into the stratosphere during the first Iraq war, or the jewelled lights of Dallas, or anywhere else, but all of these comparisons were unsatisfying, melodramatic, so that any response he had to these changes in the city was itself already channelled, polarized, emptied out.

It reminded him of one luminous scene in a seventies film he otherwise barely recalled, *Rollerball*. He'd seen the trailer and caught up with it a decade later on late night TV. Some rich party-goers, hangers on of the gladiatorial games which provided the social cement of the film's version of a media-circus future, had wandered out into the perfect night-time landscape of somewhere like Surrey to savour the fresh air and a line of sparse Scotch pines on the near horizon, began to amuse themselves by incinerating the trees with a powerful six-shooter flare pistol. Crisping them one after another until a whole line of burning trees spectacularly lit up the night sky. Laughing as each one exploded, they grew bored quickly, apart from one woman who seemed to develop a sudden headache as she realized the implications of their sports.

He was nervous. It had been his first assignment as a mobile tutor. Would he get the forty quid out of his mark? He trundled out along Canary Wharf clasping his schoolteacher's satchel on his knees, shoulder to shoulder with young commuters scrolling their just-invented iPhones. These were new uses for the opposable thumb, and the gentle flicking of index fingers, whisking through alternate worlds like fabric swatches, or tellers counting money, was striking the first time you saw it. They were the Teletubbies generation, he realized with a sick lurch. This was what had become of the last children he would ever babysit: here they all were sitting on this toy train between nearby and nowhere, nodding their heads from side to side, stroking something in unison that they held before them in mid-air, above their laps.

He met up with a Saudi boy at the entrance to Silvertown rail station, followed him with trepidation to the foot of a guarded residential tower, picked up a key from the office, and they ascended to the top floor gym of an adjoining vertiginous precipice, where they sat at a table on two plastic chairs, watching the residents work out through the glass wall of the gym. The Saudi was polite, himself a little nervous. He wanted to practice a couple of IELTS papers – he'd failed this exam upon which rested the condition of acceptance as a student in a London university, to study finance, his family's trade, for two years running now. But he was sure he would pass eventually, and hoping for success the following morning.

He'd brought a couple of examples with him. They were all about summarizing the content of statistics and diagrams in a short essay of two hundred words, whose criteria were accuracy of information, interpretive abilities and – most importantly – competent punctuation and spelling. Upon learning the customer was a Saudi he had chosen and printed out a paper on the exponential increase of women students in English higher education institutions since 1962, and another about the pros and cons of capital punishment as a deterrent to murder.

The young Saudi wasn't an apt student, but he was desperate to pass his exam the following day. He would spring up from his chair, gesticulating and speaking rapidly to this stranger, acting himself out and communicating his predicament. Graham forced him back into his chair with mind bolts, talking him through the meaning of those colour-coded columns showing the exponential growth of female student numbers, from a small minority status, to parity with males, to an overtaking of the male student population by two thirds and more. Women were everywhere in education, they were winning, and it wasn't about to let up anytime soon. At least, that's how he saw it privately. To Khalid he was strong, calm and explanatory, and little by little, by mutual applied effort and his dictation, Khalid's two-hundred word account of the statistics took shape. When they were done they kicked back for a few minutes. Khalid had totally failed to rise to his gender baiting. Good, he thought. Pass.

Capital punishment was an easier if cheaper shot, a subject matter which turned Khalid into a helplessly-flailing target of liberal ridicule, although not particularly easy to hit, as he soon discovered. Khalid just couldn't see any cons to capital punishment, it was all good, a deterrent, sure, but also in accordance with natural and religious law, an eye for an eye, a tooth for a tooth, although, he was at pains to point out, in his country the common practice was to revisit serious crimes like rape and murder tenfold upon the family of the one who had offended. That was the only way the others would really know and take seriously the consequences of acting against such a family as yours. It is an example unto others. It works well. There is no murder in Saudi Arabia, or very little, of course there is some, and that which is, is punished swiftly, justly.

He and the boy argued back and forth for quite a while, about two hours, and this time it was even harder to get the Saudi kid to chisel his words into English sentences and lay them in straight rows across a feint-ruled page. What about miscarriages of justice? And what if you weren't a member of one of these powerful families, would the law project you from them? But finally it, and they, were done. The boy paid him and walked with him back to Silvertown DLR station, offered to buy him a drink in the old docker-style pub they were passing.

He agreed to just the one, because after all Khalid would have to get back and do a couple more practice papers tonight. The rapidity with which he had pulled out his i-phone as they emerged from the tower and the number of social calls entailed in his reentry from the land of the dead into the gravitational field of his living acquaintance, quickly convinced him there was little chance of this, but still he vainly insisted. After all, it was expected of him.

They sat at a clean stacking table and he read the posters for this night and that night while Khalid expounded and demonstrated various features of his new phone. He had to agree it was incredible. Here he was, in a place he'd never been to with a person he knew little about, really, a third of his age, yet still he found himself in a version of a familiar conversation with his younger brother: agreeing something to be incredible, well-worth it, etcetera, when really … the world swept on by him, he neither wanted it to stop nor to keep up with it, he couldn't really, but all the same he was aware that idiots like the one he was now seated beside, trying to explain his own situation to suddenly sympathetic, uncomprehending ears, would be borne along considerably further than he was ever going to manage however far he managed to leap out from the tidal banks of the Thames.

Another early assignment had involved helping a young man – a personal fitness trainer in Shoreditch – to write an essay to help get him into the Army. This boy wanted to go to Afghanistan and sort out the Taliban once and for all. He had come round to Graham's flat, which was meticulously cleaned, and sat at the low coffee table working through a comprehension exercise about whether teenaged girls should be allowed to box. He was a fairly intelligent lad, and he couldn't see why he'd failed GCSE in the first place. Let alone why he'd want to go and fight an unwinnable war in Afghanistan. His sister had recommended he read *Eats, Shoots and Leaves* to help with his grammar and punctuation, but he suspected her of having a laugh at her brother's expense. He saw it as his duty to point out the dangers of the war, and its futility, but the boy was unable to see another point of view from the one he'd imbibed on army websites and from adventure-style magazines about being a mercenary. He helped him with his essay – again, his army entrance exam was the following day – and wished him luck. The luck to fail. What was wrong with being a personal fitness trainer? A nightclub bouncer? Ultimately, they were boring jobs, and this hyper-fit, dreamy young man had been determined to escape, to grow, to test himself beyond his limits.

Around the same time he'd been put in touch with Naedi Parvez, a third year linguistics student at King's College – and he had taught her by text on his antique mobile. Her lengthy, fluent messages would beg him for guidance, latitude, mercy; his brutal monosyllables urged her further along the path she had after all freely chosen. Searching for a title for her undergraduate dissertation he saw a black girl spitting in the street. How disgusting, he thought, but incorporated it immediately, knowing by some instinct 'Girl-spit' was an important term: it was going to prove crucial to the future of Hip Hop, to its credibility within the academy as a subversive, counter-hegemonic weapon against the dominant cultures of black misogyny and white liberal feminist condescension.

Her extended essay was on irony in some dopey sub-satirical website aimed at post-adolescent middle-class smartarses who were none too bright but liked a patina of pseudo-sophistication shining on their puerile sense of boredom and entitlement. Naedi herself enjoyed this site, more than hip-hop, if she was honest, which had begun to bore her considerably; but – as she said, with an indifferent shrug – "I guess that's my generation for you."

She was a whip-slender young woman, Arab-American, but could have been a Latina or anything else, wearing heavy-framed spectacles, just an American girl, exuding a sense of semi-athletic lassitude and now last-minute panic. To Graham she looked a bit like a young Nana Mouskouri. He thought he discerned a sense of desiring to be punished for her laziness, and he tried to satisfy it by extending demands and insisting on payment for texting her and waiting for her to fulfil them. She brought out the bastard in him. He wondered if he should wear a mask. He decided yes. This seemed to work well. She lived with her mother in a flat near Victoria station, chosen for its proximity to the burned out pleasure centres of tourist London.

He ascended from the underground and wended his way past *Billy Elliot*, now in its twenty-fifth triumphant year, to their place above a supermarket, to ring the entry bell, climb the dingy stairs, and enter their small, rented living room with an assumed air of absolute authority. Naedi would emerge from the bedroom, her hair gone greasy-grassy, her shapeless clothes dishevelled, as if she was somehow heaving off the weight of long hours of fruitless intellectual toil. She turned on the laptop and showed him what she'd done, meekly asking him for suggestions, hesitantly explaining the meanings of a few recent linguistics buzz-words which happened not to be familiar to him. He gave her an hour of his time to the minute, then she was on her own again, trying to implement his mild instructions.

"I'm panicking," she'd say as her deadlines rushed towards her with spanking paddles.

"Don't panic," he reassured her softly. "Everything is going to be okay."

He thought of these assignments as the honeymoon period of his career as a personal tutor.

How much of teaching was just trading on the ignorance of the young? Encouraging their and their parents' false hopes? A lot of it, that's how much. He knew very well that he was caught up in it all whether he liked it or not. Doing his little bit to sign people off on architecture degrees who would never have the ability to nail together s henhouse in a hurricane; great actresses who would always be stuck at the selfie stage. Indigo children. The bruised purple fruit that must be picked up as quickly as possible before it rotted, before the wasps got to it. Part of the coming race who were going to make the twenty-first century so much better than the last one. He wondered how people could believe such nonsense, but remembered being brought up with similar stuff himself. Aspire. Achieve. Ascend. Accelerate. And what were the indicators of indigo children?

Autism, attention deficit, the tendency to express themselves better in bubble diagrams than old-fashioned hierarchical prose, because after all that's how everything was totally really linked, by arrows, circles and lines of flow. And while you're at it why not decorate your notes with silver sparkle and key-in a few links made out of the spare wool to be found in the let's improvise box in the corner of every undergraduate classroom. He was tempted to blame the French, although he knew enough to realise they would never entertain such educational liberalism. But actually, he thought, people pursuing those kinds of practice were actually the okay ones, the ones who were genuinely responding to the wider social intake, rather than those featherbedded revolutionaries having conversations with each other about whether or not certain categories of other people should be allowed to speak at all, and on what terms, that's if they actually existed. Yep. Academics were nasty, complacent, cynical little shits, the more successful – *a fortiori* – most likely to be smiling backstabbers in it for international travel and a good pension. You just had to hang onto the hope that your children were going to turn out to be indigo children. Every child an indigo child! He was waiting to see this slogan appear on banners roped to the railings outside schools, alongside those A* GCSE percentages which you could bet were going to break more or less everybody's back before school was finally out forever.

THIRTY

Christian greeted him with a withheld smile of knowledge, his neat moustache bristling slightly, and told him he was about to publish his first novel on Kindle. Looking steadily at the screen as he scrolled through his client's job applications, he described the process of writing it, rapid and fluent, and how his wife had been astonished by the ease with which all those organized words had tumbled from his fingertips.

He spoke again of the importance of following one's passion, and when Graham politely asked for the title Christian told him didn't want to spoil it for him. However, he did discreetly slide a folded sheet of paper with the web address across his desk, which he pocketed with a promise to look at it later. He congratulated his sustainability consultant, who had turned out to be another life coach in effect – after all, he could do nothing else but admire the marketing technique of a man who insisted he was indifferent to sales. He just wanted to see what would happen.

Christian's novel – *I Am God* – was linked to the important job getting questions he had asked himself, and others, because, well, he had decided it was so and therefore it was. His answer, to defeat all punishing social overseers, was to declare himself to be God, and thereby he hoped to overcome every obstacle by force of will alone. In his Kindle auto he was a surgeon, with the power of life and death over others, and by writing his book he was "adding value to the world" whether anyone wanted to read it or not. This fable of breaking through to realize one's full potential was an absolute value in itself. Naysayers, for him, were simply to be ignored, avoided – there was no way you could ever prove yourself right in the eyes of one of them, any more than the devil could be persuaded he was your friend, not just your tempter.

It was a devilish voice, but its temptations were false. Be average. Fit in. That's what they were saying, according to Christian, and who needed it? In other words this devilish advice of your friend and neighbour was the precise opposite of what the devil usually offered – absolute power, without responsibility. Adding value to the world. That was a good phrase. He liked it, but he wasn't in any position to argue his points with his life coach. Christian had to be appeased, not told he was barking up the wrong tree, that he had fallen for the devil's blandishments without realizing it. "Hell is a fable," Christopher Marlowe's Dr Faustus declared confidently, just after he'd made his own deal with Mephistopheles, and not so long before the Hell's Mouth, that standard property of the Elizabethan stage – expensive but necessary for Marlowe's immensely popular play – was dragged into position for the final denouement. Christian was of course reading from his empowering self-help manual, he didn't believe in any of this shit – just the counter-shit which said you could do anything you wanted if only you set your mind to it. This is probably what Marlowe himself believed, or something like it, and for this the Elizabethan secret service had killed him. He wondered if Christian might suffer a similar fate; but no, he decided, probably not, not in this day and age. Nowadays his fantasies of world domination were considered to be suitable advice for the jobless.

"Graham," he imagined Jeremy Kyle asking prior to exposing him as a benefit cheat on afternoon TV. "Tell me, what do you like most about your job?"

He enjoyed the challenge of meeting new people, even the travelling sometimes, plus his authorized entry into a new domestic space, defined by strong diagonals and a balancing basket of eggs. The unseen poetry, the status of visiting professional. The strong element of imposture. Casing the joint. Half-heartedly weighing up the teapot. Being placed on his mettle, looking up half-remembered things in the library. Reading background texts on Elizabethan and Jacobean drama, on Chaucer, Milton and Christopher Marlowe. Edward Thomas and Christina Rossetti. Keats, Wordsworth, Dickens and Mary Shelley. Edgar Allan Poe. *In medias res. Ab ovo.*

All the same, he didn't really want to go all the way into the Pupil Referral Unit. He didn't want to really get involved and make a real difference to somebody's life. That was his problem, why he could never much sympathize with himself much less expect to elicit the sympathy of others. What was so good about making a difference anyway? And, more to the point, what difference could you really be said to be making to somebody who had forgotten about you a few hours later? At best you were a processing plant, a station along the way which might turn one kind of energy into another, a stepping stone, a sop, a rusting bunch of old machinery, somebody who might be fondly remembered by a parent. After a burst of frenzied creativity, he was ready to send off his draft of Orhan's GCSE assessment on children's literature, explaining he'd written it as a dialogue between him and his annoying younger sister. For some reason he liked the trope of the annoying little sister (or brother) and had often tried to build it into their creative writing pieces.

A Podcast on Children's Literature

Hello everybody. Thanks for tuning in to my podcast on children's literature – which I'm hoping you'll enjoy. I'm going to concentrate on two books I read very early in my life, two classic stories which have stayed with me through the years, and by talking about them I hope to make a few points about what it is children really enjoy in reading, and why stories, new or old, are important for developing a child's imagination and informing him or her about the kind of world they will be living in as adults. Here to help me is my sister, Sezin, who will be joining in now and then, as little sisters do, with a few annoying comments.

SEZIN: I don't believe you ever read anything in your life!

Well, that's where you're wrong, sis! OK, so if I never read any-thing, how did you come to know the stories of *Gulliver's Travels* and *Alice in Wonderland?*

SEZIN: I know those stories too! I read them myself when our parents gave me those books for my birthday!

No, Sezin, they were my books. I read them first, then I passed them on to you, and told you the stories too, or maybe just explained the pictures, before you could read them yourself.

SEZIN: Are you sure? I don't remember that at all. I seem to remember unwrapping them and being delighted by the bright shiny covers, and the drawings – a man in old-fashioned clothes pinned down on the beach by a lot of tiny people with needles instead of spears and bows and arrows … um, and another one of the same man with his mouth wide-open, putting one of the little men inside … like he was going to eat him! It was frightening, actually. Not suitable for kids, I'd say.

They were Lilliputians, Sezin. That was Gulliver's first voyage. He left his wife and family behind in England and was shipwrecked on the island of Lilliput. I found out later it was written by Jonathan Swift, an Irish writer in the eighteenth century. It wasn't really meant for children, but as a satire of his society and the cruelty and stupidity of human beings. But in time it became popular all over the world as a story for children. Of course, they had to tidy it up a bit and cut some parts out. The children's version was about Lilliput and Brobdingnag, the Land of Giants.

SEZIN: I remember now. I think the land of giants was a television programme as well. So was the land of the little people. I must admit I didn't realize it was so old. Also, what do you mean by satire?

Satire, my dear sister, is when a writer criticises his or her society by means of comical exaggerated stories or jokes. Sometimes they do it in disguise, for example when there is censorship, and these kinds of jokes are usually forbidden by the government. Jonathan Swift wrote another satire called 'A Modest Proposal' in which he suggested one way to overcome the Irish potato famine would be for the Irish to sell their babies to the English lords and ladies to be eaten. He went into a lot of detail about how they should be prepared for the table.

SEZIN: That's disgusting!

Yes, but he was only joking. Anyway, back to Lilliput. In the land of the little people you may remember, there were two factions at court, the little-enders and the big-enders. They really hated each other, and sometimes wars broke out over their quarrels.

SEZIN: Little-enders and big-enders? That sounds rather rude …

It was their boiled eggs, Sezin dear. Some thought an egg should be opened by slicing off the narrow end, but others insisted the wider end should be bashed in with a spoon. And the King of Lilliput had to wear one high heel and one flat heel to show he was on both sides at once, which meant he hobbled everywhere, bobbing up and down, and made a laughing stock of himself.

SEZIN: That is funny – and stupid. What happened in the end?

Oh, Gulliver liked the little people, so he helped them fight one of their wars against a neighbouring island. Then they helped him build a giant (but really small) boat and he sailed away – to his next adventure, in Brobdingnag, the Land of the Giants.

SEZIN: I remember that one better for some reason. There was a girl in it. He was the pet of a girl who was in a circus, and he had to live in a cage and be exhibited as a freak for people who were always trying to hurt or kill him. It was horrible. I remember the pictures of the giant children – they looked so ugly, clumsy and terrifying. It gave me the creeps! I had nightmares about this stupid old story.

Well, maybe that's how we look to smaller creatures: to a mouse, for instance. We're built on a bigger scale. Perhaps he was trying to say something about different races, or cultures, or something, and how they often have a distorted view of one another.

SEZIN: Hmm. Perhaps. I think he just didn't like people at all, and he enjoyed the idea of frightening children. If he'd known his disgusting story would become a children's classic he would have been pleased. I suppose in those days they thought it was good to frighten kids – to make them behave themselves. In modern books the children are usually heroes, doing grown-up things better than grown-ups.

That's actually quite an intelligent thought, for you, Sezin. Pity this is my podcast. Now I'm going to talk about *Alice's Adventures in Wonderland*, by Lewis Carroll. It's a book where the child is the hero.

SEZIN: A girl is the heroine, you mean.

Yes. But it was written by a grown-up man to amuse a little girl.

SEZIN: Why did he do that? Did he have a thing about little girls?

Yes, he did. He used to take nude photos of Alice. Nobody seems to have understood about this at the time, or even thought there was anything much wrong with it.

SEZIN: I might have known! What a disgusting man! Just to think that generations of young kids read his books – it makes me feel like throwing up! Who was this creep?

He was a Victorian mathematician called Charles Dodgson.

SEZIN: How boring! You know, you've completely ruined this story for me. I loved it! I'm sure I got it for a birthday present too. It wasn't one of your books at all. In fact, I'm going to talk about it. It's my turn now!

I knew this would happen. Okay, go on then, if you must.

SEZIN: What I liked about it was that the girl, Alice, was so clever, and there weren't any boys in it. First she follows the rabbit down a rabbit hole – which was so funny, how he was looking at his watch and saying 'I'm late, I'm late' – and then she has to drink these medicines which make her grow to enormous size, or shrink her, as necessary. And she meets all these different characters, quite frightening ones, but they're all very polite to her. Let's see, there was Tweedle-dum and Tweedle-dee, who were always fighting on their wall to see you would be master – just like stupid boys – and the Mad

Hatter, whose top hat still had a price on it …

Do you know why he was mad? Because mercury was often used in the making of hats. It was poisonous, so these hatters were often mad.

SEZIN: You spoil everything with your explanations! I suppose I liked it because these characters were scary and funny at the same time, like the caterpillar smoking his pipe, and – worst of all – the cook and his wife, who were always fighting and beating their baby. Disgusting people! They also had a cat, or so I seem to recall, who disappeared leaving only his smile behind.
 A Cheshire cat, it was.

SEZIN: What's a Cheshire cat?

I don't know, just a kind of English cat I suppose. Now you mention it, *Alice in Wonderland*, and the sequel, *Alice Through the Looking Glass*, which had a mad Queen who forced everybody to play chess and was always shouting 'Off with their heads!', were pretty violent stories. What with the smoking caterpillar, the Mad Hatter, the bottles Alice drinks from and the fact nothing in them makes sense, really, I wouldn't be surprised if they were written under the influence of drugs, by a madman who enjoyed confusing children.

SEZIN: The English just didn't care in those days. But I still think it was a good story. It didn't do me any harm. It was fantastic, imaginative, and it made you think. I used to dream for hours about an incredible world where little girls were in charge!

Nightmare!

SEZIN: For you, yes.

Do you think *Alice in Wonderland* has anything in common with *Gulliver's Travels*? That's what I was wondering – how to tie them together and bring this podcast to an end for our patient listeners. I can't think of much, except crazy things happen, and children seem to like stories where fantastic events occur.

SEZIN: They don't know any better, maybe. Anything is possible to a child.

But there are lots of rules for children. They spend their whole time learning the rules: how to behave, how to spell, and what will be expected of them in the adult world. Children's stories are supposed to teach them moral lessons, like don't be greedy, or always obey the rules.

SEZIN: At the same time they often see adults misbehaving. In addition to which they see a mad, violent world unfolding in front of them on TV and the internet. Perhaps the children's writers seem to be on their side. Oh! I've just thought of something those two stories have in common!

What's that?

SEZIN: Well, it's changes of scale. Gulliver gets bigger and smaller, in a way, so that he can see how things look to a little person or a giant, or to an adult and a child. It's the same thing with Alice, when the drinks the potions which make her grow and shrink. One minute she's a giant goddess, in charge of everything, the next minute she has to shrink down to almost nothing, to be a little girl again. In both of them it's the child's and adult's point of view they're trying to convey. They're also saying, look kids, it's a scary world, but in a way which introduces them to reality quite slowly, with plenty of jokes.

I suppose that's one way of looking at it, Sezin. Let's face some facts: things are probably going to get a lot more difficult for these little readers of children's literature.

SEZIN: You can say that again! But I must admit that these old books you like – I liked them too. They're a lot more exciting than most of what is served up to kids nowadays.

Sezin, for once I agree with you. Now it's time to say goodnight to our sleepy listeners. Goodnight! Pleasant dreams!

SEZIN: If you are still awake.

He attached the finished document, clicked send. How in hell was anyone going to believe Orhan had written this tripe? The kid could barely string together a coherent sentence of his own. He wasn't going to worry about it though. After all, his parents were paying so much for his school fees he suspected they would turn a blind eye to anything. It was the poorer kids at the community colleges and academies who were subject to constant surveillance, strict discipline, expected to complete stereotyped assignments with dreary rote responses. The more you could pay, the easier it got.

Now it was his turn to sit back, pour himself a glass of something cool and refreshing. Edmonton's shopping centre was an indoor circus of pound shops, shoe shops, clothes shops, and cafes, which ran around an inner circle of a covered market; an uneasy space, deserted at night, from which you could be sighted from several angles.

Two weeks ago there'd been a nasty stabbing under one of the transformer-style towers that loomed over it, near Doğtaş, a big furniture and bathroom fittings emporium on the corner: an 'elderly man' (really only fifty-three) had been attacked after denying entrance to a group of thirteen-year-old boys on their way to a party. He hadn't recognized them, told them to sling their hooks, and now he was dead. One of the boys had handed himself in to the police; the others were in hiding.

It was difficult to get them to take any interest in local murders, or rapes. "Not many people believe a man can be raped," Dersdar said. "But they can – I know it's true, but other people don't know about it."

There was a level of violence in the city they took for granted. They were growing up with it all around them, accepted it totally, in a way he hadn't, and didn't, although like them he disassociated and carried on. He couldn't really afford to entertain the possibility of being stabbed on the bus, any more than they could be bothered to worry about every step they took. Much of what could be called their racism was on this level – an inherited instinctual swerve based on experience, whether their own or that of others. It protected them, as did their indifference. Their stupidity was intelligence, their fearlessness ignorance. His endless seeking of a reconciliation between these disparate factions and incompatible world-views was something he'd simply been imprinted with, like a pigeon with no real place of its own to perch.

His dreams brought him back to reality. He was sitting an exam under the indifferent gaze of his invigilator, then suddenly he grew bored with it. He'd scribbled out a couple of pages, thought he'd got the main points down, which would have to do. He stood up and left the room, vaguely thinking he could come back to it later. But once outside he realized there was no later, never would be. People were confidently shouldering past him to get into some sort of green corridor, where the invigilator, the one who bound and beat him, waited for them to take their turn, meanwhile flipping contemptuously through the sheets on which he'd scribbled out his unfinished thoughts. He found himself making excuses. He felt he'd passed the exam, but everybody who milled around the square behaved as if he hadn't.

The invigilator – and the subject of the exam paper – wrote out a series of guiding principles on the whiteboard for the benefit of future candidates. In the dream he recognized these ideas, concepts, as his own. Or were they subtly different, superior? Surely this is what he had written in his answer, what there was if it, but nonetheless they turned away from him. Wait and see. But there was nothing to wait for, not really. There were plenty of other candidates. They had replaced him. Eaten him. Shat him out. He existed no longer, nobody remembered him as he tried to flutter down onto the shit-encrusted ledge under the railway bridge ... but thankfully it had now all been ground into the carpet and forgotten.

THIRTY-ONE

Ricky looked over the menu carefully for a third time. He'd selected an entrée, a main and a possible dessert for himself and Lana – modified the entrée (perhaps a sharing plate would be a good idea, particularly if it was the squid) and now he set to tapping each of his teeth in turn for potential hollowness as he inspected the top of the dusty picture rail along its entire length with craning neck around the upper walls of the restaurant in Thames Ditton at which they'd arranged to meet, ominously he thought, since the locale if not the eatery stretched back to the very beginnings of their acquaintance. Lana had picked the place off the internet. She'd always wanted to go back to Thames Ditton; he wouldn't have been surprised if she decided to turn up in school uniform, although something told him tonight wouldn't be the night for it.

Then she was there, in the doorway, her small, pugnacious form looking around for him, spotting him and walking briskly towards his table. She wasn't smiling and he noticed immediately she was holding her neck stiff. Moving her shoulders slowly in concert with her head.

"Hello, Ricky." Lana offered him a smile as she sank into her upholstered bucket chair and her head seemed to disappear down into her shoulders, almost as if she were crouching down out of his line of fire. "Been here long?"

"Not really. How's your neck?"

"Much better, thanks."

He passed her a menu. Lana peered at it in apparent pain. "I think I'll just have a cheeseburger," she said. "And a beer."

Ricky rapidly scaled down his own order and called the waitress over. Soon they were sipping their tall beers and waiting for their food to arrive. They chatted desultorily, about her journey – it was her first long trip, down the M25, in the new car, an Astra, bigger than the Micra, with a longer crumple zone, and she had found it exhausting – and he asked how the girls were getting along. Ricky gave a number of so-so answers to questions she hadn't asked about his life, his work, and as usual skirted the subject of Hugh. He could finally contain himself no longer and asked, "Hugh?"

"Oh, he's been very good," she said. "I've seen another side of him." She looked at him frankly. "It was totally hysterical, what I was saying before. I was just distracted, in a hurry, not taking care on the road. Let me tell you, Ricky. I'm fucking lucky to be alive."

"I'm so glad you're okay." Ricky put his hand across the table without thinking and put his hand over hers, which just sat there in claw-like immobility before turning over and giving his hand a small reciprocal squeeze, and retracting into her lap. "It's good to see you!" He raised his glass to his lips, tilted it a little on the way in a toast to her continued existence, and spilt a little beer on the table. "Shit," he said.

They didn't talk too much through the meal, and Ricky didn't try to broach the subject of anything else they might do another time. Any ideas he'd had – Kew Gardens, for example – sounded ridiculous even to him, to his inner censor of stupid ideas. Lana's face was as round as ever, and her high forehead shone with its last beauty in the dim lights of the restaurant. It all belonged to the young now, he thought, everything which had passed between them, which they had done together, too old really, for it all, or perhaps just the right age. And in the near-silence with which they looked at their remaining food and at each other and into the air, it was impossible not to think about her accident and how easily, how often, such moments of carelessness robbed people of what might have been their lives, and of how the others carried on diminished because of it.

Once she had eaten a bit and got halfway down her beer, Lana became a lot chirpier, talking on about the government, her last trip, in what he thought of as her half-hearted leftie teacher's way of talking, which meant little to him, if he was honest. Ricky thought that if her accident hadn't killed her, it hadn't made her any stronger either, so that was wrong. But Lana did think it had made her stronger, and by the time they were done she felt ready to drive home.

As the evening drew to a close, both were overwhelmed by a burst of affection for each other, because after all this really was going to be the last time, and you ended up with a sense of mutual acceptance that was going to be hard to drive away from. Out on the old A3 again, back home to Hampshire. She found herself thinking, of all places, about Bognor Regis. In the library at teacher training collage, leafing through whatever they had there, picking up *The Radical Tradition in Education,* which tuned out to be the public school tradition. It must have been there she had picked up the name of Matthew Arnold, she remembered, and probably cobbled a quote or two into one of her essays.

Passing through Cobham, she remembered Graham. This particular nice boy with his crummy taste in music and delusions of grandeur, who would always be tucked away in that bend in the road. She decided to turn onto the M25 at the top of Pain's Hill, and circled towards her slip road, a brief vista that was no vista at all to speak of from the roundabout, of nothing but flaring silver birches and dark shrouding greenery, but at the last moment missed her turn-off and decided to continue to funnel along the A3.

It had been later, during her Open University degree, that she'd come across Arnold again, as part of the reading list for a context question on Thomas Hardy and Victorian thought, and realized he was, like her, something of an optimist compared to the novelist she'd loved so unreasoningly as a girl.

She settled down into the long unlit drive that would take her within a hairsbreadth of her parents' old home in Milford, where she'd grown up, and amused herself with some Arnoldian musings. There were three classes in society, she remembered. The barbarians, the philistines, and us, the people. You might be able to prise a little bit of money out of the barbarians, but as far as the philistines, the middle classes, were concerned, they had no redeeming qualities whatever. Lana herself had never known what side to be on in all that class business, she'd decided to be on no side, on neither side of the warped fences.

Then there were the bees, the busy bees like herself, flitting from cowslip to buttercup, collecting the pollen distilling it into liquor, into the delicious honey of light and goodness and culture. And of course there were the spiders. Ricky, dear Ricky. She liked him, she always had liked him. They were almost the same height – at least he didn't tower over her, like most men. But Ricky was unquestionably a spider. Oh dear. Yes he was. Spinning his endless, pointless, contesting arguments out of his bitter insides, trying to entangle her in their twisted, sticky threads. Nein Danke. Obtuse, futile, destructive of her sense of life.

Lana's neck was aching like fuck, but she had to strengthen it somehow. Driving was fucking stressful, on these roads she knew like the back of her hand, getting home to the Rhode Island Reds.

THIRTY-TWO

One long ago summer he'd placed his forearm on the open windowsill of a Morris Minor and watched his skin go rapidly brown, crisp and flake away – before retracting it to safety in the warm car. Hot wind on his face, careering along the winding lanes of South Wales for miles and miles with Jake Bugg, the owner and holder of a driver's licence, beside him. Jake's potential new girlfriend, swathed in infinite black folds of skirt in the musty back seat, cackled quietly to herself. Jake's restless energy was still burning forty-odd years later when he rented his old friend a small, sparsely furnished room on the top floor of his language school in Muswell Hill, actually the teachers' stopover room, while he looked around for something more permanent.

For two months he'd traipsed around the block of the Broadway, spotting Tariq Ali and a Channel Four news presenter in the supermarket. He bought fresh cheesecake in the bakers, scoffed fishcakes and chips from Toffs, heated up ready meals in the school's cavernous empty kitchen, bathed in a big old stained bath under an ancient gas boiler which gurgled and shuddered, apparently about to explode, and produced a thin stream of scalding yellow water. He travelled miles to do a day in a secondhand bookshop in Lisson Grove, where he'd catalogued some interesting things, such as a tiny American pirate edition of Shelley's *Queen Mab*, his youthful feminist epic, which had been neatly rebound in red boards in the 1920s and embellished with a Satanic-looking colophon of a struggling serpent. Then a month's supply teaching in a failing school in Walthamstow, until his meagre savings were done and he was pretty much barking mad. To himself he seemed to know the answers to a lot of questions: questions he asked himself. Questions that he knew no-one would ever ask him. There were times when you couldn't take another step. Couldn't get any further. Just put one foot in front of another, his grandfather had said, you'll get somewhere. But there's no fool like an old fool, that's what they'd said about his grandfather.

He left his door keys in the room and managed to lock himself between the inner and outer doors on street level, trapped there like a fly in a jar, hammering ineffectually until he managed to attract the attention of an African student whom he managed to persuade to call the police in the phone box opposite his door. Two cops arrived. One broke in through the back of the building while the other demolished the heavy glass front door, releasing him at no small expense. David had been nice about the bill for over a thousand pounds worth of damage, but it was soon goodbye Alexandra Palace and a plunge down to Cricklewood, and to Harlesden, before things started looking up. Now as the rain burned down upon his weary eyes, spinning like the Four Tops.

They had been years of degradation, struggling to keep it together, commanding his lead troops from a shoebox into which he and his memories had been horned, out of control, prowling in the park beside Hendon football ground and its corrugated lean-to sheds, running from garden to garden, and shitting in the open like a fox.

In random squattings he would feel it all flow out of him for good, an aching emptiness, purification at last, at last, wiping his behind on a handful of fat leaves from the nearest clump, their rough coolness as close as he could get to something natural, something connected, and he was still the he collected around that hollow place where waste collected incessantly, needed to be evacuated, let go of once and for all, not an idea but a process in which you shat the evil out of yourself and were made clean again for your new sins.

His landlady had come in late from her club and stood there in her fifties dancing frock and told him the terrible story of how the son of somebody at the club, a lovely feller, had hanged himself in the toilet because he thought he was a paedophile. "He wasn't though," she said. "He just thought he was; it had been suggested to him and gradually the idea took hold of him, and destroyed him. We saw it happening –" she almost laughed, as though her horrific insight somehow resolved it all. "But he wasn't one," she insisted. "He was just a normal bloke. He didn't have to die – he could have just lived out his life and been happy."

He clunked awake and wisps of his dream were sucked away, suddenly and abruptly disarmed, breaking up like formless smoke creatures from hell on their way down the drains. They had been so very real a few moments before, the usual situation unchanged, although he thought somehow this time the man had been subject to physical distortion. His torso had been of normal length and girth, but his legs were weirdly foreshortened. What was the identity of this man who stood over him?

He had resolved to find out many times, but somehow, when he was again in the middle of things, this decision was forgotten. How do you think your way out of a bad dream? You could wake yourself up, of course, which he always managed to do eventually, but what he really needed was a way to break the spell of the dream itself. What was he being punished for? And why was he considered to be forever unforgiven by this persistent abuser in his head?

He thought of some men he had known. Men he had admired, who seemed stronger than him. A boy who had lied to him cruelly and effectively at school; a colleague who had seemed to want to hate him come what may, and later proved this paranoid suspicion to be true. Men who had been full of specious advice, which they reeled off so very easily, but which, if he thought about it later, could only lead to death and disaster for the one who was stupid enough follow it. These men were willing his death, he knew that much. At least they were trying to make a fool of him. To humiliate him beyond recovery. But why? What had he ever done to them? Nothing he could remember. He really must be the most evil, or perhaps just the most annoying person on earth. Or perhaps they were just saying what they thought of idiots. And why not?

But he was not afraid at all of any of that. By and by he'd come to accept life didn't come in a pinky paper all folded neat, and he could hear muffled voices around him, the strife of happiness and pain. And it gave him that strength you get from feeling great, when it happened. He remembered a woman he'd known, how she'd planned a fierce row between them, and how he had always known somehow or other that he would again have his careless seasons.

THIRTY-THREE

They'd always met up at The Spinach Box, an eatery on the corner of a road somewhere or other, which served fresh spinach mainly: lightly stir-fried in butter and dusted with as much black pepper as you could stand. They always wondered how it kept going – which it hadn't – and stuck to cups of coffee. Rachael was now a celebrated novelist; she lived in Manhattan, it was only once every couple of years he saw her, but it was still enjoyable to hook up and rattle on as in the olden days of – how long was it? – thirty years ago, when they had been lovers, then friends, then whatever

He remembered one of their early encounters, when he'd been shocked to realize she was on the game, at least in a confused, half-hearted way. She lay there, an inert doll made of pastry, dusted with flour, uncooked and, despite her youth and beauty, unappetizing, perhaps deliberately so. Here I am, she seemed to be saying, fuck me if you must, if you can. She'd retreated from the surface of her skin, which was dry, tasted of talcum powder, lived somewhere deeper inside – if anywhere, he'd thought, taking it all on trust. He'd experienced a choking sensation, resisting an impulse to purse his lips, to cleanse the bitter taste from his tongue with his teeth, rub it off on the roof of his mouth, to spit her out and have done with her there and then.

Discarded bouquets littered the darkened hotel room, cast-away tributes of brief visitors, rank upon rank of them. The room stank of sour sex sprayed over with something ineffective, or maybe it had smelled of nothing. He didn't remember. It had been mid-afternoon in Bayswater but her curtains were drawn, creating a pleasant, cave-like atmosphere in which these tributes of her guests, all the perished roses and over-ripe pinks, rotted profusely in their untouched crackly shrouds of cellophane, tied up with ivory ribbons.

"Yeah," she'd said, "I really have to throw all this shit away."

In another of her early rooms, in Highgate, on a rubbish-strewn wooden floor you had to negotiate on tiptoe, amongst packets of untoasted Pop Tarts, beige wired bras and bloody knickers, he'd found a dried up used tampon nesting like a small red armadillo in a toppled shoe. It was a rescue fantasy which had come to fruition. Since those glory days Rachael had become a best-selling novelist, reviewer and indefatigable twitterer. How the fuck had that happened?

He was immortal in her memoirs, but so were a number of people whom he felt were less deserving. Rachael had never had any taste in men, or anything else for that matter, not in his opinion anyway. When they met he sometimes put his hand over her claw in affectionate memory. Her hands still looked picked at, and she'd never yet reciprocated his grasp, although she still babbled on like a teenager about her projects and what an idiot everybody else was, in her deeply-informed, contrary view.

"There's a lot of love there," one of their friends had said, referring to their relationship, but he had been a sentimental sort, especially about himself: a Cambridge-educated speed dealer and alcoholic who'd pissed his entire life up the wall and left only a few memories of his alleged charm. People were either 'proper people' – like Graham or Rachael – or 'taking the piss', like others who had proved less tolerant of his drunken, speed-fuelled foibles, and so, what did that blathering idiot who couldn't even stay alive really know? Nothing. Nothing.

He had still seen him sometimes, for quite a while, before the style turned back to beards, haircuts shifted definitively and there no longer men who looked exactly like him, nervously half-turning in profile, arrogant and scruffy, on his way to some dubious appointment in the roof garden of an Islington pub crammed with young pleasure-seekers, gaily swinging a carrier bag that was bursting with bags of skunk and wraps of speed.

St Paul's cathedral dome loomed whitely against a brilliant blue sky, the greensward at the foot of its portico verdant and dotted with gesticulating personages wearing dove grey perruques and other eighteenth century finery, amongst them several women peering at their male interlocutors through poised lorgnettes. The sky was dotted with fluffy clouds, and full of birds, which flew up in a joyful plume, disappearing towards the viewless horizon of ill-defined other buildings. A majority of the pillars were in place, much of the long shed-like gallery had been defined, but there were still a lot of pieces left on the carpet. Their absence from the completed jig-saw gave it a jagged look, as though the famous dome had indeed been struck by Nazi bombs and was simply hanging on, defying gravity somehow against the brownish ground of his once flowery carpet, like a giant broken eggshell.

He was hardly satisfied with the image, which he thought puerile and ill-conceived. No wonder the previous owner of the puzzle had thrown away the box. Perhaps the Frenchwomen who ran the Children with Cerebral Palsy charity shop had done so themselves in hope of making the item more saleable, although this was highly unlikely. He remembered guiltily that he had paid nothing for it, not even a song, but somehow even the thought of untreated children with cerebral palsy wasn't enough to make him finish the jig-saw completely, though it should have been quick work in these final stages. He just didn't care what the completed puzzle would look like. He already knew. He stirred the remaining pieces into a brown and particoloured soup.

Boredom returned, a most excruciating boredom, combined with frustration as he looked at the half-finished puzzle, thought of the effort of inserting the remaining pieces, the joylessness of placing the thousandth one in its allotted place, the utter lack of any satisfaction in doing so. On the other hand there was a hard to defeat impulse to find just one or two more, to fill in that scrap of sky, find the pediment of that pillar, the golden cap, the buckled foot of one bewigged gentleman in particular. There was only one way to banish those feelings. He took the puzzle apart, section by section, piece by piece, and replaced them in the polythene bag. It didn't take long compared to the months of intermittent effort that had gone into putting the puzzle together. A matter of a minute and a half. He really would have been better off making one of the model kits, but even this thought, which involved contemplating his own faulty decision-making, was too much to bear.

Once the floor was clear again and the pieces all safely returned to the bag, he took it through to the kitchen and stuffed it unceremoniously into a carrier bag that was already overflowing with empty jars and crumpled cornflakes packets. It was an easy enough thing to do.

A random consultation of the electronic chicken bones provided a coda to the wheelie bin murder. Seven years afterwards the house in Hamilton Avenue was up for sale again, this time for a price which had been inflated by £15,000, perhaps as a result of the ghoulish events which had taken place there – in other words the murder by chef Peter Wallner of his South African wife and his uninventive method of disposing of her body. Why not just take her up to Wisley Lake in the dead of night and give her a decent burial under a tree somewhere? But it was too late to change any of this now; instead there was the continual and recurring long slow fadeout of the road's notoriety. A flashback photo of the house in 2010 (it was the wrong date) with a policeman and a tent over the front drive, a recap of the whole sordid little story; another picture of the same teapot today, with a red transit van in the same spot, same tall, rather open privet hedge and a generous lick of greenery climbing across the front of the house below the three upper windows, which gave it an attractively suburban look: "a truly impressive three-bedroom home which has a wonderful contemporary feel."

Actually, it did look better than it had during Wallner's tenancy. The hedge was thicker, bushier now, and the climbing greenery more healthy-looking, more like he remembered it. For the first time he recognized the house's precise position, on the opposite side of the green from the flats: the green on which he used to fly his aeroplanes, dreaming of escape, uplift, envious of that generous fruited frontage and those windows from the perspective of a boy who shared one window with his brother, which looked out on washing lines and an identical iron-framed window directly opposite their own.

The aeroplanes were all gone from Maplin's; helicopters were still available in profusion, and four-rotor drones had gradually appeared, some with cameras fitted so you could spy on your neighbours, he supposed. If something had been invented for spying out the desert for Islamic terrorists, precision dropping of cluster bombs on their child-infested training camps, then soon everybody was going to want one to fly around the backyard during the family barbecue.

More interesting to him were the drone gliders with giant slender wingspans; these cruised the upper atmosphere, silently, economically, in perpetual motion orbits, digitally photographing all signs of life and transmitting the images back to CIA headquarters. It was one of these he most coveted; to him they best fulfilled his childhood conception of gliders: pilotless, above everything, only falling down in that they were useful. Gliders which had stealthily delivered troops to France in their swollen bellies were impressive too; low-flying and incredibly vulnerable aircraft whose light canvas and wood construction suggested the expendability of their passengers as much as anything. But those were the days of heroes, impossible to imagine the scale of sacrifice, the ready acceptance of it.

He watched an online video of men launching powered polystyrene gliders from a hillside somewhere or other, perhaps in the Czech Republic, more likely somewhere warmer: a scorched landscape above which the gliders wheeled and competed like airborne yachts on a pond. The men stood in a loose group with their thumbs on the controls of their controllers, thumb pianos on which they improvised their lines of heavenly music, feathery and oblique. The gliders wheeled like gulls, racing out over the scrubby, rock strewn hillside, soaring high in the thermals they found out there, swooping back towards the hillside, jockeying for supremacy, sheering off from one another in apparent indifference (there was, after all, plenty of sky to explore) then back onto the tailplane of a brother, twitching up there in mid-air, shimmying and breaking free to rise again in rough formation.

There were five men on the hillside. Scruffy, as usual, and it seemed barely present to themselves or each other, like husks operating virtual avatars; but actually the avatars were really husks, their operators were soft worms who had spun them, or rented them for an hour or two's solace. The men on the hillside seemed to have projected themselves up there into the gliders, that's what attracted him – they were looking out over the landscape from their sailplanes. Observing them more closely he wondered if this was actually so. Wouldn't their primary sense of it all remain in their thumbs, the planes distantly responding smudges, the other men standing nearby, closer than all this airborne activity, close enough to be physically nudged if they endangered your pride and joy radio-controlled glider?

In the valley there appeared to be a small town, or was the area of low white buildings actually an industrial estate: its mixture of low rectangular shapes and cross-hatched red roofs made it a bit difficult to identify or place. Italy, France, Spain, Germany, Switzerland, the Netherlands ... could be anywhere in Europe. A wind sock blew on the hill; a few scrubby trees stood by; a bored child stalled in free-flight; a Labrador with a toffee-cream-coloured coat browsed towards the camera, sniffing at it with a moment's curiosity.

THIRTY-FOUR

Graham used to visit the Somali internet café every day, getting to know a succession of reluctant managers: brothers and cousins from the same family who'd been in London since the early nineties, but with strikingly different personalities. Mohammed had been slender and sharp-faced, a narrow, angular head with an Arabic beard at his jawline, a porkpie hat and a traditional robe, bestowing the various copying and browsing services of the family business upon customers with a certain grace and a certain impatience of time wasters as he stood behind the raised counter at the entrance to the shop, so placed, he surmised, to prevent them running out without payment.

An indeterminate number of heavyset bearded men had hovered at free terminals, pornography police, idly scrolling the Koranic commentaries of wise clerics, hoping for trouble. Mohammed was always friendly to him, but the place had been crowded in those days. A lot of cubicles at the back. Somebody flipped out at one of them once, started ranting about race or something, a middle-aged white guy, he'd stood up and was hurling abuse at a young black man sitting next to him, and one of the bearded Somalis had detached himself and calmed him down gently, asked him to leave. The partitions between cubicles had offered a lot of privacy in those days, too much privacy, it had to be said. It was during the Iraqi and Afghanistan wars, which brought women in hijabs out in force. He would see one of them racing up the hill in an electric wheelchair emblazoned with Al Qaeda symbols, her garment flying. Once he had found himself next to her in the café where she was watching the speeches of Osama bin Laden, a small woman whose liquid eyes were usually half-closed in an angry squint. He couldn't resist speaking to her, and her voice was soft, northern English.

Mohammed moved on to a supervisory role in another business, a departure which ushered in another era, that of Osman. Osman was different. He dressed and talked local, in jeans and sweatshirts and idioms like 'back in the day, right' and 'boss' and 'bro', looked more African, bell-cheeked, round-faced. He was a little chubby, lived somewhere up under Ally Pally. Osman redesigned the interior of the internet café so now the desk was at the back and the customers sat at long unpartitioned benches in plain view. He was curious, chatty. Graham got along well with him. Heard all about his hippie English teacher, all about *khat* harvested fresh daily on the upper slopes of Mount Kenya, flash-frozen and flown in to meet the needs of cud-chewing twitchy Somalis in London; all about Assata Shakur and her daring jail-break and her long-time residence in Cuba; all about his love of Shakespeare's soliloquys and bursts of fierce invective (maybe the shadow of these was to be heard in Osman's guttural Somali tirades into his i-phone). His boredom, his plans to be a market gardener, or a trucker with his uncle in Minnesota. They talked politics. Watched YouTube videos of old anti-fascist demonstrations, far off grainy battles with the Metropolitan police in which Graham himself had participated. Watched his boredom grow into desperation. Until, finally, he left. Just jacked it in one day, refused to work; in the eyes of his family, he went mad.

Graham thought he had suffered a nervous breakdown. But at the same time there was something a little theatrical about it all, as there often is about madness. Madness is a performance, so the shrinks said, and so it often seemed. Osman had been very keen on his Shakespeare. It was the old Hamlet scam, he thought. Feigning madness to make something happen, to force the King's hand. His instinct however was that this wasn't going to be that kind of tragic feigning which turned out to be the real thing after all and dragged everybody down to hell, but Osman was still there, in control in the middle distance, and he would come though against the combined powers of his uncles, his aunts, and the terrifying mother who had once been in the army, and had borne arms as a guerilla fighter in the service of the Russians. Osman was fighting for his life against some heavy family demons.

Barry took over immediately. "My cousin is an arsehole," he said frankly. "He has dumped his family in the shit and we are very angry with him. But I appreciate your concern, my friend."

"He'll be okay. He's a strong guy, really."

"I hope you are right," Barry replied, but at the moment, he realized, Barry's own anger was uppermost. He really couldn't give two shits about what happened to his stupid cousin.

He didn't give up, but whenever he periodically asked about Osman, how was he recovering and so on, and when might he be coming back, Barry's response seemed to contain a wince of pain. "He won't be coming back," he said, "my family is very angry with him. He is supposed to be intelligent, but what use is he really? Compared to me – who has to clean up his mess."

Barry slowly warmed up; he was another friendly, talkative fellow, and day by day they slowly became half-familiars. He seemed to feel most comfortable with the bullshittiest regulars, in particular a thin, balding guy who ran his own booking agency from the café, supplying rock bands to a range of small venues in North London and the West End. He listened to their tapes, offered them advice, highly, and he thought, obtusely critical, and if good enough booked them into somewhere for a few quid. He was jealous of him, his fluency, the endless spooling and respooling of his political flow. Graham couldn't compete with him, but he seemed to make Barry animated, to wind him up. He wasn't sure if it was deliberate or not.

There were always plenty of cousins in the café, browsing the Puntland Times and keeping an eye on the flow of customers, which at the café's height, was continuous. The Puntland Times, a Mickey Mouse online newspaper for a Mickey Mouse country. Even the name told you it was cheap. Poundland. "That is my country," Barry said once when they were left alone at the tail-end of one of his sessions with the freelance band booker. "How do you think this feels? Knowing your country has been given away by the English to the Italians, like a piece of trash? Here, free gift. Take it please. I'll tell you, it makes you know you are not considered to be very important in this world. You are the inferior." He was glaring into his customer's eyes, as if he bore some responsibility for this, which he may well have done, partly by knowing nothing about it.

But mostly he was as relaxed and easy-going as his cousin, and like Osman he had his schemes. He wanted to build a website which would bring together every Somali restaurant in London, advertise them, make them pay for it, and be a great new initiative for the community. "It can happen, my friend. Somali is the new Indian. Vegetable is the new meat." He was to write brilliant copy for the whole thing in good English. He offered to do it for nothing, but it never seemed to get to that stage. Barry was always still gathering support, interviewing website designers. Another idea was to import fancy Arab menswear such as you seldom saw in London. He showed him some photographic spreads from magazines of handsome young Arabs posing against a desert backdrop beside expensive cars, wearing elegant James Bond style *kurti*, the shorter of the male dress-like garments with high collarless tops, finished with excellent details. Tasty threads. If you were an Arab. Barry thought they were so excellent, they might catch on with Westerners. Either way it would be better than standing around in the internet café all day long.

On the other hand was the seemingly endless flow of the days, strange customers who wandered in and out, and the incredible rudeness of many of them – and their amusing antics. He had been there when a real life troll, a spotty half-French boy, permanently stoned, jumped into the seat of a dapper young black man who had just stepped outside to talk importantly on his mobile, and rapidly sent spam to everybody on his immediate contact list, including an Italian girlfriend with whom he had been carrying on a conversation. UR SO UGLY, the boy had speedily typed, BUT THAT OK COS I JUXT WANT TO FUCK YOU. Upon arriving back the rightful occupant had shooed him out of his seat, and seconds later various WTF messages started pouring in, not least from the Italian girlfriend.

The black guy furiously typed apologies. His girlfriend wasn't sure whether to believe him; she seemed bemused but not particularly upset. He rounded on the boy, who was still typing at the next computer, flatly denied he was responsible. "I should take you outside and beat the shit out of you," the man said quietly, menacingly. "But … no, no, I'm not going to do that. I'm bigger than that. I've had to learn control, to discipline my emotions – I'm not going to let you destroy that achievement." He sounded like the most rational person on Earth, a real Vulcan, but also just slightly mad.

The troll-boy continued calmly to deny his involvement in any wrong-doing, despite the fact that both himself and Barry had witnessed his daring escapade. Barry banned him from the shop, told him never to come back, but after he had left and the black guy had stomped off into the night, Barry couldn't stop laughing. A few days later the boy had been reinstated as a customer, with honour. Graham wasn't too happy about this.

"Just make sure you close your account properly," Barry said. "Look. He is a customer. What he did was funny. That black guy is never going to come back. What he did was funny." He turned away, ending the conversation.

But month after month Barry's appearance began to deteriorate, just as Osman's had before him. His long, crisply elegant white traditional garments had given way to shapeless jeans, ragged at the bottom, a filthy sweater. Always with the small round pork-pie hat jammed on his head: a grubby, embroidered kufi. He had run into him as he was wandering across the edge of Tottenham Hale Retail Park. Barry told him to hop into the decrepit Astra with a floting passenger seat he was piloting back to Hornsey. They drove back through T-town, where Barry resided, near Bruce Grove station, down West End Green, and out onto Turnpike Lane. The trip was marred only by Barry's continual scheme-spinning.

By the time they arrived he had elaborated a whole Somali Saturday school for kids, in a cheap to rent community centre he knew of, with his favourite customer installed as the sole teacher on a reasonable hourly rate. Like Osman he was a creature of North London, and it was difficult to imagine that one day Barry with his Arab profile, crooked teeth and pendulous lower lip would be dying his beard red like the older generation, even though, like Osman, he did retain a certain hauteur about him, a sense he had somehow been born for better things. Didn't all of us, though.

And then, one day, Osman reappeared behind the counter. This time it was he who wore an elegant white *thobe* and had a *kufi* perched on his head. But he was painfully thin, remote and seemingly unable to speak except for a few halting words. He had been in Egypt for the Arab spring, studying the Koran. There'd been a flicker of recognition for him, but Osman was saying nothing.

He felt a little hurt as he remembered their ironic high-fives on Tottenham Lane as they'd parted company on the corner of and Osman had continued on down the hill to the Mosque for Friday lunchtime prayers. There had been an easiness between them, an ease and confidence such as he felt not to be there between himself and Barry, although he realized now it was just the superficial camaraderie of shopkeeper and customer. He remained convinced he had been feigning madness, inspired by the Prince of Denmark, but next day Barry said; "He is changed. He is a completely different person. It's ... weird, my friend."

"He seemed to recognize me," Graham said hopefully.

"Yes, I noticed. I think he wanted to talk to you."

Osman had looked quite haunted. His face had been pinched into another, harsher shape as though it were clay, and had become that of another, remote person; but on another day the errant cousin appeared again and he approached the counter, determined to prise something or other from him, some acknowledgement. All that remained was an ironic twitch at his lips; then he looked briefly at him, his eyes alight. Haunted? Mad? Eventually he brought himself to utter a few words.

"Remember I told you how I was looking for adventure?" Osman seemed to wink, as in a novel, or play. He leaned forward. "Well, I found it."

"Really?"

"Yeah man!"

Barry's restaurant scheme spluttered into life again then seemed to peter out, likewise his idea of importing traditional Arab menswear. Barry didn't even know the names of any of the garments he wore. Osman never reappeared again and the place was deteriorating fast, almost as though somebody had pulled a switch and no-one round here needed an internet café anymore. Barry would be glad to see the back of it. The kids all owned laptops, the drifting in of passing trade had dwindled to nothing and only a couple of nutters were left, including Graham, who suddenly decided he wanted to buy a second-hand computer from them.

"Is this a good computer; it looks alright?"

"I wouldn't wish it on my worst enemy." Barry brushed him off, in a friendly way; and now it was only a matter of days before they were gone the Somalis flitted in the traditional way, dumped the unpaid rent, and the heavy green shutters rolled down, a small possession notice taped to them. At first he missed them intensely. He stopped and looked at the shutters, peered through the punched slats at the dormant computers within, until a woman at the bus stop looked at him and said: "They aren't coming back." At home he lay on his bed under the white shadow of the glider, remembering things they had said, making them up. "We are thieves," Barry confided, "our women are so stupid. Whatever you do, whatever you do, my friend, do not get involved with one of them. They are not like you."

And so he accepted their departure from his quadrant with this stinging admonishment. He'd never been particularly interested in Somali women, although they were quite as beautiful as any other women, to him. He enjoyed the way they bustled into the internet café, their sense of precedence, their long harsh conversations with relatives in the café's wooden phone booth, and the way they always looked bundled up, folded in, like babushkas, like table napkins, their round pouting faces peeking from under the gables of their semi-conical telescopic hoods. But there you are. Barry had spoken. On the top deck of a bus passing through Cricklewood late one evening he had been disturbed by some noisy kids behind him and turned, stupidly, thinking he would soon shut them up with a serious look. "We are lions," the eldest girl said. "Don't mess around with us!" she laughed. "Somalians are lions."

Walking down Turnpike Lane on Sunday afternoon, a couple of years later, he'd decided to check his e-mails, popped into the first internet café and found a younger cousin, identical to Osman, running it from the identical glass counter. He was under twenty, fresh-faced in his white *dishdasha* and his round *kufi*, his assistant an even younger boy, who seemed to take more after Barry, while others lunged around in the back room, doing important maintenance work, and earnest young Sunday internet browsers parted like the Red Sea to reveal an empty terminal with the same screensaver he remembered from the old shop, recycled.

The front door was opened by a white woman in a hijab, a plump, intensively friendly young woman with a northern accent and an Algerian husband. Their basement flat was immaculate, with new carpets, imposing sideboard and shiny knick-knacks disposed everywhere: a traditional front parlour. She was obviously house proud, but as her thin, anxious French-speaking husband came in it became evident they were in the midst of a crisis. His forehead was crawling with nervousness and he had an air of supplication, as though he was some sort of representative of authority, perhaps his last chance. He needed English lessons, urgently, so that he could take care of paperwork, and driving lessons so that he could get a job. Their situation was not good, and, as so often when this is the case, everything seemed to conspire against them. The large window of their flat made their possessions visible from the street, and some people had tried to break in. Soon the details of their story came tumbling out of them, and while he tried to calm him down, reassure him with a basic English assessment test, he heard in fits and starts about how their baby had been taken away and how they had failed a test of competence to take care of their infant, which would be in care until five years of age: they had failed under supervision, been judged unfit parents, and they were desperate to get their little boy back home.

They lived very near another of his clients, and he was still feeling somehow pleased about this when he realized he was dealing with a situation of total need, a need to elaborate their story and be believed by somebody, but as always evident need triggered an immediate slight doubt, a scepticism of their truthfulness. Had somebody broken in through the window? Did this happen? The stronger the assertion the greater the suspicion of outright fantasy. Somehow he had the impression the woman was at odds with her family, it was her sense of determination and her belief that love will conquer all. She was remarkably cheerful and optimistic compared to her husband, especially for a woman whose baby has been taken away due to an illness.

There she stood, loving her absent child, her swollen breasts heaving against her loose hijab, which concealed nothing, heavy with the milk Allah had given her to feed her baby. She had to squeeze it out and throw it away. Her smile, her face behind her veil, her pleasure in its incongruity, her assertive rebelliousness and her force of personality – all these were winning things: an ordinary plump little woman, a thin anxious man out of his depth. Gloria and Hamid.

Naturally, they thought they were being persecuted. He didn't know what to say except to keep fighting. He took the heat out of their exchange by asking the wiry little Algerian where the nearest mosque was to be found. Hamid told him of a couple of nearby ones, pointing in opposite directions to where their reassuring brassy domes shone, beacon-like, mapping new quadrants of London's landscape, lighting up those drab corners in a different way, points of connection, geographical markers. Something to cling to in a strange land.

They needed somebody to talk to and he gave them his attention, listened to their whole story sympathetically. Hamid needed to enroll in a local college, an official one where they would teach him for next-to-nothing, and if he did Haringey would recognize he was steadily taking command of his own life. After all, he was a husband and a father and he had nothing to go back to in Paris.

THIRTY-FIVE

Over on the edge of known things, in Mortlake, Ricky had acquired a brand new helicopter, a quality job, and was slowly teaching himself to fly it around his flat. It was funny how, when you watched people flying these things, it seemed they were flying themselves. But when you actually had the three channel controller in your hand it was obviously a skill which took patience to learn: confidence, muscle control, fine motor skills, and the will-power to keep the helicopter in the air and move it around without hitting the walls or the ceiling. It was as though you were up there in the black cockpit, and would die if something went wrong. Your instinct was to back off and let it drop back onto the carpet, exhausted for a moment, as if you were holding it up with a thought-beam, or raising yourself off the ground. You had to develop continuity of concentration, ease of action. It was a little bit like learning to swim or ride a bicycle or skate. You had to do a width before attempting a length. There was fear to overcome, inertia and mental laziness; but the final reward was to be up there skimming along the tops of the trees.

Basically, Ricky thought, it was a new division of consciousness. It reminded him of his heroic failure to learn the saxophone, his success on his programming course, and the first static 3D image of an egg (it seemed pathetic now) he had produced on a computer screen. For now he gave up and definitively put the whole kit and caboodle back into the bedroom wardrobe. In the kitchen he lit a gas ring, filled a small saucepan with water and dropped the contents of a packet of noodles into it. He was eating them, drenched in Soy sauce, from a plain blue china bowl, when the phone started to ring.

Who could it be? Lana? That irritating wanker Graham, his so-called fucking twin? His idle, useless sister? He lifted the receiver and listened carefully to a rapidly-speaking voice as it began to dictate its harsh set of instructions.

Hamilton Avenue was in *Get Surrey* again – this time for a mass street brawl in the early hours of a Sunday morning two years earlier, up to twenty men with baseball bats and other weapons laying into one another in the road following an altercation which had broken out earlier in Cobham village hall. One of them had taken off in a silver van and been stopped by the police in Anyards Road, and while he was talking to them had collapsed and died with a heart attack. He was in his early fifties, cut about the face from fighting, in mid-explanation. Paramedics were unable to revive him. Graham clicked through a few articles from succeeding days. More arrests had been made, six or seven men of different ages, but mostly it had been an early twenties ruck. There was no clue as to what the fight had been about. The man who died was greatly mourned by family and friends, a self-employed builder who would do anything for anybody. Now he was up in the sky with the aeroplanes and a million words could never express how much he was loved and missed. A truly decent man. A one-off.

Graham was unable to find out any more about whatever senseless sense had been in this fight, and how come so many were drawn into it. What had to be settled in this way? He searched and searched and searched. A man had been arrested on suspicion of manslaughter, stock photos of the backs of helmetted policemen adorned the articles, their arms folded in mighty resolution, but there was none, no resolution, just the family mourning. Maybe the death itself was the resolution. He searched and searched and searched again – but there was nothing else online.

Afterwards he walked again around the estate on Google street view. It was all still there, some scaffolding erected over the front of the flats, the long green, which although it was now parcelled into a couple of playground areas, and the wooden telegraph poles had been taken down, no longer necessary, was still long enough for a decent launch. Rotate and point-and-click tools had made it easy to jump along the roads on spring heels, peer around corners, as long as there was a marked way through, some way around the back of the property; and he found it all much the same, some parts scruffier, others freshly painted, well-maintained, the streets quiet and empty. A place to bury your life, your wife. He tried to get as near the river as possible, and did, but it was impossible get through the trees and down to the long sloping meadow.

There was nothing else for it. He was forced to spring heel his way down to the edge of the estate, Spring-heeled Jack, rotating uncannily and jumping to the middle of the bridge, looking downriver with hollow, hungry eyes. The river itself was muddy and wider than he remembered, and he saw there was a split where it forked around a sizeable island in the stream before rejoining and flowing on its way around the village. Everything and nothing, like the reasons for the fight and the death of the likeable man who'd been arrested in mid-flow, looking for his son – who'd been perfectly okay, as it happened. There was a photograph of the dad astride a motorbike. All he could do was log off from his new laptop and forget about this place which had been, and obviously still was, an island, almost a law unto itself, a quiet place where events could take on an uncontrollably violent momentum.

On the day he'd thought of his incandescent egg theory, he had been lying out on the school field, one hot July afternoon, propped up on an elbow, squinting across at a small group of fourteen-year-old girls, his classmates. In their cotton ankle socks, their cornflower blue summer mini-dresses concealed not much; and he rolled away from them, onto his back, his school tie loose, and let the sun beat onto his eyelids until bright dots of light turned into deep black holes. He turned over, pressed the heels of his hands over his eyelids to shut out the too available light. The trick, as always, was to keep your eyes closed until you saw something. But what was real to him were these large eggs. The eggs were their souls. The eggs were each one forty-foot-high, gleaming, trembling above the field like tethered white balloons, no strings, these eggs were thinking them, they were thinking things – and the kids weren't real after all. If the eggs are real, he thought, I am one, I'm floating now, I'm looking down on myself; and then he was, and all across the school playing field clusters of the giant eggs were hovering where kids lolled in small groups, talking at the tops of their lungs, and at the far edge of the field, above the high broom hedges of the bridle path, two giant white eggs bobbed: a horse and rider.

The babbling broke up, broke down. The eggs animated everybody. Okay, but why? That was a good question. Their purposes could not easily be separated from his own. Even the school buildings, a flotilla of incandescent eggs, floated above themselves in the pale of the sky, and away from here the small, familiar town hovered in its mysterious air of self-possession, giant eggs moving its dead things around, and beyond this place was the countryside, the world, its far oceans and peoples, all shadows cast by the eggs, everything being the idea of itself: the universe one great big pliable shell they nestled in, yolks in the white of a giant egg. Or something. His feeble brain stretched wide open to take all of it in, a tremulous membrane, an egg-womb, an idea big enough to contain everything. He kept his eyes tight shut. The girls were calling out to him. Sure enough, they'd noticed his shut tight eyes. They knew, of course. But how could they not know? Unless … his eyes had sprung wide open. The sunlight flooded him in a vision of the unity of all things, The Great Egg of the Universe, and all the children, glooping out of eggy magma into trembling bubbles of substance, proliferating, melding, dying -pop- re-forming, and the world restabilised, for a short time, the incandescent eggs still visible above him, and the girls, and the children spread over the green carpet – and his four friends walking slowly towards him from the path by the playground fence, a laughing group of boys in their navy-blue blazers, each with a forty-foot-high egg of pearly light dangling above his head in the baking summer air.

They'd arrived together, sat around him like disciples, and he'd told them of The Incandescent Egg Theory. He expected them to laugh, but unaccountably they seemed to believe in him. Then they left – and one of the girls, Christine, a gentle six-footer who lived in the flats opposite, youngest and sweetest of a family of giants, asked what he'd been thinking. He'd told her and she smiled and said thanks, thank you. Now I get it, now I understand reality. And the other girls looked at each other, pointedly ignoring him for an irritating fool, and then they all began to chatter about bent hair clips and the theory of general relativity as the big July sun beat down on them, on their clear, shining skins, long ago, before everybody's life had turned out so unexpectedly.

There were places he wouldn't – or couldn't – go back to but which revisited him quite often to taunt him with stories of events which had occurred there, things which didn't matter much but which did matter to him. Humiliations or examples of stupid, bestial behaviour: a plethora of gone moments when you realized people weren't all they were cracked up to be, that given a choice they would always, always go for the cheapest, most unjust option. Blame the electorate by all means: they were the people who freed Barabbas and nailed up Jesus, quite easily subverted by a few murmuring agents. They didn't take much persuasion. Beyond them were the disappointed ones. Not good company. Graham knew. He was one of them himself. Get them all together and they would just be picking off one another's scabs.

A McGuffin, a panting ideal, something to protect; an enemy, a floating exemplar of all the evil in the world. Preferably a real one: a single out-and-out bastard would do, or somebody you were jealous of, more satisfying in a way than a giant unstoppable mega-corporation which could buy off anybody. Buy me! How about a noisy neighbour? A persistent litterer? A non-replier to polite correspondence? A telephone canvasser? A debt collector? Not necessarily an active force; a blocker would do nicely. Somebody to hate and blame. Your parents. Your ex. A person who was simply fed up with you or just doing their job, their sworn duty to themselves and others. The Devil. These were things you needed. They had been noticed. Noted nothings. Codified and sent out once more. He was their preacher-man, safely constrained by his role as spell checker and unfree stater of the obvious. The great dictator. His grey smiling helpful self. The person he really was, standing still, walking, passing his Oyster card across the reader in the pearly days that continually succeeded one another as the sun rose and fell like a final hammer on each day of his life.

THIRTY-SIX

In her not so distant youth, Bobbie Cainer had enjoyed an affair with a Cornishman, leaving her daughter with a potentially embarrassing name and ADHD (Attention Deficit Hyperactivity Disorder), which led to a further diagnosis of dysgraphia, high spectrum autism, and in her case combined with a fierce desire to overcome all obstacles: an array of portents which seemed to suggest potential to her mother. Her father had wanted to call her Kernow, but Bobbie had quietly settled on Donna.

Cornwall was a fabulous and remote place to Donna. She'd never been there, nor did she remember her father. She'd looked at pictures, which could be interesting in a way, but Bobbie had never really wanted to take her on holiday there. Too many painful memories. Instead they went to Barcelona, places like that. Donna remembered nothing of her babyhood. He enjoyed the baby photos of her as a cute toddler adorning the shelves on the wall unit, her large, wobbly head, her hair done up in Mickey Mouse ears, her goggling, googly eyes. They all looked so sweet at that age.

They worked together in front of the big silver Mac at whatever was to be done at school. Donna would practice her reading, he would read to her from *Great Expectations*, *Macbeth* and *Of Mice and Men*, and they'd do her homework together, her controlled assessments, and unseen poetry. Donna was a hard worker, or so it seemed at first; she really threw herself into it all, but above all she was amazingly articulate, a good talker, super-opinionated, and would chatter away a whole hour if you let her.

Bobbie had warned him about this, and so he tried to make sure they always completed something in a session, usually while Bobbie did her own voluminous homework on a laptop. She worked for a city firm where much was expected of her: complex casework outside office hours, international conference calls to America, and stress management. She could afford him.

"Donna takes things very literally," Bobbie said. "If I looked out of the window and said it's raining cats and dogs, she would run out there looking for them."

"I just don't get metaphor," the girl agreed, immediately giving the game away: she did.

It seemed to him a cliché – people produced symptoms to order from a given diagnosis – and he responded by dismissing her autism diagnosis as crap. "Well – stop taking things literally then," he said. "Or you'll never get anywhere with language."

Donna went on to elaborate on her hatred of *Dr Who*, mainly for the way the programme incessantly presented impossible, ridiculous things. "Time travel?" she asked rhetorically. "I'm sorry – that just doesn't exist."

Bobbie had long since come to the conclusion white men were largely creatures of instinct, governed by their uncontrollable sex drive and a certain pushiness resulting from their interiority complex. *Fifty Shades of Grey* – all much the same. She was fingering her hair dry in front of the bathroom mirror as he walked past her to the front door. As Donna let him out, she called: "A problem shared is a problem halved with you around, isn't it Graham?"

He'd paused to admire her as she teased her short hair into glossy spikes. "You're welcome," he said, "anytime."

It could be a good sign when they started to fight you (like Donna) but there were limits to it, and this attitude Bobbie had thought it would be good for her daughter to have, her own attitude, which had stood her in such good stead, turned out to involve her paying to listen to the raised voice as the tutor she'd hired verbally fenced with her endlessly feisty daughter. Donna knew how to put her best foot forward, did well in any argument, but her written work didn't seem to be improving significantly.

Donna progressed well in English, obtaining a 'B' in all subjects, by dint of her undinting hard work, so she thought, not his fortnightly visits, but he enjoyed his sessions with her anyway. He liked being on relaxed and friendly terms with both of them.

"My dad was white," she said. "I just came out black, that's all." She shrugged endearingly.

"That was a result then," he said.

Donna told him all about planking, which was amongst the most stupid things she had ever heard of, although some people, herself included, found it quite amusing. What it was, you had to lie on a wall, or on the pavement, maybe on an up or down escalator on the underground, and still keep very still as people were passing by, like a plank of wood, totally immobile and impassive, reclining statues, and try to completely creep them out. So stupid! The idea appealed to him, seeing all sorts of political ramifications in it. Youths were present and absent, making themselves visibly invisible, drawing attention to themselves. Donna saw what he meant, though she hadn't seen it that way. She also believed sixteen year olds should get the vote. After all, they could fight for their country, and more importantly, they could give birth to children themselves. Bobbie was right behind this as she herself had had Donna at a similar age.

"Sounds creepy," he said. "Looks good though. Sort of threatening and passive at the same time."

"I suppose so," she said. "But it's nothing isn't it, what does it achieve? Besides you could get badly hurt, lying on the handrails of an escalator and trying to keep perfectly still as you fell off the other end." Still, the thought of it was funny to her, and she couldn't stop laughing, sitting there in her fluffy towelling bathrobe, showing him the white soles of her feet as she inspected her pink painted toes. "If youths could vote it would be more important."

"I don't see why getting yourself pregnant should qualify you to choose the government," he said to provoke her. "A clip round the ear would be more appropriate in my opinion."

Donna couldn't believe what she was hearing. "I'm sorry," she said, "that's making me feel really angry."

"Oh yeah?"

"I'm boiling up with intense rage – this is the worse feeling I ever had in my whole life."

"It's only what most people would say," he said. "It's just a biological thing. Just because you could have a child, doesn't mean you are responsible enough to look after it. What about twelve year olds, some of them could get pregnant. Should they get the vote as well? Planking takes more imagination than getting pregnant. Whoever thought of that should be given a seat in parliament. They could sit perfectly still – at least they wouldn't be doing any harm."

Bobbie came through from the kitchen and joined in. She had been behind the votes at sixteen debate, in which Donna had excelled in the school public speaking competition. As for countries who'd adopted the policy, they seemed mainly to be places like Ecuador, which had a very young population due to poverty, an electorate who would die off soon enough, or countries like Germany where there was a perceived danger of a disaffected, disenfranchised youth turning to the far right. It was a way of drawing young people into social democracy.

He supposed it was no bad thing, but wouldn't make much difference politically since most young people would follow the voting behaviour of their parents. So much for the youth revolution. Goodbye Elvis. Again.

Back home he watched a few planking videos on YouTube: heroically motionless skateboarders, escalator riders, hedge imitators, pavement obstructors. It was a great thing, he thought, although the full effect probably couldn't be captured on a mobile phone. He hoped he would one day encounter some real plankers. It would be great if it really caught on, and they were littering the streets: refuseniks, heroes of labour. But somehow great things like that never seemed to happen, and the best you would ever get was a film or a novel or a poem about it, another illustration of the failure of revolutionary art to create revolutions. Donna would think he was missing the point – there wasn't one – and this time she was right. Gradually he had come to accept that Donna was always right, but she wouldn't agree even to this flattering proposition.

"I'm never right!" she laughed. "I'll never be right in my life!"

Bobbie's face had taken on a bemused look.

The crunch came at A Level, with various things she just couldn't get, the poetry of W.B. Yeats being one of them. "You know what?" she said. "I just don't care about Irish nationalism."

He tried to explain why she should try to care, but apart from the fact that she had to pretend to in order to pass her exam, she was adamantly blank. They went through the poems, on which she already had notes and background information, while her tutor failed to supply the missing spark of high enthusiasm. But they didn't capture her imagination, nothing did really.

He explained the story behind 'Leda and the Swan', the rape of Leda by Zeus leading to the birth of Helen of Troy and various other amazing half-and-half beings, from two eggs she laid, and so to the expression *ab ovo* – a story told from the egg, from the beginning. How well Yeats had captured the violence and terror of rape, and how terrifying transactions between gods and humans often were in the ancient world. But this only led to new objections from Donna.

"How could somebody think of anything so disgusting?" she wanted to know. "That's what I don't like about literature, especially W.B. Yeats. You're reading something, it seems quite interesting, but then you find there's some really disgusting, horrible idea behind it, which, okay, maybe people believed in the past, but I just can't see why we need to know about it now. Like rape is good, for example."

"But just try to imagine it, Donna," he said. "Let's act it out. You be Leda and I'll be the swan." He stood up and flapped his gigantic white wings, made some terrifying *skraak-skraak* noises, pretending to grab hold of her in his great orange beak. She cowered half-heartedly in her chair, half-heartedly laughing until he desisted and carefully put her down.

Just then Bobbie walked into the room. "How does that sound to you, Bobbie?" he asked her. "Fancy being raped by a giant white swan?"

Donna's mum pretended to consider the matter with one finger against the side of her mouth. "Could be quite interesting," she said. "I mean, if you're gonna be raped by a swan, and there's nothing you can do about it, I suppose you might as well try to enjoy the experience."

"Mum!" Donna objected, and he resumed his seat. At the end of the session he left behind some of his old Yeats books, a Richard Ellman and a Joseph Hone, but he somehow knew he was never to see them again: neither the books, nor the people.

He was in danger of becoming an expert on teenage girls – ridiculous since he'd never even had any sisters – gleaning a peculiar deluded sense about them only available to men who had had a deadening frequency of contact with the Junior Miss segment of the educational market. Girl-spit: he knew its mysteries, its truths, hidden and obvious, its half-baked potted histories of consciousness, although not as well as the average person by any means. He continued to make unsatisfactory guesses about creatures moving around inscrutably half-hidden in their interior spaces, which he really didn't mind.

Outside he walked down to the bus stop, along a bleak empty corridor, to one side the high fronts of faceless buildings with dark metal staircases leading to the upstairs flats, closed up shops opposite, for some reason a slightly threatening passage, the unfriendliest place on his route, and decided to brave the wind which funnelled between them and walk home. At the foot of the leeside of Crouch End Hill he ducked into the little park where a few men were drinking cans of Special Brew on one of the benches.

London was full of dead spots, and if you ducked into them you found they weren't dead at all, or at least there were a few people waiting to die there, huddled together. If you didn't like it, you could fuck off back to Noddyland, but nobody really cared much, not at all. He thought back to Bobbie and Donna, snugly tucked into their small, expensive flat, with their Polish lodger, a gleaming Mac and a pointless circular fluorescent electric fish tank, which Bobbie was trying to work out how to wire up to the mains and hang on the wall, like a clock which would never tell the time. It was all so far from the happy-clappy religion of her parents, a fair old trod of trials and tribulation from Reading.

He knew something already had happened to Bobbie, the death of her partner from an asthma attack when they were on holiday in Morocco, so what did he know, she'd been poleaxed by that, although she had carried on as normal, and why was it he insisted on walking through the woods, past the people on the benches, and why was he so often tempted to join them? Just another idiot, really. Trying to make something out of nothing and in the process often nixing something real.

"Why do I do this?" he'd asked once in mock-exasperation.

"For the money," Bobbie replied. "What else?"

A young woman in a stained fawn duffel coat, about ten years older than Donna, approached him abruptly through the stand of scrubby, spindly trees which provided what cover there was, and asked him for some money. Graham fished in his pocket, gave her a couple of quid, and perhaps responding to his hesitation, she asked him if he wanted something else "for a tenner". He declined and scuttled on, past their final days, happy or sad, and out onto the road again, continued up the long wooden hill to Bedfordshire.

THIRTY-SEVEN

He hardly ever thought of the acquaintance who had put him on to the agency, but since he quite enjoyed the work, he did occasionally give thanks to his shade: a troubled man he had liked, at a pinch. He had even been at his wedding, or one of them. To Rachael. But it wasn't supposed to be like that, was it? The chalice passed by a suicide should contain a heavy, spicy wine, with an underlying bitter taste, somehow leading its unwary inheritor down paths of ritual blood drinking, or some stuff so awful you didn't even want to reckon what it meant. The thing is, you knew it was all out there. A stone's throw from one of his clients a fourteen-year-old had shot somebody's sister, knocked on the door of their council flat and blown her away, an honour slaying for which the eager boy was paid twenty-five quid. Teachers ran off with schoolgirls, mothers tortured their babies, etc.

People really did these things, but mercifully his students seemed only to have to cope with *Macbeth*. The closest he himself had recently come to hell was Brimsdown – a tall, languid girl in a tracksuit collapsed dramatically across the kitchen table; he thought she'd fainted or fallen asleep, then noticed her hand was moving slowly across the sheet of paper to which her head was parallel. She was writing, laboriously, but elegantly, in some giant, loopy, but illegible script, which spiked in heartbeats as the dots over her large liquid i's exploded like the suns etched onto her fingernails, which were sinking into far off seas, into lakes of fire.

He sat alone on the shore and watched her; then, unable to bear her beauty any longer, he watched every appliance in their newly-fitted kitchen, until she was done and in silent contempt pushed the filled up sheet of paper across to him.

St John's Wood. Nearly an hour early for his appointment and there wasn't a café in sight. Not a district he'd visited often. As darkness fell he walked down the hill towards Abbey Road, featuring a round-the-clock reenactment of the most famous road crossing in world history, four people frozen in exaggerated walking poses, one of them grimacing and holding up her hands like a member of the black and white minstrels, while another took aim from the roundabout with a large telephoto lens.

He'd come prepared to teach a session on Allen Ginsberg's *Howl*, which he'd printed out and anyway knew like the back of his hand from years ago. The student attended a super-pricey private school on the way to Cambridge, the sort of the place where they flopped around on bean bags and negotiated their learning outcomes on a varied vegetarian diet. Her parents were both psychoanalysts, and it was with her slim, elegant father he'd negotiated the class. He was worried about her ability to focus and draw together her coursework in the limited amount of time before her deadlines.

His daughter was curled up on the couch. A feline seventeen-year-old, she smiled and extended a warm limp hand. "Hi," she said. "Everybody seems to call me Tatty."

They were friendly, pleasant people, Peshi and Tatiana, and it wasn't long before he and the girl were immersed in the possible psychoanalytic contexts of Ginsberg's poem. Tallulah took notes on her laptop; Peshi searched the cupboard in vain for a tea bag, Graham blathered on and on about Wilhelm Reich, Naomi Ginsberg's madness, and the type of treatment Ginsberg had been under for his homosexuality. Ginsberg's shrink had told him to accept his sexuality and his visions, which had been a help. He talked a bit about the difference between radical and conservative Freudians at the time, and partly making a stab at getting Peshi involved, mentioned R.D. Laing. Peshi, it transpired, was quite a fan, and taught at the Tavistock Institute. Soon an old copy of *The Politics of Experience* had been located and Peshi was dictating a few germane quotations from it, about listening to the voices of the mad. Then there was the question of whether the so-called 'holy madness' propounded by Ginsberg was really madness at all, or just the posturing of a few rich kids with therapists.

He found himself talking about Ginsberg's propensity for taking his clothes off in public; maybe he had started that sixties fashion for pretending to be Mr and Mrs. Blake reenacting the Garden of Eden in their own back garden in Lambeth. Perhaps it was Abbey Road which had prompted this thought. John and Yoko on the cover of *Two Virgins*. Peshi thought it was all about infantile regression. Toddlers often pulled their pants down as an attention getter, and he had noticed something like this in the behaviour of very drunk young people in the street. Girls often lifted up their tops inappropriately. Graham chipped in with the fashion for young boys to wear their trousers halfway down their backsides. Tatiana appeared to be familiar if a little bit impatient with these digressions.

At the end of the two hour session he mentioned that most poets didn't achieve the level of media celebrity Ginsberg had enjoyed, and often found him overrated.

"Ah, Poet-envy," Peshi chuckled.

As he prepared to leave, Peshi mentioned Tatiana might need help with another of her coursework essays.

"It's on *Lolita*," Tatiana's wide mouth lifted at one corner. "I like a bit of controversy," she said. "I just need a bit of help with my perspective on it. Like, it's great, but what to say?"

"You do realize it's supposed to be a highly moral tale?" he hazarded vaguely. "Or so they say."

Tatty told him she wanted to compare it with *Memories of My Melancholy Whores* by Gabriel Garcia Marquez. "It's about this ninety-year-old bloke who decides to give himself a twelve year old girl as one last birthday treat," she explained. "Y'know, so it'll be nice and tight." She held out a small, brown fist, which she clenched tightly as though attempting to contain the giant manhood of Garcia Marquez within it, her eyes crossing, her lips distorted in mock-effort.

"Sounds like a book I have to read," he said. "I expect they'll have it in my local library – if it hasn't been stolen."

"I mean, honestly. My school is full of real dimbos. I mean, when our teacher, Kath, asked us to choose our books for our personal study, several people asked if they could do Harry Potter. How thick is that?"

Peshi had walked in in time to hear the last bit and made some silent shushing noises.

He remembered furnishing his current domicile from the surrounding streets, dragging back carpets, a mattress, some chairs, a high stool, a couple of mirrors, bookcases, a computer stand, a standing lamp, a two-ring hotplate, a microwave, a portable TV from the eighties, and two pale framed prints from an old Chinese restaurant: a pagoda, blossoms, the ridged, shushing sea – and multiple cranes in flight towards or away from the sun, one of them turning back in anguish. There were also some empty frames, a haphazard dinner service containing some nice pieces, items of cutlery, and an upright enclosed tower fan which swivelled and blew out a wedge of lukewarm air; it had worked for quite a while until it burned out last summer.

In the dead months of the summer he missed them, and thought about them a little bit. In July and August his top floor flat could grow at times unbearable even with the windows wide open. Whatever attachments he'd formed in his life, distant or recent, hung around uselessly in the air. Everything seemed as dead as a doornail. He had nothing much else to think about, no companion, and couldn't afford to go on holiday. What did this sense of attachment amount to? He wondered. Did he truly harbour any unhealthy desire to take possession of somebody else's sacred teapot?

He mainly saw the most agreeable aspect of other people's home life: the bustle, the routines, the hour or so after mealtimes, when people were together, in concert, rubbing shoulders in their shared domestic spaces, and, since he was there, behaving well. It was the idyll of togetherness. Bobbie and Donna, he thought with half-serious envy, would be off somewhere. Barcelona maybe. Portugal. Would they like it there? But this time he knew he wouldn't be seeing them again.

Bobbie had called to say Donna had only got a D for her AS level coursework, and how she had come home crying. He had been practically in tears himself, choking with disappointment, and guilt, as he thought of her tears. It was so unfair! She'd deserved to get a B for the essays they'd worked on together. She'd worked hard for it. The teacher was obviously a grade A* shit, that was for sure, a stuck up officious little woman. But, he thought, a perfectly justified invigilator of a concept of justice. The first thing you had to learn as a teacher, he had once been told by a more successful one than himself, was how to disappoint people.

But there you go. He wasn't Donna's father. He couldn't be there to comfort her, nor did he have the power to countermand this heinous decision. She would be giving up English, he knew, and yet to listen to her on the subject of time-consciousness in *Mrs. Dalloway* had been to sit back in genuine pride and pleasure at the way she had put it all together. Bobbie had said something to twist the knife, to suggest it was all his fault: she had trusted him and he had hurt her daughter. So that was that, realistically that was how it was nearly always going to turn out. What would be the point of thinking about it too hard?

Different kinds of attachment, different kinds of loss. He thought vaguely of John Bowlby's ideas about attachment in infancy and wondered if he was inappropriately over-emotional and clingy due to some inadequacy in his early upbringing. It could've been worse – he might have been programmed as the affectless psychotic type. In other words, a normal man. What a load of bollocks it all was, he thought, or probably nothing important to worry about now, anyway.

For years now he had been trotting around these streets like a too-late rabbit without a watch, so long that he sometimes recognized addresses in Finsbury Park and Holloway. He seemed dimly to remember visiting them in two generations on consecutive days. On long featureless roads which had seemed to lead somewhere, and did, looping back to years ago when the pub on the corner was still a pub and not a squat with scribbled tag-lines around a defunct doorbell. On the door pillar somebody had written their never to be forgotten memories of somebody else who had gone away, gone on years ago, way up into the Headgate, and the person answering the door was recognizably a replica of somebody he tutored back in the days of mods and rockers and two-tone music and housy-housy. Would it always be like this? Granny's little girl or boy, granny herself grown-up and nodding along to her borrowed iPod, her teapot repossessed for not pouring straight, her spout broken off and fixed with superglue, leaking still leaking stars around the joint and the nectar of togetherness he had tasted once or twice, as a new boy on the chopping block.

Soon after her retirement he'd watched as his mother burned some papers in a galvanized wheelbarrow, noting her grim and glittering satisfaction as a life's paperwork went up in flames. She prodded at each overstuffed folder and ring binder of invoices, each row of neat double entries in the books, until they were all thoroughly carbonized and crumbled before their eyes to glowing piles of paper-shaped ashes. Gone forever was her shadow career as the unpaid, unwilling book keeper of BAJ motors. What had been her problem, really? After all, it was their living.

Still, life went on. Benny died one day and their last greying Persian kitten turned into a scuttling Andy Warhol wig even he wouldn't have wanted to wear. How they'd loved poor Blissy, his remaining twin, and they'd buried her in turn in a homemade shrine in the back garden, according to a ritual of their own weird devising, under a trellised canopy with a hand-painted sign, and beyond that, to the breakdowns, the agonies, the unseen final frames.

Londoners were good at looking the other way, keeping themselves to themselves, and suddenly, unexpectedly reaching out to you, as though you might have all the answers to what perplexed them, for sale, or buckshee. Meanwhile new ones were swarming into the country down the channel tunnel, clinging to the undersides of lorries, or crammed inside them, concealed breathlessly in containers, detained in Oakington or somewhere not yet closed down, interrogated, subject to deportation, discovered as speechless children mysteriously bleeding from the anus. French *sangliers* had definitely reestablished themselves as a species in Kent; washers up and waiters were recruited in London; winkle-pickers in Margate; prostitutes everywhere; and those with some money behind them waltzed in without a murmur of protest, to buy premises, open restaurants or internet cafes, operate import-export businesses of every kind. Offering legal advice to newcomers on how to overstay their welcome, with worthless degrees printed off by the fair's fair Universities of Old Londinium.

Services had been expanded to cater for them. The luckier children were at this moment pursuing university courses in cutting out paper doilies as well as forming a new cadre of lawyers, doctors, and gangsters. Earlier immigrants were bewildered survivors of decades of racism, discrimination; being loved to death by liberal educationalists and arts administrators – and still they kept coming, and changing, and changing us in the process of being half-assimilated into the general mulch of Britishness.

It was really bad, a nightmare – or was it? He liked to watch them at the open windows of upstairs flats as he passed by on buses through Tottenham, sniffing the fresh spring air, whiskers twitching as they in turn watched the various world perambulating past on the crowded bank holiday streets below. Actually, it was great, and if asked he would have pointed out there were still vast unsettled tracts of land – Dartmoor, for instance, had been good farming country in the Iron Age and could be again – should London or the big northern cities or the decaying seaside resorts of the south coast run out of habitable space – maybe there could even be a new Iron Age.

So he could easily relate to Mark Duggan's desire for revenge, if that's what had driven him to pick up his battered police-planted skeng, locked into some Fifty Cent Billy the Kid fantasy – but they always seemed to pick on the wrong people. He himself would've liked to buy a gun off the Dark Web and to blow the mayor's head off as he ostentatiously cycled home from work over London Bridge. But there you are, he was kidding himself. Actually he admired Boris Johnson's chutzpah. The real reason he cycled was to get the blood pumping around his brain, so that he could write another bestselling book. Hadn't he made an important contribution to keeping London cool?

A police siren yawed over the bright foreshortened scape; the redundant headlights of his bus were just about useful for people to see them coming but failed to penetrate very far into the wide region of night: it was like the blurred fringe along the unexplored spaces of Google street view. Out there among the documented tribes a woman was giving birth, rats and foxes tore at black sacks of rubbish, a young boy was dying of an overdose, two people were seeing each other for the first time by the light of a scented candle; but nothing in that darkness was of such importance that his journey home could not equal it – the violent superficial chase of the youthful crowds, their nightly adventures, over now, crawling at twenty miles an hour along the edge of the profound common experience, and good sense, of a solitary middle-aged man.

He felt a longing to get away from this world, as well as the other one he visited so often: the world of homes and children and struggling to love them; all the ordinary unspecified fears and

anxieties their neighbours shared.   He carried the thought of a
young girl he hoped would one day grow into a normal married
woman like a concealed letter promising just that: his longing
to get away was like the first stirrings of maturity when a rare
experience suddenly ceased to be desirable; but, he realized, if that
was adulthood, he was never going to get there. His mother had
been right about one thing: he was selfish to the core.

THIRTY-EIGHT

Jim Dale was looking out of the conservatory window at his bird-feeder. Tip-Top Tutors, absurd as the name sounded, had begun as a teachers' collective: a small group of friends who found themselves sick of working on the part-time fringes of the education system, as supply teachers, daily cover merchants working catch as catch can for rapacious, crooked agencies to whom head teachers of city schools, so often finding themselves without a body in the classroom due to the stresses of the job, often picked up the phone. Tip-Tip Tutors would be different, working one-to-one, giving directed help where it was most needed. They would cover for each other, where necessary, but they were all classroom practitioners, with no phony bullshitting middle men creaming off a fat percentage of their money.

Things had gone on alright for a few years. Tip-Top Tutors were flying around all over the shop, bringing quality tuition wherever it was required, and many of them had been able to sign off, at least they were supposed to do so. Jim had met his spouse Mary through the agency, a dark haired, slightly scatty primary school teacher who just couldn't hack it in a classroom environment. No killer instinct, but absolutely fine for home visits. Jim remembered the day she'd looked deeply into his eyes and said she didn't know how long she could keep on lying about how improvement was just around the corner, which, in his eyes, had been the sign of a nice person. After discussing it with the others, he'd told her they were looking for somebody to answer the phones full time, co-ordinate the tutors and do a bit of general office work. Mary had jumped at the chance, and after a while the basis of their relationship had changed – for the better, he always thought.

That, in his experience, was how good things often happened. You had your head down, nose to the grindstone, concentrating on something for all you were worth, and you looked up suddenly, in the middle of it, realized you had forgotten yourself for days, sometimes weeks. Just blinked out of existence for a while, or perhaps into another, more purposeful kind of existence. And when you came to unexpectedly you felt very happy, happy in forgetfulness, and sometimes there was somebody beside you, because it was quite a magnetic effect, but sometimes there wasn't anybody, but it didn't matter much either.

Anyway, so it had been with him and Mary, although you could also say he had arranged for things to turn out that way. Anyway, the point, the real clincher, was that after this discovery had been made by one person, it had to be impressed upon the other, without delay and often very insistently, so things generally worked out a lot better if they had been deliberately and thoroughly planned by the two people involved. He wasn't sure this made sense, but somehow, he thought, this self-forgetting he remembered was part of his luck, his general happiness.

Jim looked out of the window again at a few remaining flashy nuthatches and dull sparrows which were clustering around the bird-feeder, dimly aware of Mary pottering somewhere in the house behind him. Nuthatches were overrated, he thought, with their sleek heads and black racing trim striped masks, vaguely red-flashed breasts – clever little clockwork creatures designed for eating nuts and seeds. Give him a sparrow any day.

Like a lot of teachers he and Mary didn't have children of their own – they'd seen too much of other people's, as the pleasantry went. His had been a life of moving around, the companionship of his wife, and now his looming retirement, ever deferred. Why not keep going forever? Why not indeed, as long as the commission kept trickling in from his carefully-vetted team, none of whom were part of the agency's original cohort.

Trickling was the right word: into the water butt. Neither of them were keen gardeners. The break-up of the first agency had been inevitable, he supposed, like all such schemes … but after all, they weren't exactly teenage utopians. It had been the business with Raphael – and his partner Jeanette. They'd done well to survive that little debacle of threatened court action and God-knows-what-else (although the girl had clearly been lying, exaggerating), but Owen had never really accepted the necessity of getting rid of them altogether. He'd turned into a sort of one man fifth column, in a way, finding fault on Raphael's behalf with every perfectly reasonable decision which was made by himself and Mary, whilst the last remaining member of the gang of four, Kevin Murphy, had always been on his own planet.

Between them they'd robbed his London memories of any pleasure which might have accrued, and he missed them all like a hole in the head. He'd always wondered what that particular cliché meant, but never bothered to find out. A place where your dreams and your trust in people leaked out into the atmosphere and blew away. Oh well, good riddance to bad rubbish. And then there were people like Sister Emmanuel, or Sister Higgins as he'd insisted on calling her, her real name. She was a fearsome creature, a bit of a monster. But the parents had loved her. She had sorted the kids out alright. She was dead now.

What were they playing at, these Pupil Referral Units? They had all these great new purpose-built premises, a staff to student ratio which would be the envy of Eton, but the tossers couldn't even get the controlled assessment question to him in good time for him to prepare his student to sit it. The girl's regular English teacher had copied him in on the correspondence as he went through the motions of getting a password or something, then the whole thing was put on hold or forgotten about, until he raised the subject again, the girl became confused and dispirited, and any benefit she might have gained from her grandfather's generosity in paying for extra tuition was at least partly wiped out. And yet he and other private tutors had the reputation for being incompetent, not proper teachers etc. It was fucking obvious. The girl could write fluently, but she had no context in which this was particularly valued, or distinguished her from most of her contemporaries, and once she'd flown off the handle a few times, uttered wrong words, been referred, the whole mentality was punitive.

Even though she was in reality a little devil who had punched another girl in the face, a blacker girl who had been taunting her. Even though she had been taunting the other girl and had been punched herself, she deserved more help than grinding her through citizenship lessons, getting her down off her high horse – and now, it seemed, preventing her from recovering sufficiently to do well in English Literature GCSE, which they didn't even do in the pristine PRU. Kids were amazingly buoyant. It was still almost incredible how much their over-estimate of their own abilities and possibilities seemed to help them bounce through it all. But, unfortunately, this tendency made it easy to fob them off with a pep talk or two when what they really needed was proper coaching, detailed attention, preferably in an environment where free play wasn't given to disruptive permanent illiterates who would never be able to do anything except waste everybody's time.

Most teachers seemed to live in a fantasy world. He thanked the lord of hosts he wasn't one of them, because all things considered the Pupil Referral Unit was probably just what Althea really needed.

It's not what you know, it's who you know. They'd dinned that catchy little number into his head throughout his childhood. In other words, it didn't really matter how talented or knowledgeable you might be, what was really ultimately necessary for success was to crawl up the backside of the right people, which you couldn't do anyway if you were the wrong sort. They all knew one another already you see, just as C. Wright Mills had explained so clearly in *The Power Elite*. If that book was right, there were plenty of people who knew it was right without having read so much as a page of this American sociological classic of radical positivism. The thing to do, therefore, was to give up any ambitions that might have been forming in your developing brain and prepare yourself for a life time's nay-saying and cat-calling of those who had triumphed over you by illegitimate means and always would. And there was a further wrinkle to be smoothed out of this half-truth.

It's not who you know, it's what you are. OK, so if you're the wrong type you'll never get to know the right people. The right people being of a higher social class or group in whatever sense you liked. The insiders. Even if you know them, or try to, this will only ensure that they will judge you as their unworthy inferior. You're opening yourself to identification, when a far better strategy for success would be to hide yourself away, to work in secret and in contempt of the controlling parties. Unless you happen to be the right things for them. A middle-class woman perhaps. A person of colour. A homosexual. A Jew. Name it. But it really existed, this 'what', just as any discriminated against group was right to believe. There were some groups it seemed to whom right-thinking society never stopped saying sorry. Give us the money and we'll say we're sorry, we'll let you into our school, our newspaper, our university, our professions, and we'll pretend to believe that you are equal to us.

No, he wanted to say, it really is what you know, or rather what you can do with what you know. It really is intelligence that determines your place in the arrived-at scheme of things. But he knew, everybody with any thread of honesty knew, this wasn't actually the case in real life. Just an idea that couldn't be relinquished, something upon which the whole ball of wax was founded, the true grit in the lobster quadrille. Yum-yum. Or was that oysters. The world is your oystercard. Some real genius had thought of that name.

THIRTY-NINE

Ray Davies had decided to try out the new Turkish restaurant on Tottenham Lane. Sumak, it was called: a vast, glittering brown and gold palace on a site which had proved difficult for a succession of bars, late night drinking holes, pick-up joints. Even a family-orientated Russian social club had foundered there. The new restaurant however seemed popular, and since he liked the odd kebab, and it was near the studio, Ray thought he might as well give it a whirl.

He rapid-scanned the menus, wondering whether to have the Mercimek, hot or cold mezes, or just stick with a lamb shish and salad. He looked across at Rob, the sound engineer at Plum, wondered what he would be choosing. He couldn't help noticing the prices, pretty reasonable really, so he hoped Robbo would be springing for this without too much grief. Rob was a good bloke, let's face it, he had to be: thin, trembling, bald, but still with some traces of ginger hair and a faint Scottish accent, that's when he said anything. Actually it was like he wasn't there at all a lot of the time, which was what Ray liked about him.

Ray always found it difficult to say what sophistication was, to define it, but he knew he possessed something, a sensibility, which people had defined as being sophisticated, whereas Rob ... would always be a fucking idiot: a nice idiot who knew how to turn a few knobs. Sumak reminded Ray of Yma Sumac, the iconic Andean princess of exotic music who'd turned out to be Puerto Rican. Martin Denny and all that. He liked a bit of the exotic, even if, in the early days, it had only been a bar of Fry's Turkish Delight, as exotic as it had got on Muswell Hill Broadway in his day – still, at least he was really that which he was cracked up to be, that was something at least to be proud of, like the gold standard.

"Think I'll have the fishcakes," Rob interrupted his train of thought. "It's down as a starter, but I'm going to have it as a main, with chips. Should be alright, eh?"

"Interesting choice," Ray agreed absently.

"Eh? Eh?" Robbo hadn't quite caught his last words. He was turning his head to the right in order to advance his left ear into the sonic line of fire, but ironically it was his deaf ear he was putting forwards, the very ear his brother had struck off with a cutlass at a late seventies recording date; in other words, he was turning a deaf ear to Ray's comment.

"I'm having a lamb shish with salad," Ray said.

"Really pushing the boat out, eh?" Robbo had caught his drift this time. Really he loved the two brothers, who had at least kept him in intermittent work for more years than he cared to remember, Ray always joking that with Robbo's mixes there was no need to worry about losing the original authentic feel of a mono recording, no need to rush outside and listen to it on the car radio. But all that was strictly *sub judice* nowadays, in the hands of the lawyers. All what? Nobody really knew.

"I think I want to try the Rulo Borek," one of the living companions said. "I've always liked that one."

Ray reexamined the menu, carefully checking the price. "I had it once. It's a bit like Swiss roll except it's Turkish and a bit glutinous."

"That's the wrong word, Ray," said the other living companion, the younger of the two. "Besides, it's absolutely nothing like Swiss Roll. It's a savoury, made of filo pastry."

"Well, chick pea salad for me," said the first living companion glumly. He or she exhaled, a wistful sigh. "Maybe a few falafel and some lightweight tangy dip."

"Corbasi," Rob muttered with an air of grim decision. "Tavuk corbasi."

A really beautifully turned out young waiter in an immaculate white shirt and a silk waistcoat came up to them; fresh-faced and eager, his eyebrows knitted together not in consternation but as the simple inheritance of a child of the Bosphorus, naturally as it were; and he was smiling, ready to take their order, and they were prepared to give it. Living companion number one took command, smoothly conveying their dish ideas from their own vacant brows to his open pad, and everybody ordered a half of lager to go with it.

There wasn't much small talk as they waited for the food to come, but what there was largely originated with Robbo who, whatever his social challenges, was polite to a fault, especially on an occasion as rare as being invited out with Ray and his two mysterious living companions.

Ray was wearing his long, elegant cashmere coat which he had refused to surrender. Now he shrugged it off and draped it over the back of his chair, leaning forward over the table on his thin elbows to whisper something to one of the living companions. Rob strained to hear what it was, he was fading out again, a trace memory of being somebody else stiffened his spine for a moment, an assistant in Essex Hall, a long gone hospital for imbeciles by North Station, Colchester, but even this was attenuated. Cut off. Like his ear. By that bastard, Pete.

They'd all got about halfway down their lagers before the food came, and then they all tucked in. Robbo had some strips of pitta bread to go with his Tavuk Corbasi, which he was dipping in, whilst the younger living companion pronounced the Rulo Borek to be delicious, eating it with a small fork. The older living companion quite enjoyed his or her plate of falafel with a light creamy dip, although as always he or she couldn't help noticing there was always something a bit dry and endless about falafel, there would always be a few left over, he or she seemed to remember suddenly from previous restaurant visits.

Only Ray was unoccupied by his food, which seemed to everybody else by far the nicest deal; but although their famous friend appeared to want to do nothing but pick a little at a piece of lamb, a chunk of pepper, a spoonful of salad and rice, he wasn't ready to relinquish his food to the others, despite their envious glances, especially Robbo who had found the Corbasi a bit unsatisfying as a meal.

"I really like the new number, Ray. It's your best new song in ages. Hair of the Dog, wasn't it?" said Robbo, eyeing several untried cubes of meat on his boss's plate. "What's all that about, then?"

The living companions laughed, almost in unison. "Don't you know what *Hair of the Dog* is, Robbo" the younger said. "It's a programme on our satellite, a sort of reality TV show."

"It's our favourite – we're both totally hooked on it.," explained the older living companion. "So Ray's written a song about it, has he? That's beautiful. But Ray –" He or she turned to the distracted Kink, who immediately skewered a piece of lamb and stuffed it into his mouth. "You've never even watched a single episode of *Hair of the Dog*. You really hate it."

"I don't hate it," Ray protested. "How could I if I haven't even seen it? But I have heard enough of it through the ceiling." He smiled, twinkled. "You know, it's kind of a shaggy dog story, that's all."

"So what's it all about, this programme?" Robbo persisted. "Dogs?"

The others sighed, turned away, lapsing into a moment's silence.

"It doesn't really matter what it's about," Ray said at last. "It's more the sound of it – I just liked the sound of the phrase, my own associations with it, and Bob's your uncle. Another song." His long smile snaked up, and then it fell again, his mouth drooping down in a way all of them were familiar with. When Ray went down he really went. He actually looked as though he was about to start crying, and sometimes he really did. Living companion number two reached his or her hand across the tale and placed it over Ray's bony wrist. He visibly relaxed, shivered, then withdrew and slipped back into his coat, the capacious sleeves of which were lying open, gashes of silk, ready to receive his spindly arms.

He shrugged it back over his shoulders. "Getting a bit nippy in here," he said.

Which it certainly wasn't. Sumak was gradually filling up, flames were leaping at the charcoal grill, and couples and families were filling up the new Mediterranean tiled tables, smartly dressed, most of them, ordering and receiving fine, interesting looking meals and bottles of drink. The speakers were playing, although not loud enough to hear, some heavily accented bouzouki music, which was very like Greek music, but much darker, and even crazier. Ray felt the sweat start from his brow, involuntarily lifted his arm and wiped it across his forehead, as if to banish some unwanted thought of yesteryear.

"I was wondering about the programme itself, like," Rob continued. "Just curious." He looked across at the two living companions, who looked blankly back at him, making it seem even more of a ridiculous secret, perhaps a sort of game they were playing on him, a joke at his expense maybe. It was quite possible everybody in the world had heard of this thing except Robbo. He wouldn't be at all surprised. "It's a game show, is it?" he asked, brazening it out, forcing it out one final time.

"Something like that, yes." The second companion replied appeasingly, and the subject was then effectively closed.

Ray couldn't really have cared less. It didn't really mean much to him what Robbo thought one way or another. But he did sometimes let himself get easily annoyed by things, he had to admit. He knew there were always several levels of his response to anything, so it was important to him to be around people who understood all this about him. Robbo and the living companions were definitely people he could handle, more than that, people he liked and could rub along with on a regular basis, even loved, maybe, but actually it was more than half-true.

Robbo, on the other hand, sometimes made it difficult for Ray to remember he'd ever loved him, really, or why, and he found he had to try and sit on his annoyance while he was bombarded by negative feelings about the useless bozo he relied upon in his studio. When it came right down to it, Rob just wasn't good at anything. Which really meant he was no good at all. A bit like the Five Skills Rat, or Mole-Cricket, in that little poem from the *I-Ching* which Ray had always loved but kept to himself, believing it to be part of the real inspiration, that peculiar mish-mash of semi-secret lore that had led to his early success as a songwriter:

It can fly, but it cannot pass the roof,
It can climb, but it cannot reach the top of a tree,
It can swim, but it cannot cross a gorge,
It can dig, but not deep enough to shelter its body,
It can run, but never outrun a man.

Robbo all over, it was exactly who he was: an idiot. Some commentators thought the Five Skills Rat was actually a large Chinese water rat: a creature of considerable accomplishments. Others had suggested the flying squirrel as the true identity of this mysterious rodent, since the animal in the verse has many of its features; but finally the humble, despised mole-cricket was identified as the true culprit: pathetic, useless, in other words a fucking pest, like Robbo. You could drown him, stamp on him, knock him out of a tree, overtake him, easily catch and kill him, but where was the fun in it? The clueless bastard should have died fucking years ago.

Ray's opinion was you really did have a moral responsibility to help out and encourage the lame ducks and Five Skills Rats of this world. All of the humble brooding mole-crickets, who were trying to keep silent, vibrating with fear and so giving away their positions on the ground. Robbo was fucking useless, it had to be said, and even worse he was a mole cricket who answered back and thought he was in charge of Ray's creative process (if you wanted to call it that); and then he just lay there waiting for you to pick him up when all you wanted to do was put your Cuban heel through his delicate carapace and have done with him once and for all – but … but …

By and by they were all finished with their food and ready to leave, taking their cue from Ray, who was sitting there motionless in his loose cashmere coat, feeling replete but slightly anxious. Robbo put his finger up for the bill and their waiter busied himself preparing its short addition. "Let me get this one, Ray," he said, pulling his battered wallet from his greasy back pocket. "On me tonight."

Ray put his hand across the table and placed it on Robbo's bony shoulder. "I really love you, man," he said. "Thanks for being here for me all these years. I appreciate it more than you'll ever know."

The two living companions beamed in happiness, and they all touched one another's backs affectionately as they were leaving the busy, happy restaurant where another Turkish family were making an unexpected success of their new venture in the crowded restaurant market of Hornsey. They were working hard, but everything was turning out fairly well for them, for now, as it usually did, in his long experience of urban life.

FORTY

He was back in his corner café eating his usual breakfast. Coffee and sausage-in-a-roll. He supped at his bowl of creamy coffee, took a huge bite of the roll, put his reading glasses on and pulled *The Sun* towards him. It was his usual breakfast, but not his usual state of mind. He hadn't slept yet, just laid on the bed for a few hours, listening to biographies of the Beach Boys, John Lennon and Atlantic soul on the radio through the TV. Churning over nothing in particular, not wanting to do anything which would keep him awake, he knew damned well he wasn't going to be able to sleep anyway. He'd got into a nocturnal cycle, he didn't know exactly how, and at sixty years old he still didn't know how to get out of it.

He'd gradually taken to talking to foxes. "Alright foxy?" he would call softly if he happened to see one rooting around when he was on his way to buy cigarettes at the garage, and the fox would often look up briefly in acknowledgement before continuing on its nocturnal patrol with a calm and arrow-like purposefulness. A new family of young foxes were quartered below the wooden deck with which some neighbours had paved their back yard, and these were particularly pretty and frisky: you saw them frolicking about the streets at night, play-fighting and biting one anothers' fluffy ears, keening like baby banshees, while their elders, bony and October grey, foraged more widely, heading downhill to the bin liners of Crouch End, pausing only to be blessed at the wayside shrine of the Holy Innocents, to piss in its small adjoining park. Well, it was nice somebody cared. They stood around in twos and threes in the back alley beside the Chinese takeaway on Tottenham Lane, watched him steadily, motionless until he had passed.

The café was full of early morning coppers from Tottenham Lane police station. They kept the place going, tucking into their breakfasts, stoking up for a full day of assisting he public, young and neatly turned out in their white shirts, bullet-resistant vests, handy snap-on handcuffs sheathed in black hip-holsters, radios at the ready. He often watched them, listened to them without hearing a particle of intelligence escape from their lips, and for all his curious staring none of them ever glanced in his direction. An exclusion zone surrounded them. At this stage in the day they only had eyes for each other, interested in who was sitting next to whom, realizing he supposed that their attentions – friendly or otherwise – would be forever unwelcome.

Up with the lark, up with intrepid masked men in bright orange overalls, urban spacemen who used their trigger finger operated picking sticks to inspect each of the previous evening's discarded roaches, stowing them for later recycling. Back at the sorting office teams of trained roach dismantlers were ready and waiting to select and grade the juicier ones. He rapid-scanned the paper, looking for an indifferent new horoscope writer who'd recently taken over from Mystic Meg. Poor Mystic Meg – she just didn't see it coming. And yet she'd diagnosed his own problems bang on the button, day after day, year after year – she deserved a rest, to be fair.

IT'S DOG EAT DOG
IN THE WORLD OF THE COCKROACH

Namby-pamby pinkos have long claimed the cockroach is a co-operative critter. Colonies of these disgusting beetles live together in peace and harmony, they claim, only occasionally quarrelling over how to divvy up a nice piece of pizza crust.

Now our exclusive pictures give the lie to the myth that led loony London teachers to suggest they should be kept as classroom pets. The so-called friendly cockroach is a fierce, armoured cannibal – ruthless and rooting for the blood of its neighbour.

BUT – it's true they do band together to bring down larger prey. Amazing telephoto shots – too explicit to print in a family newspaper – show cockroaches swarming up the hind leg of an unwary pet pooch which chose the wrong lamp post to do its business against yesterday in horrible Haringey.

Its irresponsible owner was unavailable for comment.

The Sun says: Yes, by all means, cockroaches MUST be available in our schools (though not in the kitchens, eh Jamie?) – BUT ONLY if they're used to teach the right lessons!!

His brain was fried eggs, sizzling and spitting in its pan; struggling to retrieve a few helpful images of cannibal dogs from its memory banks. Plenty of wagging tails in there, some stick-fetching, a few nasty dog fights – but no episodes of same species canine feasting flashed up before his inner eye. He folded the newspaper in half and tossed it neatly to the far edge of the table, fresh for about as long as his breakfast roll, which he devoured immediately with ragged, broken teeth.

The teeth were becoming a serious problem: they announced him as probably a drug addict or what have you, and as he smiled on the doorsteps of his clients he tried to keep his mouth closed as far as possible, and to remember always to be positive, never to complain. People with full-time jobs, people who could afford him, were always a bit funny about that. To incite pity guaranteed their rejection. After all, he was supposed to be competent, to be able to do things they – and their children – couldn't do. And this was more or less true. His teeth, although broken, had a certain jaggedness which thereby made them effective for chewing and tearing recalcitrant materials.

The Turkish kids had been a pain in the neck with their impertinent questions about his love-life and his solitude and his sexuality, and he had had to tell them to mind their own business. You only had to be out of sorts a few times, even once was a hazard, and it was probably going to be bye-bye forever. Sezin hadn't called him for some time. Others, even friends, made remarks about 'choices you have made' and 'your lifestyle' – he wasn't aware he had one – and that was the nub of it – until they pointed out what they didn't like about his attitudes.

Everything was meant to be a matter of choice, a glorious option you were exploring for a while, and if things had gone wrong – well, shucks, they hadn't necessarily started with a full deck themselves; they had traded themselves into their present teapot, and somehow, by daring to moan, it was as if you were asking for an extra slice of fruit cake, or trying to make them feel bad about something they'd worked hard to achieve. It wasn't always easy being middle-class! So: chirpy, smart and well-prepared. Remember: a private tutor is on a permanent zero hours contract, so the minimum wage was a dream as far off and impossible to attain as a farm full of rabbits.

But you had to know your onions, they were the basis of your usefulness, your tearfulness. Keep your mouth shut. Tooth whitening didn't really work – but you had to carry on with it as if it did. These were lessons which needed to be learnt. It was difficult when you realized you weren't necessarily acting, your brain just wasn't going to clear, you had forgotten some important stuff you were supposed to know like the back of your hand. He drained his coffee cup, stood up and walked out with a backwards shoulder wave at the Turk behind the counter – and staggered back home, where he undressed, flopped onto his groaning bed and passed out at last, waking up as crepuscular darkness was edging in over the back gardens.

He noticed the glider on his ceiling, still above him. He tried to dismiss it, but however he tried to see it – a glider is what it was: stuck up there standing on a long wisp of cirrus cloud for good, tantalizing and transcendent. Turned on its side it might have been an angel holding wide its shining wings, standing on a long wisp of cirrus cloud.. Otherwise it was nothing except a glaring reflection, but since his brain was wired to see a glider there, a glider was what he invariably saw. All you could do was look away from it, turn it off like the lyrics of a song that was still purring away from years ago. Jesus, I like your angel, he said to himself. Thank you for sending him to look down over me.

The difference between a radio-controlled helicopter and a glider is that you let go of the glider and it flies of its own volition, or rather by virtue of its design, it glides on the air, whereas there was always something artificial about a helicopter – except there wasn't. It was just a glorified dragonfly but like an insect it had to keep buzzing to stay aloft on its little motor; it was purposive, directed, whereas a glider just glided, possibly under some sort of control, but floating on a whim, on the cushion of the lower atmosphere and the currents of the air.

His mind wasn't at all clear, he was groping through fog. There was a message on his mobile phone. He dialed 123 and entered his code – but it was nothing, just voice-spam about an unpaid bill from years ago: no vital news of Keisha's controlled assessment tasks. So how the fuck was he supposed to prepare her for them? Basically he was going to have to make up the question. He sat at his computer and looked up 'dog eat dog'. This contradicted a Latin proverb which maintained that dog does *not* eat dog, first recorded in English in 1532. Nevertheless, by 1732 it had been set down by Thomas Fuller in his *Gnomologica* as "Dogs are hard drove when they eat dogs." Which is still how it should be, he thought. A desperate expediency, not a routine, not the prime fucking directive

He lifted the blind and watched dusk take hold of the gardens, the tree tops, the windows and roofs opposite. Propitiation. Shadows deepened, a light or two came on, yellowy evidence of the other beings moving around in their parallel dwelling-places. It knitted everything in the visible world together, at the same time unclasping his mind so tensions were resolved and the patterns in everything came clear for a short period before dissolving and descending into nothingness.

He very much liked watching those moments register in his field of view, and his own thought moved out amongst the upper branches, finding itself surprised in the shadows in the cornices, the grooves in the rooves, the chimneys with obsolete aerials strapped to them, and the holes in the rows of upright tiles marking their summits peeked over them like the eyes of a row of owls, and the deep blue fell behind them, and how this part of London, just in case you'd missed how nice it was, always seemed to be cheerily exclaiming: *Tu-whit! Tu-whoo!*

Stephen the Evangelist managed to stop him halfway down Rathbone Avenue, veering towards him across the tree-lined autumnal street where they had once discussed the roof-top nesting habits of gulls, looking up until one of them, a large female herring gull, had begun to dive bomb them. Stephen was immaculately dressed as usual, a dapper little man in a three-piece suit: a seventy-five-year-old on a permanent mission for the Lord. His tan satchel was similar to Graham's. He pulled it round his body and flipped open the worn leather flap, carefully elected and extracted a recent copy of *The Watchtower*. "Graham," he called. "Graham: I've got something for you here."

Stephen could easily have been accused of going through the motions, but Graham somehow thought that that didn't quite define what he was doing, what anybody like him was really doing.

He was trying to make contact, trying to communicate something, and he had seen him on the corner of Turnpike Lane approaching people at the bus stop, lurking outside Budgens, talking to some person he'd accosted, usually a woman, in much the same way as he talked to him; and quite often there was somebody who would take him, or themselves, seriously enough to give him a good argument.

Not that Stephen had any particularly good arguments, but then he wouldn't would he. "Look at this, Graham," he said sometimes. "Read it to me – just this part." And he would pass across his bible, pointing to a passage in the Book of Daniel.

"Ah, Daniel in the lions' den," he said knowledgeably.

"Yeah, yeah," Stephen exhaled, "Daniel in the Lion's Den. But this is something different. Read it Graham, read it to me now, please."

And so, on an occasion he dreaded to repeat, Stephen tricked him into engaging with the prophecies of Daniel. They were obviously important to Stephen, central to his faith. Daniel was a clever man, cleverer perhaps than Shadrach, Meshach and Abed-nego, who had relied on the brute strength of an angel of the Lord of Heat and Coldness to protect them from a fiery furnace so hot – seven times hotter than normal – that it had caused vain king Nebuchanezzar's henchmen to combust instantaneously, and four men were seen to walk around unharmed in the furnace. He had actually enjoyed hearing this story again.

Daniel deflected Nebuchadnezzar's insanity not merely by interpreting his dream, but by knowing, without being told, exactly what dream he had dreamed, or alternatively by convincing him that he had dreamed the dream Daniel had told so persuasively. He knew because he was a master psychologist. He knew Nebuchadnezzar's not so secret fears – that he wasn't as all-powerful as he thought himself – in fact they may well have been obvious to everyone. The dream he told was the dream of the giant statue of gold, silver, brass and clay, and how the lines of succession it symbolized, of dynasties each less valuable but stronger than the last, would be shattered at last by a giant unhewn rock hurled by Jehovah himself, which would destroy and replace these false kingdoms. And so it was Daniel had learned that he was able to improve upon his own position but not to divert the course of history. Nebuchadnezzar had been impressed, convinced by Daniel, and had rewarded him with power; but being as how he was such a vain, nasty homicidal megalomaniac, he had decided to prove this Daniel and his admittedly impressive Jehovah to be wrong, wrong, wrong.

Stephen the Evangelist had succeeded at his task of making him reconsider the word of the prophets, and the strength of the Old Testament, and the collective wisdom of the ancient Hebrews – not to rely so much on his own puerile ad hoc symbols of a personal Jesus. It was just that he didn't want to repeat the experience today. Fortunately, Stephen let him off with a dire warning about global warming, which he'd heard before – "Hailstone in May! What is this?"

"At least they're not frogs!"

"Things are getting better, Graham," he said now. "Things are definitely going to get better for you."

FORTY-ONE

Ray, Ricky, Jim, Yemi, Lana, Sezin, Christian ... whomsoever he could think of at that moment. Various kids. Their loving parents. Stephen the Evangelist. Every one of them was a different kind of poet. Each lived in a world of their own making, bleeping out a code: I am here. This is what I want. From you. From the world. In upturned voices calling out after the passing carriages. Painting their wooden idols with their enemies' blood.

Ray was a kind of poet, we all knew what kind: the kind who could write about dead end kids with a kind of fey obliquity which made you think he knew what he was talking about, until you'd actually paced out Muswell Hill Broadway. Ray Davies was aspirational, looking up in a way, seemingly unaware he was already at the top of the hill even as pink pigs pranced by on their hind trotters to his outpourings of pure untrammelled melody. His brilliant brother, whom Graham had recently seen in a documentary guzzling a Costa coffee on Fortis Green Road, gesturing towards St James' church where his sisters had got married, would probably have said, yeah, he was always a snobby bastard, Ray.

Ritchie had always been a skilled skater, a poet of leaps and arabesques. Charlie Parker survived and grown even more languid, relaxed back into Lester Young, but he was still an angry young poet who wanted to expose himself, or better still, for others to expose themselves to him. All his scenarios ended with you begging him for mercy. Yemi was into the poetry of holidays and questionnaires. Easy to answer, leading to success in your heart's desires. She herself was the true poet of mobility, ageless, and inscrutable to her co-workers. How old was she? Married? A man in her life? Always about to step onto an aeroplane, which had only briefly touched down on your planet.

Jim's was an anti-poetry of crisply-imparted information, rising to lyric occasionally in its slightly anxious fussiness: he was a totally straightforward person who could insinuate somehow that the boggy outer-reaches of Enfield weren't so drastically beyond your usual orbit. Persuasive, insistent, methodical, he slid things past you. Sezin was a poet of self-sufficiency, community, autonomy, and of control, and of short-sighted greed.

Lana had become the poet of her daughters; she'd made quite fantastic creatures out of them: speakers of languages, assumers of names and identities, creators of podcasts, engravers of exotic designs upon stone and clay and leather. They were full of themselves, with a confidence she hadn't possessed at their age, struggling with her silver flute and a thousand and one parental expectations. She'd worked at her poetry of experience, gathered up her scribbled masks and her pictures of bantam roosters and leghorns and gone for it. But, it seemed to him now, he had never really known her at all, and could only remember her now through a few old pop songs.

Somewhere out there was a half-timbered pink Tudor house whose single protruding gable lopsidedly put down a hand to rest on the shoulder of its front door like that of a small child. This or something like it was perhaps the house he had always wanted to own, his teapot of ultimate reassurance, of heart's desire; and he might even have done so had he had the gumption to pursue it to the exclusion of anything else; but it was obviously too late for such nonsensical dreams.

Christian: a poet of the civic godhead, although he didn't need any such justification. He was in his own way a proponent of the second self, that part which must always remain hidden.

Saturday morning last, near Friern Barnet, one of his friendlier families had stood chatting on their doorstep, the dad offering an Irish tip for the National: a bet he'd rushed away to place, but which remained untaken. There they were, tucked away in their lovely little teapot with a kind of red plank on the wall which said REVENGE in curly lettering, a humorous touch, near an old deco factory undergoing desultory refurbishment, above a small friendly signposted wood, on a branch off a climbing feeder, which led up from a busy dual carriageway midway between New Southgate and Bowes Park. They were always pleased to see him, to share the school's indifference to their dyslexic daughter. Was it maybe because she was Irish?

Everything started out from London: what a shitty little proposition. Impossible to believe if you contemplated its vast spew from the top deck of a bus, or knew anything about its much vaunted movers and shakers; but more or less true nonetheless.

Not everything rippled out from its original stone's impact to the provinces, but whatever did make it onto a poster on the outside wall of a supermarket in a small town in Essex was going to be taken to be the result of an inevitable justice, a just inevitability they were going to be nodding their heads over forever, missing as always the accidental quality of everything, as well as the inevitable finger on the scales which had produced the result long inscribed as an indelible grade on your leaving certificate. Teachers loved that sort of thing – so often the enforcers of an apparently unforced social fate, and the biggest snobs on earth.

Unlike the man on the corner angrily throwing dismantled scaffolding clasps into the open back of a flatbed lorry, Graham had too little to do with his time. A little bird told him, a little bird of ill-omen with its warning chirp. Wouldn't it be terrible if, if such and such should spoil your fortune, only trying to be helpful, to help you take advantage of your very last chance. An oxymoron, an example of foreshadowing. But he knew he was lucky to have this work – at least it was a more interesting something to do than be a Pole who dismantled scaffolding.

He was hurrying on his way to deliver a cargo of Jane Austen to another needy child, who not being of her persuasion lacked the powers of concentration and the means of social identification to make a cult of her. It wasn't her fault, nor was it his. It was just time for Althea to consult her personal tutor. He would perch on a dolls' chair by her bed and sing to her as he strummed on her small plastic guitar. She hadn't so far proved to be a violent or difficult child, but as her mum had pointed out, he hadn't really seen her in action.

He mounted a couple of steps and firmly rang their taped bell on a front door in Finsbury Park. Althea had experienced a major problem with the unseen paper: "If I see a Osprey, I will kill it," she announced with a theatrical flourish. But there was always literature to redeem her.

He set to work explaining poems one after another; she made rapid copious notes, her eyes bugging as she covered page after page of her file pad in a loose scrawl with a felt-tip pen. In a couple of hours they were finished with poetry – and drama. *An Inspector Calls.* The most obvious play, to complement the easiest novel. She thought Mr. Birling had been right to sack troublemaker Eva Smith for demanding twenty-five shillings a week. Well, she wouldn't get away with it nowadays, would she?

He was too tired to explain it all again, this worn-out pipe-puffing parable of the evils of capitalism. How could it be that the exposure of the most shocking abuses of the past and present was so tedious to everybody? Like most of the books on the syllabus it was worn out. But he could easily see why one of the educational great and good had once thought it was a good place to start.

He packed up his things, said goodbye and left their place with his bag on his shoulder. Althea ran after him quickly, catching her tutor up in the street as he headed back to the station. He thought he might have forgotten something, which he did sometimes; but the girl stood there hopping on the spot and smiled at him happily, bless her cotton socks; and she pushed another ten pound note into his hand, from her mother, for luck.

FORTY-TWO

The new job came up quite unexpectedly through a personal contact, just as Christian and Yemi had said it would. A scanned business card arrived in his inbox, forwarded by a friend to whom he'd been describing his agency work; following a couple of gruelling three hour interviews in a branch of a franchise restaurant, in Stratford, high up in the rafters of the glittering Westfield Centre, which he'd prepared for with an hour of quiet contemplation in the faith room, he was soon signed up to a zero-hours contract with an organisation which mainly dealt with children excluded from school. The idea was to reinclude them. A safety net. Their idea was to keep on defying, denying.

His first assignment involved a long daily journey to Surbiton, a town where – he learned from a wall display in the local Wetherspoons – Thomas Hardy had written *Far from the Madding Crowd* – to visit a demented young arsonist who was being held in a secure care home. He had his own special memories of Surbiton, such as splitting up with Lana in a pub next to the station, but they didn't trouble him overmuch. Instead he concentrated on getting to Berrylands Road on time and writing his reports in the evenings. These were dashed off somewhat, performances of what he thought his Australian manager might like to hear, and he was too embarrassed to read over whatever feeble nonsense he had written in them.

It was during a freak heatwave five years earlier, a dog-basking, balmy couple of weeks in early spring, that he had started working at a temporary job as a census collector in Tottenham. He'd snagged this position by filling out multiple choice scenarios online. You had to decide which combination of letters to circle if somebody was out when you called, what kind of household it was, and so on. He got a high mark, went to an induction day at the Holiday Inn in Bloomsbury, and it was a done deal. By the beginning of April he was out with a stack of forms, banging on doors of slow responders throughout T-town, which had one of the lowest rates of response in the country, something like fifty percent. In some cases this turned out to mean they had difficulty filling out the forms, in others it was a kind of exploratory go slow, or tentative refusal.

Winifred and Patrick MacBride and their six children had now settled in the area for life. Neither could read or write nor did they seem to have worked, ever. If not exactly proud, they seemed bemused by this condition. "Unless you'd count picking up a few bits of scrap metal in the road," Patrick explained, with a wink. It took three visits to get the form done, maybe four. On the last day he found Patrick working on his van in the road. As Graham passed by he had first one wheel then the other off. He held his blackened hands up in alibi, smiling.

Later, cleaned up at their dining table, he told Graham he was a left-hander like himself. "Wouldn't it be that you'd always smudge your writing by dragging your hand on it?"

He admitted this could happen sometimes if you weren't careful. Patrick said he was actually stronger in his right arm, but he did most things leftie. Every surface and wall in their flat was covered in Catholic pictures or statuettes – Christ, angels, lambs, all the faded beauties of fifties and sixties Ireland. He noticed not for the first time a faithfulness to the precious details so many people kept. All mothers, knowing their children's dates of birth, will take some sort of pleasure in remembering them. There was something old-fashioned, timeless, about these two people. Winifred had been born in '72 and Patrick in '77, or the other way around. He found her beautiful, charming, with a hard to define flatness, or was it just the directness and lack of side of some illiterates. But they were both likeable people.

"Would you like a glass of water?" Patrick was in confident, generous charge of the tap. "She's no qualifications," he informed the collector. "A good housewife, that's all."

They'd come over from Ireland – she from the North, he from the South – in the mid-nineties, all the kids were born on succeeding years. At last she'd smiled, showing her dimple: "There's so many ways to spell Bridget," she said.

In a charming little hobbit cottage tucked away at the bottom of Bruce Hill had lived Altimon and Delzie, pottering along with the gentle aimless friendliness of retired people who have paid off their mortgage. Altimon had been a forklift truck driver, Delzie an auxiliary nurse. He told them his name, which they both repeated, smiling at him. They liked his name.

"I hope you don't mind the smell of West Indian cooking," Delzie said.

What if he had? Underlying this was the suspicion he was going to try and stop her cooking it in her own kitchen. She was a large-breasted woman, slow to smile, married to a shivering whippet of a man who'd lost most of his yap. Both were in good health, although diabetic. Altimon looked washed-out. Delzie was darker and solider and more questioning.

He said he was just there to count people, but when he asked if they had a car, she pointed out that "a car is an object, not a person." A bit stern. "What *is* this for?" she asked him again.

As he trotted out his rehearsed spiel, Altimon repeated, "We've done nothing wrong. We was British before we came here."

Nice freshly decorated kitchen dining room, wallpaper which had been old fashioned back in the seventies when it was designed, and the whole place was full of the feel and furniture of those blurry years. "Our two sons lived here – but now it's just us two." Time-encapsulated, like all of us, he thought. They reminded him of his own parents, who were about the same age but not quite as healthy, especially his mum. Always lived in the same area? Yes. Delzie had once worked for Camden Council, Altimon drove a forklift for a wholesaler – called The Rubber Company, but which had dealt in everything from medicine to wood.

The invigilator sat at a large dining table beneath faded fifties postcard views of the colourful beach landscapes of their youth, places no longer there, or for all he knew exactly the same; photos of their grandchildren, grinning into their long ago moment, grown-up now. Delzie at pots and pans, hovering, a little shy, diffident perhaps, but more willing to ask questions than her husband. She liked to be asked, he thought, liked transmitting these details of her life – as nearly all did, he imagined – as though he was some sort of approving witness to their being; or perhaps it's difficult to sort the memories from the facts, and just more interesting to leave them mixed together, where they always are. Altimon was egging to tell him the whole story, but there was no real excuse for it, unfortunately.

Further across the quadrant he'd been assigned, Beverley and company were usually enjoying a bevy. There seemed always to be a big party going on in the front yard whenever he passed by her corner, a hill of empty beer cans, a fragrant and inviting barbeque in preparation. There was a young woman who lived in a shoe with her seven children; she was busy, she knew what to do, smiling at the top window, her arms in suds: baby bathing, suggesting he call later. Later he sat at the table, worked through her forms, her children's names, her employment history, her husband who'd lost his hands in a motorbike accident, her dormant catering business. Bellyfull. Soon tiring, Bev handed him over to her eldest daughter, who sat down opposite him and spelled out all the names, and the little ones came in to gape; they wanted to do it too. Her daughter insisted she was noted as 'Black-British' instead of 'Caribbean'.

"She has to be," Beverley laughed, "*different.*"

"He's writ it, he's writ it!" she cried in delight when she saw he'd misspelled one of their beautiful first names. Aaliyah. Calista. Estefania. Fidelissima. Julissa. Shaunene. Thembisa.

Earlier the same day he'd come across a sadder case, a tale of two sons, although he had filled in all the details easily enough. One was in an asylum in Jamaica, the other had been cut on his twenty-first birthday over in Stoke Newington. She was a part-time care-worker, a full-time carer. A large plasma TV to get lost in, to be taken away from it all, a distractor for her four children. Her daughter sat on the opposite couch, texting, texting while her mother talked out her sadness, her urgent sadness, to the only person who, for a few minutes, was listening to her. It was all too much for her – and for him.

The upper flats behind the little rows of shops on Phillip Road had been difficult to access – rickety outside staircases, smashed doors blocked off with planks – and when he got up there a jumble of laths behind dusty panes; down in the yard there was an abandoned keyboard from a stalled career in synth-pop, a stiffly sprung letter-slot in a blank wall, a twisting fire escape down which all occupants seemed to have fled. Anyway, he'd caught the eye of a guy ascending one of those ramps into a rumouredly inhabited nowhere, and they'd filled his form on a wheelie bin lid at the end of the track. One room, him and his grown-up son, no kitchen.

Bulgari, no English. Signs were enough. Building, house, all work in building house. No. No building house now for a year. He'd been here eighteen months, his quick look held a sufficient force of explanation. Easy, easy, they know we are here.

An old Turkish man who could speak no English at all called for a young woman who didn't speak it either, and they started shouting angrily at each other. "NO," she said, slamming the door. He rang again, the old man beckoned him in. They sit on his rumpled bed, and the old man picked up his mobile and dialled his carer. They passed the phone back and forth, to and fro, back and forth. He was laughing now, enjoying himself. The woman poked her head around the door. He shouted at her in Turkish to fuck the hell off. The invigilator had smiled, and put his hand on the old man's to reassure him.

All those little things people had given him, what did those things signify: a banana, an orange, a cup of tea?

One of his first customers, a nightclub bouncer who worked in Shoreditch, emerged from his small council flat and escorted them both to a Turkish café. Graham watched him slurp his Turkish soup and he drank a Coke which the enormous West Indian bruiser had bought for him. Later, at a ground floor window, appeared a naked man. "She's out at work," he said, smiling. "A bird, obviously. No, no, I don't live here." A pair of bikers expressed their disdain for all forms of government by unleashing their Alsation onto him, their strain of clemency, their sense of proportion, by whistling him off just as he vaulted over their front wall.

Hugged by a Romanian gypsy granny. Quite pleasant. She didn't quite manage to get her teeth into his neck. Plus there were always those who wouldn't speak. He had looked into the pale eyes of an Albanian and seen one of his brother's scruffier friends, or perhaps even himself: an Englishman.

Two Frenchwomen in early middle-age were quietly clearing out the home of their recently dead sister; a black Church of England vicar snatched open the door of his excessively timbered mock-Elizabethan teapot when he banged on it with the iron ring, and glared at the invigilator with hostility. He had been preparing his sermon, had forgotten to complete his form.

Somewhere along there a woman had appeared from behind a curtain and spoken through her closed downstairs window.

"I returned my form weeks ago." Her voice far-off, hard to make out. "I obey the laws of this country, unlike some people."

He tried to avoid offence by not disturbing Tottenham residents who happened to be celebrating Beltane; he trudged around long crescents with Boer-war names, criss-crossing the area like veins in the back of an old woman's hand; empty settings, a scimitar, a chopped sickle, diamonds confiscated by the black sky. Undergoing no refurbishment, derelict, boarded up, tattered dirty curtain, a tiny light showing high up in a tall Edwardian corner building, where somebody was hiding from him, at dusk.

After it was over and the final late form was forwarded for processing, what were to become known as the Tottenham riots had kicked off without warning. Initially a spontaneous response to heavy-handed policing of a crowd which had gathered outside the Police Station following the shooting of Mark Duggan, a local bad boy who had or hadn't had a gun in a shoebox in the car they were tailing, the fierce summer rioting spread quickly across the capital, and then the country; disaffected kids torched their areas and went on an opportunistic thieving spree co-ordinated via their Blackberries.

Many pairs of go-faster trainers had been acquired and long built-up businesses were blazed to jagged cinders as the mobs rampaged briefly out of control, arousing panics and terrors and calls for stiff penalties in the rest of the population, soon answered, and a mighty spouting forth of opinions and instant analysis in the contorting liberal media – these were consumerist riots, devoid of moral purpose – before it all died down, or was contained, within a month, running its course like a summer fire, boiling up like a kettle and blowing off steam. Leaving T-town permanently scarred, but not for very long; T-town, with its prosperous Conservative Club (unharmed) and never to be reopened Working Men's Club was soon repaired as if it never happened. The local youth who had predicted the whole thing in a vox pop interview on Wood Green High Street, as a likely outcome of Government withdrawal of funding from youth clubs, no doubt felt vindicated, but this insightful hero boy was never approached subsequently for his opinion. I told you so would have been a legitimate response, from him, if they'd bothered to ask him for a further comment.

As it all unfolded he lay back on his bed, flipping between news channels. He watched fires flaring up on Tottenham High Road and fierce pitched battles between brick-tossing youths and riot-shielded police; he remembered how, during a period when he had been bunking off from door-knocking, he'd popped in to Bruce Castle Museum for a look around. This impressive building on the site of a castle built by Robert the Bruce housed Haringey's municipal collection. Including exhibits commemorating various industries which had once thrived in the Tottenham area. He couldn't help fantasizing about the riots as something of a missed opportunity.

He would like to have been the only looter to break into Bruce Castle Museum. He would've liked to steal their pristine JAP speedway bike, taken in a can of petrol with him, just wheeled her out, juiced her up, kicked her over and sped away down Bruce Grove, like his great uncle, family legend Allen Kilfoyle, who had ridden at Harringay Stadium in the early thirties. Straight into Tottenham High Road – look out this ting ain't got no brake – dodging between the shields of the cops, swerving burning cars: shaking a fist at any aggressive juveniles, up on the pavement, *graaaah*, in and out of the gleeful mob having its few days of rage, crackling away over splintered glass as if it were strewn barley-sugar.

On Facebook somebody posted a wildfire clip of a large herring gull stalking in and out of a shop with stolen food in its beak, an opportunistic looter. But something kept nagging at him, a memory he couldn't quite locate properly or bring into focus. Somewhere, at a front door along those long, curving avenues, a young friendly guy had handed him a completed census form. Handsome, lean, just getting into or out of a child-bright, candy-coloured dream car of some sort, and at that point still alive.

High on the brickwork of the boarded up Working Man's Club, a blue plaque commemorated Luke Howard, Namer of Clouds. Graham looked up at some neat rectangular scrapes of low cirrus which looked like they'd been applied with the edge of a palette knife, some high up dabs of over-boiled cauliflower florets. The highest floated above, an aristocracy of clouds, wispy, refined, barely touched into existence in the upper air; the second comprised a stolid middle-class of clouds, a second degree, holding their own, shouldering out the sun with their sense of entitlement; and below them ever-burgeoning masses were boiling up into strange, beautiful shapes: these were the truest of clouds.

Lightning Source UK Ltd.
Milton Keynes UK
UKHW04f1655221018
330966UK00001B/52/P